© PLAYING GOD

Many asked for the Second Coming of Jesus Christ.
Few thought it possible...

Authors: Nelson Bustamante and Carmen Victoria Pardo
🔘 *@nelsonbus / @soycarmenvictoriapardo*

Editor in Chief: Andrea Vivas Ross
Art Director: Raquel Colmenares Ross
(Become Creative Studio *@become_ studio)*
Graphic Designer: Raquel Colmenares Ross
Translation and proofreading: ©Helen Hadley / ©Oliver Greaves / ©Translinguo Global
Book adaptation: ©David López Jiménez / ©Translinguo Global
Proofreading: Pat Stanford

Publishing house for independent authors:
Paquidermo Libros *@paquidermolibros*

First edition: March, 2023.
Miami, USA.

ISBN: 978-0-9995523-1-5

Many asked for the Second Coming

PLAYING

of Jesus Christ.

GOD

Few thought it possible...

*This is a true story
based on fictitious events..*

NELSON BUSTAMANTE & CARMEN VICTORIA PARDO

"In order for crises to be overcome, the Church advises not prudence and caution, but courage and decisiveness. There is no reason not to side with the truth or to adopt an attitude of fear before it. The truth and all that is true constitutes a great good, to which we should tend with love and joy. Science is also a path to the true, for in it reason is developed; that God-given reason which, by its very nature, is not determined towards error, but towards the truth of knowledge."

Pope John Paul II

THE SECOND COMING

"So, Christ also, having been once offered to bear the sins of many, shall appear a second time, apart from sin to them that wait for him, unto salvation."

Hebrews 9:28

—*December 21st, 2025.*
11 p.m.
The streets of "The City That Never Sleeps" seem to be back on their feet after the pandemic.

The famous Rockefeller Center Christmas tree lights sparkle. Its lights are usually switched off at midnight. It is decorated with five miles of lights. Under this sixty-six-foot-long structure are those who take the opportunity to capture the moment with selfies and make it last forever. Boy, will they remember this!

Not everyone experiences the city the same way. While some have been resting, others have just put their heads down for the night. Then, there are those who have not yet realized what is happening, those that cannot even imagine that everything will change.

In a small apartment, in the south of Long Island, Camilo is walking around like a zombie. At seventeen, and like every teenager, he thought he had seen it all. He had not. Cell phone in hand, he walks into his parents' room. They are sleeping. He switches on the lights and stares at them. He doesn't say anything. Seconds pass. They seem like an eternity. Carmen, his mom, opens her eyes and gasps.

"What are you doing there? What are you doing there? Are you okay? Pedro, wake up, something's wrong with the boy!" she yells at her husband as she shakes him.

Pedro wakes up. Both parents wait for Camilo to say something. He says nothing. The screen of his cell phone is on.

"Camilo, could you tell us what's going on?" "I told you, woman, this boy is glued to that damn device... all day long. Look, he looks like a zombie!" his dad remarks.

Without saying a word, Camilo hands them the cell phone and gestures for them to read what is on the screen. Pedro grabs the cell phone. Reads the news. As he cross himself, he says to his wife:

"We're fucked, Carmencita, we're fucked!"

He drops the cell phone.

It is a fact: Jesus Christ has been cloned.

The rules where broken. In Times Square, New York, the screens quickly switch to show the details of the big event.

The news immediately goes viral. Around the world, everything seems to be in chaos. Telephones ring. There is no one who is not looking at their cell phone, keeping note of what is happening. #cloningofjesus is trending worldwide in a matter of minutes.

The Vatican is in an uproar. It's nine o'clock in the morning in the heart of the Catholic Church. It's a sunny, if slightly chilly day, like any other. Inside the world's smallest city-state, silence has descended.

Some are astonished, others outraged. The news had been rumored for months, but no one believed that these scientists would dare to cross the line. What a way to celebrate Christmas time! Science has won the battle against religion. The shock is worldwide.

CHAPTER I
THE BEGINNING

1

Arnaldo Romero is part of the Roman dome. A scientific priest. Mexican. He comes from a working-class family. His passion for science and religion blend seamlessly. He loves science as the way to test what escapes human understanding. He loves the Eucharist and recognizes it as the living presence of Jesus among us. He speaks five languages.

On December 12, 1994, the Day of the Virgin of Guadalupe and his 28th birthday, he was ordained a priest. This ingrained in him a certainty that everything concerning Mary marked his life.

His ambitions did not reach joining the Vatican's close circle. When he was young, he just wanted to serve his people face to face, to serve the neediest. However, his passion for science and his speech, led him much further in the curia of the Church. At the age of 39, he was summoned to Rome to serve in the Pontifical Academy of Sciences of the Vatican, the only international center of sciences in the world made up of 80 eminent and pontifically appointed individuals, among the most notable scientists in the planet.

The perfect place where his two greatest passions would come together: science and faith. However, it was also a place where they would collide.

In the beginning, he was the second in charge.

He spent long hours studying Gregor Mendel, who was considered the father of genetics and was also a priest. Arnaldo obtained a Ph.D. in Mathematics and

Sciences. He was part of various research projects in Genetics at the Roslin Institute in Scotland.

On April 9, 2005, he arrived at the Casina Pio IV, in the Vatican City, in the gardens of the heart of Rome. The headquarters of the Pontifical Academy of Sciences are pinpointed there.

A week earlier, the night before Divine Mercy Sunday, Pope John Paul II had passed away. An aura of mourning, sadness, and uncertainty hung in the air. The conclave to elect Peter's successor had not yet gathered. You could sense the turmoil.

He always used to dress in black and wear his clerical collar. The Ford Focus that transported him to the Academy was of the same color.

"Visiting, Father? I'm asking because of your suitcase," said the driver.

"No," he firmly denied. "I've come to work. To stay here."

The car arrived at the entrance of the academy, where there were rectangles, friezes, and reliefs. It was a typical trend within the Medici's circle at the time of Leo X, around the year 1513.

He observed the coat of arms of Pius IV in the center of the façade and, towards the lobby, a bas-relief of Artemis of the Ephesians. The same Greek goddess of nature, who not only gave life but also took it away.

He climbed out with confidence. When he took his suitcase, his suit stretched and left visible a cross tattoo on his left wrist. In the upper right and lower left vortex, appeared the letter c in each quadrant.

The driver could not help but ask.

"Excuse me, but this is the first time I see a priest with a tattoo. I didn't know you could do that!"

"Ha ha ha! This happened before I took my vows. I was young, you know how that goes."

"Of course! I got tattooed when I was young too!"

The driver quickly rolled up his shirt sleeve to proudly display the artwork on his skin.

"I got this one on my forearm for a girlfriend. And this one for another. After that, I stopped getting tattooed. If I'd continued like that, I would be marked by more girlfriends," he said confidently and mischievously. "You've wanted to be a priest since then? I saw the cross."

"It was a coincidence. I guess the call was already in me. I don't even remember why I had it done!" he answered quickly, trying to change the subject.

Of course, he clearly remembered the moment and the meaning of that tattoo. A flashback of that night came to his mind. The first one in which the alcohol made him forget even what his name was. When he kissed Alma, the girl he liked, but also tried to feel up, which got him punched in the eye. That is why he didn't go home that day: so neither his mom nor his dad would notice. On the night he got the tatoo, it was the night of the covenant.

In either case, there was the cross, calling out to him, sealing his life.

As the driver continued chatting to him, with effort, Arnaldo cracked a smile. Discreetly, he pulled down the sleeve of his shirt.

"It is time," he said out loud. He touched instinctively the crucifix on his chest that had accompanied him since before his ordination.

He entered the enclosure. He identified himself. He was immediately escorted into one of the rooms.

The director of the Academy of Sciences of the Vatican, Dr. Arner, was waiting for him. He was a Swiss microbiologist. He had followed Father Arnaldo's career closely. He had heard a lot about him.

They had spoken over the phone. It was the first time they would see each other face to face. There were also some researchers and the prefect of the Vatican Secret Archive.

"Father Arnaldo! Welcome!" said Dr. Arner at the same time he extended his hand enthusiastically and gripped Arnaldo's hand firmly. "It is a pleasure to have you here with us. The Pope held you in great esteem."

"What a joy that we finally meet each other! I am honored to be here!"

"This is Giacomo Ronconi, Prefect of the Vatican Secret Archive, and Alberto Benítez, who was the personal secretary of our beloved Pope John Paul II, may he rest in peace."

"My pleasure!" said Arnaldo as he shook their hands.

"I also heard about you a few times from the Holy Father," said the late Pope's personal secretary.

"I insist, it is an honor for me to be here and serve you," said Arnaldo.

"You've arrived at a particularly complicated but transformative time. We'll catch up later. In any case, I wanted to welcome you and show you your office. Come with me," said Arner.

It was at the end of a corridor. A medium-sized space. There was a mahogany shelf filled with books at the front. On one side, a white wall where only hung an image of Christ.

"In this computer, you have access to all the papers, research, and work done at the academy. There are the passwords. Make yourself comfortable. You can take a walk around the place if you wish. I'll be back later to talk to you," said Dr. Arner.

Certainly, the history of everything the academy had researched and followed closely was there.

The wheel was just beginning to turn.
That man, who in the beginning only wanted to serve his people, was inside.
His presence would shake the foundations of everything he touches.

2

The Catholic Church has been a perfect target for conspiracy theorists, who exist not only outside but also within. From immemorial alliances with secret societies and Judeo-Masonic plot theories; to the well-known *thesis of Cardinal Siri*, which throws out the idea that the chair of Peter has been occupied for decades by false Popes.

Once again, a new conspiracy theory comes to light. According to it, within the Catholic Church, there are infiltrators in the higher ranks. They are an important part of a select "club" that seeks absolute control.

It also includes heads of government, presidents of multinationals, tycoons, bankers, economists, royalty, and heads of the world's media.

It consists of an exclusive list of globally influential figures who are united not only by money but also by power. If true, the gaze of some representatives of the Church is not centered on Jesus as is well professed. The information is confusing. It's not clear what's true and what's a lie. It's not clear who is an ally or an enemy.

As a result, tensions began to escalate, disrupting the functioning of this ecclesiastical body. Chaos broke out.

It is said that this "club" seeks to bring down the Church, among other things. They want to build a new one, tailored to their needs. The reality is that, beyond these theories, the group does exist. It established its bases in the 1950s, after World War II. Since then, they coordinate a meeting every year, attended by the 120 most influential people on the planet. The location varies from year to year. They alternate between North America, Europe, and Western Asia. The meetings last four days and are held in luxurious seven-star hotels and palaces. The press has no access whatsoever.

Its name is "Nuremberg Club."

Each meeting is a glorious party where the safety of the attendees is considered a priority. Generally, the army takes charge of security where the meeting takes place. They are accompanied by the most exclusive private security team in the world where the smallest details are considered.

While the potentates meet, the airspace is closed in a range of 31 miles. It cannot be any different. The masters of the world are all reunited in the same place. They are billionaires. Powerful. Some of them blinded by something more dangerous than greed: their eagerness to rewrite history.

The logistics are not simple. The parlors where they meet must achieve rigorous requirements. They must be spacious, with high walls. They must have large windows that allow natural light to enter. All of them, dressed on both sides with long beige silk curtains. The tables must be rectangular. Long. Light table linen, very delicate; with lace in the same tones as the curtains. Simple, exquisite. In the center, there are bouquets with kadupul flowers.

Chairs should be uniformly dressed. In perfect symmetry. White glove services are a must. Among the women, there is a pattern that distinguishes them. They highlight simplicity, elegance, and good taste. They don't flaunt many accessories, but each piece is a work of art by itself. They all wear branded clothes: Oscar de la Renta, Gucci, Prada, Alexander McQueen. The most daring combine their outfit with denim. To pass by is to be impregnated with the most exquisite smells of perfume.

Men tend to be elegantly more conventional. They wear suits by brands such as Ralph Lauren, Brunello Cucinelli and Alexander McQueen. On their wrists, Rolex and Chopard 201.

The atmosphere is one of dark secrecy. Perhaps that is why what is said about them gains additional significance: that they want to establish a new world order and a universal Church. Their final objective is to control absolutely everything. They have the power, the money, and the means. They cannot only change the course and history of a country but also of the world.

Theories show that in these meetings they plan the events that irremediably, later, happen.

They pull the invisible strings that govern our destiny. From the spheres of power, they shape our way of thinking.

To what extent do we believe that our thoughts are our own?

Just the thought of it makes the skin crawl.

Some of the people who are part of the Nuremberg Club are Freemasons. They no longer wear aprons or meet in lodges; that is done by the lowest ranks. They are at another level, exquisite in every sense. They also belong to the so-called *Order of Malta*. They know the Church inside out and know how to implode it.

Every year, they reunite under Chatham's House rule. It states that, at the end of each meeting, although those present may discuss the results of the seminar with the outside world, under no circumstances may they mention who attended or tell what a specific individual said. Who they talk to is '33rd degree'. It's confidential. When someone attends, they cannot leave the place.

Even if someone has enough power and money, they cannot participate in these meetings. They must be summoned by its members. Their movements have been stealthily followed by investigators. By journalists. By the Church. And by a former Russian counterintelligence analyst, who for the next years will focus his studies on this power elite.

His name: Anatoly Stuling.

He speaks Russian, English and Spanish. He belongs to an extensive family of men linked to science. His father, Mikhail Stuling, is a scientist as well, and was invited to join the Club of Rome, a non-profit organization founded in 1968. This non-profit organization is considered a first cousin of the Nuremberg Club, composed of scientists and politicians concerned with improving the long-term future of the world.

In the case of Mikhail Stuling, the invitation was coordinated by the renowned Russian scientist Dimitriv Basov, who was part of the club's board of directors. Years earlier, he had shared some important research in the field of science with Anatoly's father. They became close friends but drifted apart due to some political and even religious differences. It was time to meet again.

The annual Nuremberg meeting was only a week away when Mikhail received the invitation. He was not part of this prestigious Club, nor did he know about it.

The special missive was signed by his old friend Dimitriv Basov. He was incredibly happy to see his name. The only decision Mikhail had to make was whether to attend. With expenses covered and such an interesting opportunity, he did not give it much thought.

He traveled from Russia to Milan, Italy, on Aeroflot Airlines, one of the oldest airlines in the world. Estimated flight time: 3 hours 22 minutes. Seats designed to make the ride pleasant. He had never traveled first class before. He was surprised that these chair-beds could be transformed into a work-study. He had never seen anything like it.

The beauty of the flight attendants enchanted him. Elegant and tall. With red skirts and jackets. White gloves. Exquisite. A scarf of the same color tied around their necks gave them a distinguished air.

He thought of his wife, Ivanna. About what she would feel like if they could travel one day like this. They had been married for almost 40 years and had a love that made envious young and old alike. As a good Russian, he believed that to have a successful trip he had to sit quietly for a long time.

"What do they want? Maybe Dimitriv needs me to join him in some important research," he said to himself.

The flight attendant thought she heard something. She approached him.

"Is everything alright, sir? Do you need something?"

"Yes, everything's fine," he answered nervously. It was then that he realized he was speaking out loud. Fortunately, the seat next to him was empty.

Minutes later, dinner time arrived. It was served in a glass and porcelain tableware set. First dish: *borscht*, a vibrant red vegetable soup, which includes beetroots. Second dish: delicious *pelmeni*. He felt like a God. To drink, vodka was a must. He could not believe it. Time really flew by. He heard the flight attendant's announcement. They landed in Milan.

He arrived at the hotel at almost ten o'clock at night. He was assigned a suite on the eighth floor. It was furnished in a modern Milanese style and the terrace overlooked the city. He placed his luggage on the floor. The bed was king-size. He sat on it. It was much more comfortable than the one he used at home. The event would be held in twelve hours.

He picked up the room phone and dialed the operator.

"Good evening. Could you please connect me with Dimitriv Basov?"

"Just a moment, I'll connect you."

The noise of the telephone woke Dimitriv. He did not expect any call. He answered, shaken.

"Hello! Who's talking?"

"Dimitriv, it's Mikhail! Sorry I woke you up, I'm already here at the hotel."

"That's okay! Welcome! It's a pleasure to have you here! I'm glad you could come. How was the flight?"

"It was great! I'm excited. I don't know what this is all about, but thanks for the invitation."

"We'll catch up tomorrow. Is it okay if we meet at seven and have breakfast together?"

"Sure!"

"We can meet at Palazzo Parigi. The restaurant is located at the back of the hotel. It consists of a terrace with a private garden."

"Sounds perfect to me! See you tomorrow then!"

He left everything organized and got ready to sleep.

As it did every day, his biological clock caused him to wake up at five o'clock. However, it was only four in the morning. It was impossible to go back to sleep. He decided to get up, take a shower, sit on the terrace of the suite, and wait for sunrise.

Seeing that the sun was already showing its first traces, he took his brown briefcase, put on the id card included in the welcome packet, and went down to the lobby. As he exited the elevator, he paused to observe the majestic spaces in detail. An exquisite blend of marble and rich woodwork. There were works of art and antiques everywhere. A magical and enveloping illumination was filtered through a huge central skylight. It was a luxury to which he was not used to, and which amazed him like a child.

The signaling was delicate. It showed the way to the spa, restaurants, and event rooms. The Golden Palace, the Club of Rome's meeting site, was on the right. In that same direction were the halls of the Golden Supreme, where the Nuremberg Club would meet. On the left, the way to Palazzo Parigi. His long-time friend was waiting for him there.

He saw him from afar. It was impossible not to. His corpulent body, now with a little more weight, always stood out. His hair was already white. Years do not pass in vain. He was reading some documents while smoking his third cigarette of the morning.

"My friend and colleague!" said Mikhail excitedly as he approached him.

Dimitriv placed the documents on the table. The cover clearly read «*Progetto ROMA – Nuovo secolo, Nuovo uomo*». They embraced each other affectionately. As they took their seats, he hurried to stow them in his leather briefcase. On the lower part were embroidered the initials DB in gothic letters.

It was November 1997.

Two years and a month for the change of century.

They talked about what had happened in their lives during the nine years they had lost contact. Finally, they got down to business.

"Well, tell me a bit more about this club. Why the invitation? For which I thank you in advance," said Mikhail.

"Having you here is a privilege. For several years now, we have been bringing together renowned scientists and leaders from different sectors to discuss issues of global interest. Nobel Prize winners. Personalities from the highest spheres. We talk about the changes occurring on this planet because of our actions. We anticipate events that may be feasible and present reports so that measures can be taken, or impacts can be minimized around a specific issue. We do not always achieve consensus, but this is done up to the implementation of the projects."

"Who puts them into operation?"

"Final decisions are made by an organization known as the Nuremberg Club. You could say they sway several projects. They evaluate them and oversee their implementation. We suggest them and they decide."

"Are they here?"

"Yes. Two meetings are held in parallel here: Nuremberg and Rome."

"Sounds interesting"

If you put it like that, it certainly, was.
He would soon have a radical change of heart. Not only would it be a shock to his paradigms, but it would also be a shock to his life and the lives of his loved ones.

Hours passed rapidly. The clock was close to striking ten o'clock in the morning when they looked at it. They hurried to charge the expenses to their rooms and headed to the hall.

For the Nuremberg event, about 100 people were present. 52 participant countries. The *crème de la crème.*

The group of attendees for the Club of Rome was smaller.

In both cases, participants were required to sign a contract or legal document that obliged them not to share, under any circumstances, the information about the persons who spoke in the meetings. To do so would entail significant international sanctions.

Mikhail didn't see anything wrong with this. He signed without giving it much thought.

Unfortunately, he had no malice.

The main discussion at Nuremberg was held in the Supreme Palace, a large hall dressed in floor-sweeping silk curtains and hanging glass chandeliers made of rock crystal. The topics of discussion varied between the crisis of institutions, the models of social simulation, and the general changes for the new century.

In addition, private rooms are arranged for certain meetings of Nuremberg Group. The access to these is limited. The number of participants reduced. It is the most exclusive of exclusiveness.

The issues addressed here are entirely controversial. They can call into question the values of any ordinary mortal. In these halls the discussions become heated and chilling.

On the third day, between ingenuity and a security error, Mikhail managed to get into one of these rooms. The meeting was just starting. There were fifteen persons. A renowned sociologist and economist was the speaker. He was talking about Malthusianism, a demographic and social theory that emerged towards the end of the 19th century, which poses the problem of overpopulation of the poor and working class. One of the solutions: limited procreation. However, this time there was an extra element to this theory. They spoke of the importance of broad social cleansing. Something like modern eugenics.

"We are already living overpopulated. There are too many poor and unskilled middle-class people."

"At our previous meeting, we raised the importance of reducing the world's population by 75% by the year 2045. In other words, 4 billion people must not only disappear, but it is imperative that they are not replaced."

"We have great news! The club has approved our application. It is estimated that the first phase will take place by 2019-2020. They will let us know how they are going to do it."

Those present applauded enthusiastically.

The more he listened, the more surprised Mikhail became.

What was all that about?
What was he doing in that place?
He did not know what to think.

In the adjoining private room, a much darker idea was being discussed. Fortunately, Mikhail did not listen. The certain possibility of human cloning. The cloning of a man that could change the course of history.

Again.

Mikhail was torn between shock and awe. A beautiful, tall, and athletic woman approached him. She was in a black blouse with a skirt. A very thin, fuchsia-colored strap that emphasizes, even more her tiny waist. She looked about 22 years old. She touched him gently on the back. As he turned around, he is impregnated by her scent and mesmerized by her black wavy hair. She belongs to the security corps. He had to accompany her; he could not be there. He had broken the rules.

Dazed and disoriented, he apologized. He did not know what to think after what he had just heard. He started walking through the corridor. The place no longer looked the same. Now, it was shady. He wandered. That sounded like a nightmare.

He decided to go to the bathroom to wash his face. As he entered the toilet, he bumped into someone coming out. To his surprise, it was Dimitriv.

"Hello, my friend! It's you! What happened to you? I lost you when I entered the Rome session," said Dimitriv when he saw his guest.

"I was wandering around and entered one of the small rooms."

"How did you do that? They are restricted!" he said, astonished.

"It was a mistake. I realized that afterward. They removed me after a while."

"Everything okay?" he asked to calm his friend at the sight of his distorted face.

"Yes," he hesitated. "I'd like to talk with you."

"Of course. Let's meet at six o'clock at the hotel's bar at the end of the talks."

"I'll be there! I need a good drink."

Dimitriv left and Mikhail took zombie steps towards the sink. When he turned around, he saw a briefcase somebody had forgotten. He recognized instantly the embroidery of the initials. He knew it was his friend's. There was no doubt he had left it behind. A flashback came into his head of the nervous way Dimitriv had put the report away the day they met. He then recalled the word *ROMA*. In a fraction of seconds, the complete text *'Progetto ROMA - Nuovo secolo, Nuovo uomo'*.

Was his friend engaged in all of this?
The threads were beginning to weave together. It
could not be.

"*Nuovo secolo, nuovo uomo,*" he said out loud as he remembered.

What was in that report? After what he heard, his scientific instincts told him something was up.

His heart started beating rapidly.

He took the briefcase and went into one of the cubicles in the bathroom. He closed the door. His hands started sweating. He lowered the toilet lid. He sat on it. He opened the briefcase carefully. With trembling hands, he began to rummage. He found the document. The title was no longer an image in his head, he could see it before his eyes. He started reading the first lines. The more he did so, the more his heart raced.

A secret with traces of death.

"It can't be! This must be a mistake. This is crazy!" he thought.

Insanity is said to be a reckless, foolish action.
That is exactly what he would do.

He decided to close the briefcase and run out of the place. That is literally what happened. He ran away. He went up to his room and packed everything into his carry-on luggage. Without warning. Without saying goodbye. He took his things. He left.

Hours later, when he was on the plane back to Russia, he realized what a crazy thing he had done.

"What happened to me? How could I have stolen Dimitriv's briefcase? What am I doing?"

It would have been easier to stay and continue as if nothing had happened. To corroborate if everything was true. Not to let impulse dominate actions. To inquire further, to seek the truth.

What was he to do with what he had in his hands?

When the plane's signals went off, he got up from his seat and opened the head compartment. He took down the suitcase and pulled out the report. He began to read it carefully. He would have just over three hours to devour it.

The more he read, the more he was tormented by it all.

In his mind, he was fixated on the idea of dismantling what these people were up to.

He never considered who he was dealing with.

Among the hypotheses through which he rambled; he never conceived the fate that awaited him. If what was written there was true, the apocalypse itself was in the making.

Humanity, the Church, and history itself would change forever. A Machiavellian mixture between the return to the dark ages and Dante's Divine Comedy, which would definitively open the gates of hell.

CHAPTER II
FLESH AND BLOOD

1

Man is always seeking the truth. His truth. The one that gives meaning, origin, and destiny to his existence.

Who, in one way or another, has not undertaken this crusade?

"...and ye shall know the truth, and the truth shall make you free..." reads the Biblical passage.

Some seek truth in faith, others in science. There are people who combine both territories. A truth verified by science and based on faith becomes a solid foundation.

Also a sure stir.

Jesus Christ's story is, without doubt, one of these truths. A man of faith, of proven existence. A transgressor who came to transform humanity.

His life is recorded in the so-called Canonical Gospels. Those that the Church recognizes by apostolic tradition as inspired by God.

These are the allowed ones.

But there are also the forgotten gospels. Those forbidden by the Church. They are known as the Apocryphal Gospels. They include hidden details of the events recounted by the Evangelists. One of them is the gospel called 'The Doctrine of Judas Thaddeus', which narrates the legend of the image of Edessa or

Mandylion; known today as the Holy Shroud. It tells that the Image of Edessa, which wrapped Jesus, was more than a piece of cloth.

Thaddeus narrates how King Abgar of Edessa, whose health was fragile and delicate, had written a letter to the Messiah asking for a miracle for his healing. Jesus answered him that, when his mission on Earth was finished, he would send someone to cure his illness. After his resurrection, the apostle Thaddeus took the Shroud to King Abgar, along with a letter from Jesus telling him to keep it for good health. Thus, the king, after being cured, converted to Christianity, and the precious mantle was kept hidden in Edessa until the conquest of the Persians in 609.

Since then, the itinerary of the Holy Shroud has been traced back to what is considered its presence in our days.

This Shroud of Turin is a linen cloth, 14.3 feet in length. On it is printed the image and blood of a tortured man, with wounds and physical traumas. A man who died by crucifixion. That is why it is considered a relic of the first order. Hence the fascination that surrounds this piece of cloth; a symbol of life.

Of eternal life.

One of the people who had access to the Shroud of Turin was Dr. Max Frei-Sulzer, a botanist and director of the Scientific Service of the Zurich City Police. Also a Professor of Forensic Science. A Protestant. A relic skeptic.

However, in 1973, this man of great international reputation obtained the approval of the authorities to extract dust samples from the Shroud of Turin and to carry out some analyses.

The result of the report showed that the Shroud contained pollen dating back to the first century. Around the head and abdomen of the image of that mantle, they found 28 different types of flowers. They correspond to flowers that were found in the surroundings of Jerusalem at the time of Jesus.

How can we be certain that the image really belonged to the man from Judea who changed history?

They repeated the study in 1978. During that time, it would be examined by a group of scientists to look for new data to prove its veracity. The Vatican allowed access to the Holy Shroud for 120 hours.

The project was called STURP (Shroud of Turin Research Project) and was developed to analyze the Shroud of Turin, in which the body of Jesus is believed to have been wrapped after his death. More than thirty experts in various fields were convened for this research project: scientists, thermal physicists, forensic pathologists, and chemists. In short, true eminences.

Among the scientists who were part of STURP were Kevin Davis, Ph.D., a biochemist, and Darnell Mullis, Ph.D., in biology and an embryologist. Mullis was sagacious, intelligent, calculating, and quiet. Tall, fair complexion, almond-shaped eyes. He had worked at the European Molecular Biology Organization. He was 49 years old.

There he met Dr. Davis, who stood out in the study group for his sharpness and tiny size. Kevin was the youngest. Simply brilliant. He could create algorithms in his mind that could decipher the results before even capturing them on paper. He was, in fact, a prodigy, a genius. That extreme intelligence was mixed with his personality. Sometimes he was eccentric; always agreeable, talkative. He was one of those kind people.

The investigation began in Turin on October 9th. Kevin had a long trip ahead of him. It would be the most sumptuous laboratory he would ever work in. Nothing less than the Royal Palace of the House of Savoy.

He arrived in Northern Italy on October 1st, from the mountains of Silicon Valley in California. The next day was the start of the preparation phase, so he would only have one day to overcome the jet lag. It is not easy to adapt to nine hours of time difference.

According to the schedule they sent him, it would be a tight one. They should participate in a previous congress. The days of investigation where the Shroud was going to be analyzed would be from the 9th to the 13th.

That sunny day of October 2nd, Kevin was in the central square of the castle at ten o'clock in the morning; enraptured by the sober and baroque *façade* of that palace, a World Heritage Site. To the left of that majesty was the Chapel of the Holy Shroud.

Even for a skeptic like him, that place was surrounded by an indescribable mystical atmosphere; one of those that cannot be explained but can be felt. He walked in with characteristic confidence as if he had known the place forever. He marveled at the paintings of cherubs hanging on the high walls.

The central corridor served as an entrance hall. A large number of men were conversing with each other. They were the scientists with whom he would share in the days to come. They were mostly Americans. They had taken with them 72 boxes of the most sophisticated research equipment.

Some of them seemed to know each other. Others met on site. Kevin was no exception. Being the youngest, outgoing and friendly, he did not go unnoticed.

"Glad to meet you! I am Dr. Kevin Davis. Excuse me, your name?"

"Mullis, Dr. Darnell Mullis. My pleasure!"

"Your face looks familiar. Do you work at Lawrence Berkeley National Laboratory?"

"No," he answered kindly. His brashness reminded him of himself when he was young.

"Then I know you from somewhere else. You look familiar."

"Must be from life. Maybe you were my double," Mullis replied, smiling.

Finally, the long-awaited day had arrived. They divided teams into twenty-four-hour shifts. While some slept, others conducted research and then switched. This way, the work would continue uninterrupted.

Mullis and Davis were in the same shift.

The STURP organizing team had allocated seven rooms for this purpose. The equipment stood out against the carved wooden furniture, and silver and gold ornaments that adorned each room.

All were called to the precinct. On a tilting aluminum table, the most studied Christian relic in history was spread out: the Holy Shroud. Without wasting time, they began the evaluations in small groups. The analyses were diverse: infrared, ultraviolet, X-rays, scientific photography, and thermography. The list was very extensive.

As a way to protect what was about to be evaluated, there were no security cameras on site.

Everything went as planned.

Although the work did not stop, they had a few breaks for coffee and stretching. That was the day Darnell Mullis and Kevin Davis stopped by to talk about the experience.

"The days have gone by fast, don't you think? I think it's been interesting." Mullis pointed out.

"As for me, I think the investigation has been simplistic," Davis replied, coffee in hand.

"What do you mean?"

"Don't you think another type of observation is missing? We are supposed to be here to determine the veracity, or lack of, this sheet. It has been four days and we still do not have an answer. We have all this equipment and I feel it has been unsuccessful."

"Why do you say that?" insisted Mullis.

"We know that it is not a painting. Thus, we discard the hypothesis of art: How did this linear image that starts from the front and ends at the back appear on the canvas? It is anatomically correct. It is impregnated with the blood stains of a tortured and crucified man—"

Mullis interrupted him.

"But we have not finished yet. We are arguing that the image could be a product of the body's exudations between the embalming ointments, right?

"Yes, but when we say that the man on the canvas had contusions, more than 120 lacerations on his back, legs, and shoulders, it's also worth asking 'can any "normal" human being endure that'?"

"What's wrong with you? Now you're being romantic about it."

"I'm just asking myself questions."

"In the past few days, you told me that you did not believe in this Jesus. I listen to you now and I wonder if you have changed your mind. Dr. Kevin became a believer," he said with sarcasm.

"There are several things in this evaluation coincide with the Biblical account, even if I do not believe and neither do you. But at some point in this process, hasn't doubt been planted in you? Let's face it, this is out of the ordinary," claimed Kevin.

"You're right about that! But I insist, our job is objective. These are our conclusions. The printed image could well be a photographic negative," said Mullis, trying to convince himself. He wanted to erase from his mind Davis's reflections.

"Explain this to me. Are there any conclusions for you? I feel that we have not reached the bottom. If it is a photographic negative as you say, we would be in front of the first proto-photograph in history. If so, it could get worse. We have to ask ourselves other questions." The tone of the conversation became intense. "Besides, that man's blood is real and belongs to the AB group," Kevin insisted.

One of the investigators was following the discussion from a distance. He did not intervene. He had Asian features and wore large black rimless glasses.

Another of the scientists who was listening to them approached. He decided to interrupt them very respectfully:

"Excuse me, colleagues, for butting in. It was impossible not to overhear your conversation. I am a man of science as you are, but also a man of faith. Have you heard about the Eucharistic miracle of Lanciano?"

They both shook their heads. They looked at each other, surprised by the comment.

"That happened more than 1,300 years ago. By that time, a Basilian monk was celebrating Mass while doubting the presence of Jesus in the Eucharist. At that moment, before his gaze and that of all the faithful, the host became flesh and the wine became blood. Even today, thirteen centuries later, they are preserved as the flesh and blood of a living person."

Kevin and Mullis paid attention with skepticism.

"Of a living person?" asked Mullis.

"Yes. Alive! Seven years ago, in 1971, a professor of Anatomy and Pathological Histology named Odoardo Linoli made a study on that host. The result showed that it is myocardial tissue from a human heart that is alive and... do you want to know which blood group it belongs to?"

"AB group?" asked Kevin.

"Exactly! The same one as the Shroud. If you stay here for a few more days, I'll invite you to visit the Franciscan church in the center of Lanciano. You could see it there with your own eyes."

They did not know what to say. This man took them out of context. Mullis's expression started to change.

"I can only tell you that in the things of God, sometimes the explanations of science do not exist. I studied science because I wanted to somehow prove the existence of God. I understood it doesn't work like this. Science requires certainties and religion requires faith, but sometimes both can go hand in hand."

A profound silence reigned in the air.

At that moment, they heard the voice of one of the coordinators. It was time to return to the research rooms. They said goodbye. The man was heading to the adjoining room where Kevin and Mullis would be going.

Although those days had made him question himself, Kevin Davis remained a man of science alone. Faith was not his thing. However, there are questions that, as they make their way into your psyche, open up new possibilities for what would not have been possible before.

"What would Jesus be like today?"

"Could science ever create a God or even surpass it?"

Those were the questions that began to swirl around in Davis's head.

There was only one day left to conclude the investigation.

Both his curiosity and his scruples knew no bounds.

New questions kept appearing.

"What if there really was Jesus and that was the blanket that covered him?"

"How can I check it without time constraints?"

"Will I be able to stand again in front of such an indecipherable relic?"

He did not ask any more questions. He decided to go one step further.

Mullis was talking to one of his colleagues in the room (he was the scientist with the big black rimless glasses who was listening to them outside). They were in a corner of the inn.

Kevin walked to the opposite corner. He took some notes. At least, that was what it looked like. He slid his hand into his left pocket. Subtly and stealthily, he pulled out a tiny pair of scissors. As if he had rehearsed it a thousand times, in a kind of magic act, he cut a minimal portion of the sample where it was impregnated with blood.

It happened fast. A question of seconds.

Just as quickly, he put everything back in his pocket. Nobody saw it.

At least, that is what he thought.

2

Not only American scientists participated in STURP.

Jun Lee is also a renowned researcher from a humble Asian family. He was born in North Korea, four years before the end of World War II. Although much of the population in North Korea is atheist, he comes from a Christian family. Believer, although not practicing, since Catholicism cannot be practiced.

During the Korean War, his mother met a very sweet and supportive neighbor. The woman was a Catholic and they quickly became friends. In the midst of the nightmare, they prayed together in secret, pleading with God to put an end to it all.

But she carried another cross on her shoulders. Several crosses, to be more honest.

She thought her son had been born with some defect. When he was inside her belly she did not feel him move. He spoke his first word when he was four. So, between prayers, she not only prayed for the end of the war, but also for her son's health.

This is how she met Jesus. But this was as close as she and her loved ones came to any religion.

Three years later, her prayers bore fruit. At least partly. Lee was already talking and the war was over. But another battle that was more intense, cruel, grotesque, and unimaginable broke out inside her own home, annihilating everything in its path. The woman was devastated. Without thinking, she grabbed her things and decided to run away with her son. She went to the United States.

They arrived in the District of Columbia, a poor, ugly, and dirty neighborhood in the middle of the capital of the most powerful country in the world. Nearby was a park with rusty swings. Dry grass. It was a place where rats were confused with squirrels.

Children hung out in gangs. Some of them were colored, others were Caucasians. Almost all of them were untamed mischief-makers. Jun Lee stood out for his Asian features and transparent white skin. As soon as they saw him, they would pick on him. They pushed him, spat on him, threw stones at him, and made fun of his glasses.

"Four eyes! Chinese four-eyes!" they shouted to him while they laughed.

His glasses were too big. The black plastic frame matched the color of his straight hair. That is how his mother had bought them so that they would last a long time. Lee was a laconic. He learned to use silence to evade his pain.

The pain he harbored on the inside was heartbreaking.

He had a nervous tic, and, to top it off, the poor guy was short in stature. In other words, he was the perfect target to suffer bullying.

As Jun Lee grew older, he became more reclusive, introverted, and sullen. He locked himself in books. He studied all the time with delirious obsession. With everything he learned, he awakened, even more, the genius that lived inside him.

This is how he discovered that science would be his life.

He graduated with honors in 1970 with a degree in Molecular Bioscience from Washington State University. He quickly began working at one of the largest research centers in North America, the Institute for Advanced Study in Princeton, New Jersey; the same one that served as Albert Einstein's work center.

Eight years later he was assigned by the research center to participate in a study commission to examine the Holy Shroud.

He considered himself an agnostic, which made his participation in the STURP evaluation ideal, as it guaranteed impartiality in his observations.

In fact, it was the first time he heard about the Shroud of Turin.

He decided to find out about that giant cloth. He frequented the library in search of books that could help him know a little more. That is how he learned the story of the Holy Shroud. He read that Hitler had entertained the idea of appropriating the Shroud. Since then, his curiosity has been piqued.

"Why the obsession with this Shroud?"

"What does it hide?"

"Is it true?" he asked himself.

During the Second World War, Pope Pius XII, who ruled the Catholic Church, decided to send this Sacred Mantleto to the sanctuary of Montevergine to save it from bombing. Not for nothing has it been the subject of debate among the most renowned researchers, theologians, scientists, and historians over the years. It is the same Holy Shroud spoken of in the Apocryphal Gospels.

Lee could not wait to embark on that journey. It was time to put science to the test and remove the veil of mystery against the dogma proclaimed by faith.

He could never have imagined the destiny to which this investigation would lead him.

A package arrived in the mail. It included the schedule of their stay in the Italian city, as well as general observations on the use of the operation plan.

The organization was impeccable. Every detail spoke to the success of the program.

41

All team members had to be familiar with the plan by Monday, October 2. The manuals were extensive and detailed, which included blank pages, where they could take notes or make last-minute changes.

> *STURP Schedule:*
> *First week: October 2-6. Negotiations. Process of preparation.*
> *Dry experiments.*
> *October, Saturday 7 and Sunday 8: worldwide congress.*
> *October 9-12: physical evidence.*

It sounded interesting.

The organizers also warned that after their arrival in Turin, the press would try to approach them.

> *We do not anticipate any problems, but please do not complicate our situation by giving interviews to the press or even giving 'innocent' information to reporters of any kind. Reporters can put two and two together, and get four just like anyone else.*

"Interviews? For the press? Me? These people don't know who they have invited! Now, that's funny!" He laughed as he read it. It was one of the few times he did.

By the end of September, he landed in Turin.

The day arrived. He could rest. He stayed in his room and did not come out. He called the room service.

They would meet at ten o'clock in the morning.

He woke up early. He took out a beige three-piece suit from his suitcase. It had thin brown stripes that simulated squares. The shirt had a long collar and a very wide lapel, as did his pants. He had a high brown vest hidden underneath. He bought it to look presentable for the occasion. It was not his idea. The truth is his mother insisted so strongly that he had no choice.

The power she had over him was immense.

He was used to being punctual; sometimes excessively so. He was ready almost two and a half hours early. He went down to the hotel's reception and requested a cab. As he waited, he looked at the newspapers. There were some in Italian and others in Spanish. They were stacked on a pair of small round tables of thick glass, right next to black leather sofas. He took one. The Spanish newspaper *El País*. He began to read, and in less than three minutes the cab arrived.

"Can I take the newspaper?" he asked one of the bellhops.

"Of course, sir! It is all yours."

"Thank you so much!" he answered quickly.

He walked fast so as to not lose time. The taxi driver was waiting for him with the door open.

"Good morning," he said kindly to the driver. "My name is Dr. Lee."

"*Buongiorno!* Where do I have the pleasure of taking you?"

"To the Royal Palace of the House of Savoy, please."

He started reading the headlines in the newspaper.

He did not see that the newspaper was from the previous day.

The funeral of John Paul I is scheduled for Wednesday. The election of the new pope will begin on the 14th ... The practice of an autopsy to establish more accurately the cause of his death was excluded...

"These Church people are incredible! How can they not perform an autopsy? How can they not? Did he die of a heart attack or was he poisoned? That's crazy! If so, they won't even know! How absurd!" he commented out loud.

He was not far from reality.
Many years later, the truth about the death of that pope would be discovered.

"Excuse me, sir, but did you say something?" pointed the taxi driver.

"No, no. I'm sorry," he said apologetically, lowering his eyes and hiding behind his big black glasses.

He arrived so early at the Royal Palace of the House of Savoy, that only the place's security guard was there. He approached them, introduced himself, and was immediately looked up on the list. They let him in. He was the first one to arrive.

He entered the main hall and was engaged in observing the way the wooden furniture was carved, and engrossed in looking at the silver and gold ornaments. Half an hour later, one of the main event managers arrived. He went straight to introduce himself.

"Dr. Lee! *Benvenuto!* Andrea Rizzo of the Center of Sindonology of Rome. I'm one of the organizers of this meeting!"

Andrea approached effusively. He had to bow to greet him, as he was very tall. Meanwhile, he gave him a kiss on each cheek as is customary in Italy. Lee did not know what to do. It was the first time he had been greeted in this way. He got nervous. Andrea noticed. With his two hands, he took him by the shoulders warmly to make him feel confident, and looked him in the eyes while smiling.

"Ha ha ha! It's common to greet people like this in the area. Every foreigner always makes the same face when we kiss them on the cheek."

"Excuse me, I am not used to it," he answered almost inaudibly.

"Don't worry, over the coming days you will surely get used to it," he said with humor. "By the way, all the boxes have arrived. Very sophisticated equipment! They are in the halls. I have some business to take care of. This is your house. See you again!"

A few minutes later, the other invited researchers began to arrive. Lee had retreated to a corner. He waved to them from far away without saying a word, just nodding.

He saw a young man arrive who, in a few seconds, became the life of the party. He was another researcher. A bit too crazy for his taste. He was perhaps as extroverted as he wished to be deep down.

He listened to the way the young man introduced himself to those present.

It was with ease and self confidence.

"Glad to meet you! I am Dr. Kevin Davis. Excuse me, your name?"

"Mullis, Dr. Mullis." "My pleasure!"

The two researchers continued their conversation. Lee thought about approaching and breaking the fence that distanced him from the world. His imagination traveled through moments back to the time when he was a child. He no longer heard the voices of men of science; instead he heard those of the neighborhood children playing when he had decided to engage in conversation with strangers, for the time. There they pushed him, spat on him, broke his glasses, and mocked him.

He refrained from taking the initiative. In his anonymity, he felt safe. He preferred to stay that way.

Dr. Kevin saw the tiny researcher from a distance. He was approaching to introduce himself when Lee turned around. He slipped out of the room. He did not extend his hand to anyone.

From then on, he preferred not to be so punctual. In this way, everyone would be ready to start the day and there would be no time for chatting or greetings. Neither for embraces nor kisses.

Each day, before starting and as part of the protocol, one of the coordinators explained how the data would be collected.

"The X-ray source will operate during the test at 50 kVp, 20 mA. The ADC will be configured as well as the memory for 1,024 channels."

There, Lee was free.

There was no fear or anxiety.

Within the work environment, everything he heard was music to his ears.

He was born for science.

On a daily basis, the scientists met in small groups. They were to rotate between the different rooms according to a prior grouping made by the organizing team. That is why he did not meet that young man who greeted everyone until the last day.

That day in the room they were assigned to, they would be working with a potentially dangerous 50 kVp X-ray tube.

Dr. Darnell Mullis took over. He had already faced a similar team. He was in a corner next to Lee and another researcher when Kevin entered the room. Lee was afraid of being approached by that young man, so he concentrated on the analysis.

"Any results from the image analyzer?" asked Mullis.

"What it tells us is that the image has unique, three-dimensional information encoded in it," said another of the scientists.

"It is a fact that the Shroud has been in direct contact with a body." "That would explain the presence of the blood and the marks that are imprinted from the flagellum," Lee commented.

"Yes, but there is no way to explain it. At least, not with what we have now," another scientist mentioned.

Lee saw Kevin move to the opposite corner. He preferred to avert his gaze to avoid any eye contact. He concentrated on the conversation he was having with his two other colleagues. He said nothing more. He noted down his thoughts:

The image is an ongoing mystery and until further chemical studies are performed (perhaps by this group of scientists, or by others in the future), the problem will remain unsolved.

Hours later, the study ended.

In the main hallway, they were celebrating the work done.

Lee left without saying goodbye, ready to pack his things and catch the first flight back home.

Deep down he felt a bit empty. He was expecting a more convincing result.

His previous expectations had been higher. The debate was internal.

Had the veracity of that holy mantle been proven, then he would have had no choice but to accept the resurrection of Jesus. And for an agnostic, that was not easy.

Despite what Andrea said upon his arrival, he did not learn to give two kisses when greeting people. Fortunately for him, there were not many people in the airport lounge. He took a newspaper:

Swiss man and two Americans awarded Nobel Prize in Medicine.

American scientists Daniel Nathans and Hamilton Smith, and Swiss scientist Werner Arber were awarded the 1978's Nobel Prize in Medicine yesterday. Sweden's Karolinska Institute reported that Professor Arber discovered restriction enzymes; chemical compounds that allow scientists to understand the genetic character of organisms. This research raises hopes for genetic manipulation...

Although he does not know it yet, that will also be his destiny.

He will genetically manipulate.

He will be recognized.

If anything had remained in Lee after the STURP experience, it was the fervent desire to see face to face the one who years earlier had become his greatest enemy.

The enemy who did not save him as a child.

The one who let his mother suffer.
He wanted to complain to him, to demand answers.
And in due course, eliminate him.

(3

"The bread which I will give is my flesh, for the life of the world."

John 6:51

It did not take long for Father Arnaldo to learn all the mechanics of the Pontifical Academy of Sciences, nor what was handled there. On his computer, he had access to all saved papers and research.

Sometimes what we are most looking for may be right in front of us and we do not see it.

For some years he had been doing research on some topics that he had to approach with caution. Within the ecclesiastical institution, it is not easy to consider as "true" some facts "outside the rational." The task of validating them is a long one. To do so, they must be governed by canons or tests determined by this Roman body.

In any case, a scientist who is a priest must proceed with much more discernment than a layman. Discernment requires inner silence, and this has been difficult for Father Arnaldo lately. He knows that he has violated some internal rules.

He sometimes finds it difficult to navigate the Vatican bureaucracy, and his vocation has been challenged.

That is what happens when you open the door to fear and it embraces the spirit. It makes you doubt. It made him doubt.

That torments him.

The noises inside him scream louder.

In that state, the silence required for discernment cannot exist.

Arnaldo is keeping a secret. One that is shaking his foundation.

He has thought about revealing it but is afraid to do so. It would put him outside the ecclesiastical structure. At least, that is what he believes. What his spirit is experiencing is "the dark night of the soul" of which St. John of the Cross spoke. He can understand it better now than when he learned it in the seminary.

He kneels down.

Once again, he takes in his hands the crucifix hanging from his neck and asks for forgiveness.

He does not want to think about what he has done.

For this reason, there are days when he prefers to escape. He wants to be alone. It was one of those days.

He discovers that when he sees tourists passing by, his mind wanders. He doesn't think, he becomes abstracted. As he contemplates them, he wonders where they come from, what they are thinking, where they are going... What each of their stories is. He spends hours this way, simply watching.

He left the academy around noon in search of a café. The one he likes is located in Via della Conciliazione. They already know him there. Since his arrival, he has been going at least three times a week.

"*Buon pomeriggio,* Father Arnaldo! The usual?"

"Yes, the usual."

From his first visit to Italy, he was captivated by the flavors of *espresso* coffee. It was the strongest he had ever tasted, and he liked that. He liked to savor the coffee and to pass the time watching the tourists. After extracting the scent of that moment, he decided to go for a walk. He did so in the direction of Castel Sant'Angelo.

His mind could not stop wandering.

How do you live between two parallel realities and try to appear congruent to the world? However, amid the confusion may be the most luminous answer.

He stopped, paused again and then continued. Arnaldo walked guided by his instincts.

He did not feel worthy.

Like Judas, he had betrayed Jesus. Squarely. That was his torment.

In a store window, there was a decorative sign with the verse *"God doesn't call the qualified; he qualifies the called."*

The message was before his eyes, but he could not see it. He was being talked to, but he could not hear. That was probably what God was doing with him: He was preparing him.

He stopped in front of the Apostolic Palace in Vatican City. The secret archives reside there. There are more than two million documents that hide the movements of the Roman pontiff's pastoral activity, as well as other information hidden from the public light, which gives a veil of mystery and secrecy.

He decided to enter that underground bunker. An imposing structure of reinforced concrete, located in the bowels of the Belvedere courtyard, in the north of St. Peter's Basilica.

He was impressed by its extensive aisles, the almost 53 linear miles of shelving, and the insulated rings that protect it. It was impossible not to think about what those two floors held. The most crucial moments in history are there.

How many were plunged into deep obscurantism?

The enclosure was gloomy. The halo of mystery and suspense that covered it seemed like something out of a Hitchcock movie. Still, it was fascinating. He stared at the multiple warm ventilation ducts and rectangular neon lamps that were arranged one after the other.

The place was not full. There were about five people seated, all with various reference books.

He decided to look for something that would allow him to make sense of his life. He wandered through all the aisles, lost among thousands of titles. He did not search with the eyes of the scholar, the erudite, the priest; he only searched with the desire to find an answer.

How many clergymen had had an experience like his? What did they do?

Among hundreds of tomes, one title caught his attention: *The Magician Pope.*

"The Magician Pope...Maybe there's something of him in me," he thought.

He requested it.

He began to read about Sylvester II. He was an esoteric medieval sage of the year 1,000 who reached the throne of St. Peter. He immersed himself in his history, magical knowledge, and mystical experiences. They say that the man made a pact with the devil.

He looked at himself. Has he done the same?

On one hand, he felt identified. On the other hand, he felt like a heretic. Little. Unworthy.

Once again, guilt and fear gripped him. He lost himself in the shadows created by his doubts. He became paralyzed.

If you are not prepared for the answer, it is better not to ask.

He heard his name.

"Father Arnaldo! What a pleasure to greet you again! I am Giacomo Ronconi. Remember me? I was with Dr. Arner the day you arrived at the Vatican Academy of Sciences."

"Of course, I remember you! It's good to see you," he greeted as he tried to catch his breath.

"Are you okay?" asked Giacomo.

"Yes, just that I suddenly got short of breath," answered Arnaldo, while holding on to the chair.

"Do you want something? Do you want some water?" Giacomo pointed out as he saw his face turn pale.

"If you don't mind, thank you."

"It looks like a drop in blood pressure. While I go to look for something sweet to help, can you make it to my office which is at the exit on the right-hand side? It's the first door. Eating and drinking are not allowed here."

"Yes. Thank you so much, Giacomo. I'll catch up with you," answered Arnaldo.

Giacomo quickened his pace and left the library. Arnaldo held on to the chair again trying not to faint. At the next table, a man who was sitting with books and reports did not take his eyes off Arnaldo. He looked hard at him.

He got up and approached him.

"Do you want me to accompany you? Do you need help?"

"Don't worry. You're too kind. I'm better now," answered Arnaldo.

"Are you sure?"

"Oh, yes, really. Thank you."

The man, still worried by Arnaldo's pale face, returned to his table. There was a binder. Its title: *"Progetto ROMA - Nuovo secolo, Nuovo uomo."*

Arnaldo stayed a few more minutes breathing deeply. He fixed his attention on that title just to calm his mind. As he left, he said goodbye to the kind man who tried to help him.

He was a bit wobbly as he walked away.

To the right was Giacomo's office. The door was open. There was a large library, full of books and pictures. Some pictures were with his family, others of him at the side of the late Pope John Paul II. The walls were lined with diplomas and awards. He had a large, comfortable black leather chair and two other less pretentious ones for the visitors. On the large pure mahogany table were a computer and a glass of water on a metal cup holder.

Giacomo had already arrived and was on his back reviewing some documents. He was a man of great wealth. Very great wealth. After a spiritual encounter that transformed his life, he had simply given himself to the Church. He was a committed layman.

When he noticed that Father Arnaldo was already at the door, he invited him to take a seat and drink the sugar water he had placed in the cup holder.

"Thank you so much. I don't know what happened," said Arnaldo, now a little calmer.

"Have you eaten?", asked Giacomo.

"Who eats breakfast when one has such an inner turmoil?" he thought.

"I didn't. Maybe that's it," he answered warmly.

"Nor even coffee? Do you want some?" asked Giacomo.

"I did have coffee. You are too kind. I cannot begin my day without it! Also, I must confess that I have found the best *espresso* coffee of my life here. I go so often that they already know me!" he said with a smile. He was recovering.

They talked for a while. Arnaldo told him about his experience after those months following his arrival at the Vatican. It was a warm conversation; the kind that makes you feel like you have known that person all your life.

Giacomo wanted to try the coffee that had so charmed his new friend. He would have no problem remembering the name. The place was called Caffe Giacomelli, in Via della Conciliazione. They agreed to meet on Friday afternoon.

They said goodbye as if they were old friends.

As Arnaldo left the library, so did the kind man who had wanted to help him.

"Feeling better, Father?"

"Yes, thank God!"

"To tell the truth, I got scared when I saw your face. I thought you were going to pass out!" the man said.

They both smiled. Arnaldo extended his hand.

"My apologies for not introducing myself earlier, I am Father Arnaldo. If you ever need any help, I am at your disposal at the Pontifical Academy of Sciences."

"Thank you. My pleasure!" he said as he extended his hand. "My name is William Murrow. If my father was still alive he would surely take your word for it. He was a scientist, a very special man. A great father and a great man of science."

"I do not doubt that we would have had a lot to talk about. I'm a scientist too!"

"A scientist? But aren't you a priest?"

"Yes, a scientific priest," he smiled again.

"I could've never imagined," said the man. "Well, it was nice meeting you!"

Arnaldo left the place, but not before touching the cross hanging on his chest. He got startled when he saw his watch. Time had flown by. It was 2:45 pm. He quickened his pace. It was time to go back to work.

He arrived just at the hour of mercy. Before entering, he decided to smoke his respective cigarette.

"Routines must be respected," he thought.

The walk had done its part. He managed to relax a little. At least that was reflected on his face.

However, the torment continued inside.

4

"...that the submission of our faith might nevertheless be in accordance with reason, God willed that external proofs of his Revelation should be joined to the internal helps of the Holy Spirit."

Enchiridion Symbolorum, DS 3009

Although believing in miracles is part of the Christian life, being in front of them does not always give us certainty. Our human nature sometimes requires more than one confirmation. As happened to Peter.

Santa Magdalena de Jicotlán, in the state of Oaxaca, has less than 100 inhabitants and about 40 houses. Arnaldo was born and raised there until he had to go to high school and was sent to his uncle in the city.

In that town, most of the houses are still the color of bricks and adobe. In the area of the "well-to-do" people, their homes are coated and painted in bright colors. They also have beautiful gardens and are close to the town hall. Arnaldo's family is very humble and does not live in those houses. However, they have a cozy home. Modest. Warm.

The silence of the streets is only interrupted when the children go to or leave the only school in town. It is also interrupted when the church bells ring. Besides that, only the birds and the sound of the wind can be heard through the leaves of the trees that surround the place.

The silence is only outside.

Inside the houses, there is always noise. There is always a well meaning neighbor visiting at all hours with the latest gossip.

Santa Magdalena de Jicotlán is a village that always has "something to talk about." It may well deserve the top score for communication: in less than thirty minutes everyone knows the story.

From an early age, Arnaldo showed great interest in mystical subjects. He could not be any different. His parents were very involved in the Church. His mother, Mrs. Ana, always cleaned the sacristy and helped the priest organize his things.

As in every small town, the stories of images sweating oil and the tales of miracles gave rise to long lines of locals willing to witness and take advantage of the occasion to ask for "favors." Anything unexplained was the talk of the town, including tales of diabolical possession.

The head priest, Father José Luis, claimed he was also an exorcist and that more than half the town, at one time or another, seemed to have been possessed. Everyone would go to expel their demons.

One of the women in the village said that she had had "revelations." According to her, the Virgin spoke to her and warned her that frightening things would happen if they did not pray the rosary. Within seconds, the inhabitants of Santa Magdalena de Jicotlán were praying fervently in the church. Never before had so many rosaries been sold in such a short period of time.

That Sunday, the sermon revolved around her and how God communicates with us in many different ways.

One night, when Arnaldo was nine years old, he woke up agitated. He felt that "a voice was speaking to him." He was not sure if he was asleep or awake. It seemed so real.

"Arnaldo, son, my bleeding heart waits for you. Don't let me down."

At that time he was studying catechism.

He preferred not to comment anything about it.

He was dying with worry at the thought that the priest would talk about him at Mass if he found out. At the end of the day, it was just that, a very real dream.

However, that *'don't let me down'* was imprinted in him.

He was experiencing the fear of God. The thought of not fulfilling His expectations frightened him.

A week later, a host bled in the middle of consecration.

The commotion at Mass was total.

"A miracle! A miracle!" they yelled.

The priest put it on display in the monstrance at the end of the service. The town began to fill up with visitors. The silence was only a distant memory. The collection began to grow.

Faced with these cases of Eucharistic manifestations, the first thing the priest should do is to communicate it to his superiors. On this occasion, the priest left this detail out.

Arnaldo grew up in the middle of it. He was the main altar boy. In catechism classes, Father José Luis always emphasized the importance of confession.

"It is God's way of pouring out his mercy to a repentant heart; the medicine that frees us from the disgrace of sin," he said.

That is why Arnaldo always wanted to go to confession. Although he had not yet received communion, the priest allowed him to do so. He had deep regrets, as he liked Margarita, one of the girls at his school, and thought of her differently. He felt guilty about the little white lies that he sometimes told his parents. He even confessed to stealing some chocolates. They were from the priest himself. He had found them in his drawer.

As usual, searching once again for the mystery of grace, he arrived one day at the parlor. The day of confession was over. Arnaldo was the last one. He knelt down. He crossed himself. The voice of the priest could be heard through the window.

"Hail purest Mary," said the priest.

"Conceived without sin. Bless me, father, for I have sinned."

There was no answer from the other side of the tiny window, just a terrifying silence. Eternal.

"Bless me father for I have sinned," repeated Arnaldo.

A deep sob was heard. Arnaldo felt the Father's soul tearing.

From that small cabin of old, gnawed wood, a voice answered:

"Arnaldo, my son, forgive me! There was no miracle! There was no miracle!"

A thud made Arnaldo stand up. The father collapsed.

The boy dragged him out of the confessional. He tried to wake him up.

Seeing that he did not respond, his heart began to race. Next to the priest was a small jar.

Something was wrong.

From the ground, not knowing what to do, he looked up searching for answers.

There, in front of them, the wooden Christ seemed to be watching them from the wall.

The answers did not come.
The priest had no vital signs.
He had taken his own life.

On the day of the burial, Arnaldo returned to the sacristy.

In the old wooden crate, he found a letter that the man had left for his parishioners. In it, he confessed that the miracle of the bleeding host had never existed. He had cut his finger on the edge of one of the Bible pages.

For this reason, the body of Christ had been defiled, and so that the fervor of the believers would not be diminished, he never said anything.

Neither would Arnaldo.

He tore up the letter and kept the secret. That man had taught him to love God and the Eucharist.

The subject was no longer discussed in town.

There was no Mass for a long time.

However, his mother kept cleaning the sacristy.

As soon as Arnaldo entered in the seminary, a different ordeal began.

Seeking to understand the inexplicable mysticism that had befallen him, he turned to science.

On the one hand, his rational side needed answers and "certainties."

On the other hand, the raft that saved him was faith.

One day, at the seminar, he told his story.

He confessed how in his toughest moments the phrase *"don't let me down"* would come to his mind again. He told about:

When he got tattooed.

When he first had sex.

When he smoked marijuana.

When he and his friends burnt down a car.

When he tore up the letter from the village priest.

He thought that by taking his vows there would no longer be any reason to remember anything from his past. He could not let God down.

How could he if he was already His?

But the Devil always tempts.

While he was preparing for consecration, in parallel he did his doctorate in mathematics and science. His performance was outstanding. His professors involved him in areas where science and faith were mixed.

One of them was Father Angel Martínez, director of one of the medical schools in Rome.

An honorable man who also belongs to the Congregation for the Causes of Saints, one of the nine congregations of the Roman Curia.

One of the seven experts who meet biweekly to evaluate potential miracles.

He was summoned to Venezuela. He was asked to evaluate a possible miracle. This time, Eucharistic.

A commission was to analyze the event. He could bring a student to go with him. He extended the invitation to Arnaldo because he stood out and showed particular interest.

However, the young Mexican's experience with this type of event had not been the best. He was filled with skepticism.

The report indicated that, in the chapel of the Betania Farm sanctuary in Cúa, Venezuela, Father Otty Ossa Aristizábal was celebrating Midnight Mass on December 8, 1991. At the moment of consecration, he divided the host into four pieces and placed them on the paten. As he looked down, he saw that one of them had a red spot. From that Eucharistic bread, a liquid began to emanate, just as blood flows when a person is wounded.

There were no words to describe it.

On this occasion, they followed protocol: to check that the priest had not cut himself and report what had happened.

A first commission of inquiry then took part. The host was subjected to various analyses. The results? The blood present in the host was type AB+. It was the same one that was found in the Shroud of Turin and the miracle of Lanciano.

A second commission was to intervene. There entered Father Angel Martínez and young Arnaldo. The host had been transferred to the convent of the Augustinian Recollect Nuns of the Sacred Heart of Jesus in Los Teques, Venezuela. It was on display. Upon their arrival in this Caribbean country, they were taken directly to the site.

That was different from Arnaldo's experience in Santa Magdalena de Jicotlán.

He was impressed. Captivated. In the center of the host, he could see a beating heart. It was the first time that he was really in front of a miracle of this nature.

He began to experience an indescribable peace.

However, he had to be impartial. To see everything with the eyes of science and not of faith. Only in this way could he evaluate the veracity of that fact that defied the laws of logic.

For Arnaldo, when science analyzes what escapes human rationality, no proof seems to be enough. A larger test will always be needed. And an even bigger one. Then an even bigger one. Everything to help to understand what cannot be explained.

To understand what is subject to debate or what is ambiguous.

Was it real or not?

This inner conflict will make Arnaldo wonder if he is an apostle like Peter, or if he is like Judas, a traitor.

The answer will soon arrive in Arnaldo's life, dressed as a woman.

5

The beauty of the Vatican gardens manages to appease even the most restless souls. Even the most soulless being manages to find peace and quiet in those 79 green acres full of vineyards, meadows, flowers, and medieval monuments.

Amidst the majesty and beauty of the site, in addition to the Pontifical Academy of Sciences, there is also the Vatican Radio. A month ago, a Spanish journalist started working for them, making the news interesting. She's 37 and has a specialization in the study of Ancient Languages and a master's degree in Aramaic. Apart from Spanish, she speaks Italian, German, and Russian. Abundant and wavy black hair, athletic build. Her name: Pilar Navarro. She is the new Deputy Director of Communications.

Arnaldo had heard the innumerable attributes of that woman, but he had not yet met her personally.

He had gone out that day to maintain his smoking routine. A vice he started at the age of sixteen and that he practices three times a day.

Cardinal Vitesse is the Vatican's Director of Communications. Like Arnaldo, he smokes. Generally, he smokes at 11 a.m. They meet and talk there.

They spent endless hours discussing the Bible and events that revealed some of the contradictions they felt were taking place within the Church. The cardinal begged him to tone down his complaints against the ecclesiastical system.

"I understand you, Arnaldo, and I understand your passion, but we can't say everything we think because we can get into trouble", said Vitesse.

In the most highly charged conversations, they even talked about what Jesus would think if he came to honor his promise of the Second Coming.

That day would be no exception. The talks would be very controversial.

One morning, Arnaldo saw his dear companion of that time of day. Next to him was that tall woman. They were talking pleasurably. She wore a fuchsia skirt that exposed her toned legs. She paired it with a white silk shirt, which swayed in the breeze and gave a glimpse of her tiny waist. She was elegant. She had a lot of bearing.

When they heard his steps, they turned around. Arnaldo understood right away why they talked so much about that woman. She was beautiful. Dangerously beautiful.

"Arnaldo!" exclaimed cardinal Vitesse, waving with euphoria and joy.

He gave him a warm, fraternal hug. It was typical of his character and perennial spirit. He hastened to introduce him to the woman accompanying him.

"I can finally introduce you to Pilar, the new Deputy Director of Vatican Radio." He turned to her.

"I don't know how many times I've told him about you!"

"How do you do? It's a real pleasure to finally meet you," said Arnaldo.

The woman approached him and kissed him twice on the cheeks, as was the European custom.

"The pleasure's mine. You can call me Pilar. All these formalities make me feel old. I've also heard your name a lot."

Arnaldo did not know what to say. He just stared at her.

Pilar looked great.

Instinctively, Arnaldo put his hand to the cross hanging from his chest. His mind recited for him:

'The lamp of thy body is thine eye: when thine eye is single, thy whole body also is full of light; but when it is evil, thy body also is full of darkness.'

He feared that the light in him would turn to darkness. His memories took him back to the days when he was not yet a priest and wallowed in every nook and cranny with his 'friend' Margarita.

That morning, Cardinal Vitesse dedicated himself to praising the professionalism of that woman. Likewise, all the affection he had for Arnaldo.

"He is a very special man. You cannot imagine how much the Pope loved him! He doesn't know how much *I* love him!" he told Pilar.

If there was one thing Arnaldo had besides charisma, it was curiosity and verbosity.

This led him to quickly learn the Catholic Church's communication system: what to say and, more importantly, what to keep silent about.

How different these green corridors are from the dusty, dirt roads of Latin America. He often made this known to his friend the Cardinal.

It was the first of many encounters. They clicked immediately.

When the three of them coincided, the get-togethers became a small party. Fifteen or twenty minutes that they enjoyed to the fullest.

If Pilar and Arnaldo were alone together, the debates and deep reflections on life, the Church, or God gained a space in both of their hearts.

The ties became closer and closer.

A friendship born quickly that would lead them down a path of no return.

Both would open their hearts to expose the depths of their feelings and fears.
This will happen much sooner rather than later.

6

Arnaldo's relationship with Pilar quickly went from simple work colleagues to close friends.

For Pilar, Arnaldo was the bridge to the peace her soul needed. That is why she enjoyed his company so much.

For him, she was the opportunity to talk freely about everything and without filters. She was approachable, talkative, and very intelligent.

They not only talked in the vicinity of the Pontifical Academy, but also in cafés, while Arnaldo accompanied her to the train station, or with some wine at the end of the day.

This woman, outgoing and talkative in appearance, was quiet and reserved at heart. Very reserved. She was especially wary of her past filled with pain, shame, and much self-disappointment. Indeed, the cross she was carrying was heavy.

And when the crosses are so heavy, it is extremely painful to carry them alone.

She decided to drop her own on Arnaldo's back.

That was the day she learned that vulnerability was a form of freedom.

Arnaldo was accompanying her to the train station at Piazza Stazione Di St. Pietro, about twenty minutes from the Vatican City. The wind blew delicately. With each breath, Pilar felt that it was God himself who caressed her face. That, with each step, it was he who accompanied her. It was the first time she had experienced something like this.

"I never imagined having a priest friend. In fact, I don't have many friends," she said.

"What do you mean you have no friends? Someone like you? Nobody could believe that story!"

"It's true, Arnaldo. Everything is not as it seems. I'm rather... solitary," she said, thinking carefully about what she was going to say.

"Solitary? You're hardly a lone communicator. Social communicators are people of many friends."

"Let's say I'm a communicator by accident," she said, smiling.

"How's that?"

For Pilar that was the starting point to show her real self. Vulnerability requires courage, and the word courage comes from the Latin *cor*, meaning 'heart'. To speak from the heart. That would be the way she would do it: from the heart.

"This is the second time in my life that I have spoken about myself. I consider you my friend and you have something I need."

"Which thing?"

"A direct line to the one up there. I don't want to burn in hell the day I die."

"I don't think someone like you will go to hell! Trust me, I come first."

They both laughed.

NELSON BUSTAMANTE & CARMEN VICTORIA PARDO

Arnaldo feared that this would be the end of him. His hell.

It will not be long before he understands that she was not joking.

"I'm all ears."

Pilar tried to relax.

"This woman you see here is the product of hundreds of broken pieces."

"We're all made of broken pieces."

"Let me explain myself better. Let's start at the beginning. I'm an only child. My mom was a single mother, so she had to play the roles of both mom and dad. Our economic situation was quite tight. She worked a lot: Double shifts, full weekends... She was never at home, so I spent my days practically alone."

"No one took care of you while she was working?"

"When I was a little girl, I was left at the house of a lady who took care of me. She became kind of a nanny. Her name was Vicky. She was a very special Colombian woman. With her, I learned to walk and to defend myself. That was pretty much until I was about seven years old. Then she had to leave to take care of her granddaughter."

"And who took care of you afterward?"

"From that moment on, I had to defend myself. Between shifts, my mom would go to the house, drop off some food and lock the door, and I would stay there until she came home again. She always came. She never stopped doing it. But many times, when she came into the house, I was already asleep. That made me grow up fast. That loneliness and fear I had only dissipated when my mother arrived. That was when I felt safe."

As Pilar told him, Arnaldo was overcome with a paternal feeling. He would never have thought that this was the past of a woman who seemed so imposing. Certainly, behind each person, each face, and each look there is an unknown world.

"At the age of nine or ten, I was already on the streets. As soon as my mother left the house, I would go out. That's how I entered the world of vices", said her.

It is incredible how events mark our destiny.

"Why did your mom not leave her job?"

"She tried, but she couldn't. She had a very strong bond with the organization she worked for. My mom was a good woman. Excellent. I remember her with love. However, there was one day in particular that changed everything. I would have been thirteen or fourteen. She arrived earlier than usual. When she came in, I was lying on the floor completely drugged. That day, she said 'No more!'. She spoke to her boss, told her what was going on, and asked for her help. The next day, I started to go to work with my mom. Without noticing, I started learning all the dynamics. Soon after, I started working there."

"And what did you do?"

Pilar thought for a few seconds. She hesitated before answering.

"Along with my mother, I was assigned to the security area. It was very hard for her at first. I would have crises in the middle of the day, as a result of the detoxification of the drugs in my body. Those were very hard times. For both of us. After that, I started to do minor jobs. My mom forced me to study. So I did both things. The days were long."

"What kind of security?"

"Let's say in private personal security."

Her dad had left them when she was born. He was a violent man, so her mom learned how to protect both her daughter and herself. Hence, giving one's life for something or someone became part of her philosophy.

For Arnaldo, Pilar's story was fascinating. They were just short of the station. He decided to slow down the pace. This would buy more time for her to tell him more about her life.

"And how do you jump from security to communication?"

"My mother always told me that, when it comes to security, information is power. She "needed" to be informed about everything to do her job properly. That's why I like that field so much. I understood the power of communication."

Arnaldo could not stop thinking while he listened, the way each story was finely woven in a subtle way. Magical.

__"But the very hairs of your head are all numbered"__
__reads the Bible.__
__How is Pilar's imperfection not perfect?__
__How is Arnaldo's imperfect life not perfect?__

"Sometimes it's amazing how God has his ways of showing us his plans," said Arnaldo, immersed in that reflective state.

"I am not sure that He has plans for me. In fact, don't be angry if I tell you that sometimes I doubt if He really exists."

"He has a plan for us all! For you. For me. Trust me."

Arnaldo was not prepared to talk about his own story.

He changed the subject cunningly.

"How long did you work there?"

"Lots of years. Lots. Let's say enough to understand some things," she smiled. "As time went by, I earned a name, respect, and a position. In every aspect. At the age of 22, I was in charge of an entire division. My mom instilled in me that when you do something you have to do it right to the end. For that reason, Mrs. Isabel's little girl was the one who gave the orders. At that time I even gave them to her. Well, that's what I thought!"

"So, the student surpassed the teacher!"

"Let's say, rather, that I had the best of teachers!"

They both smiled.

They wanted to stop time. Meanwhile, hundreds of people were hurrying to get home.

That's life, some want to slow it down and others want to speed it up.

"Do you know what?" said Pilar in a sensible tone. "I think your life and mine are a lot alike."

"Why is that? If you knew me, you would notice that maybe we are opposites. Behind this cassock, there is also a lot of history."

"I guess. We all have history."

"But why do you think our lives are alike?"

"Let's see what you think. You obey the Church, you worship God, you believe in and give your life for the Catholic doctrine. You would die for it and for the truth, right?"

"Yes," he answered.

"Well, I was also obedient in my job. I worshipped it. My superiors were gods for me. I gave my life for what I considered to be the truth. My job became my life, my call, my everything."

"Seen in that way, we might be alike," Arnaldo pointed out as he thought.

It was only a short distance to the station.

That conversation had upset Pilar. Anyone could see that she was dejected. Her past weighed on her.

Her life coincided with that of Arnaldo in something else. Both wore heavy crosses.

"Have you ever wondered what would happen if one day you realized that everything you believed was a lie that someone made you think was true?" asked Pilar.

"Yes. Of course! Of course, I thought about it!"

"I believe that the life we live is only a consequence of the truth we believe."

"For me, the truth is Jesus Christ. *'He is the way, and the truth, and the life.'* To Him, I surrender all that I am. I even go it tattooed on my body, as He got tattooed in my soul."

"There are tattoos you want to erase! Even more so if they are from the soul," said Pilar.

Arnaldo thought about his.

They arrived at the station. It was time to close the subject. Many things were stirred up on that walk.

"Pilar, don't you think that those tattoos that you now want to erase from your soul are the ones that have made you what you are today? Doesn't it make you proud to look back and discover the person you have become?"

She said nothing. Each of them had a tattoo that they could not get rid of. They certainly had more in common than they thought.

"So," said Pilar, taking up her question and slipping away from Arnaldo's, "what would you do if you suddenly discovered that everything you believe is a lie?"

"You didn't answer, I'm going to respect that. I'll answer your question all the same," he stayed a few minutes thinking. "I don't know. To find out that everything I have believed is a lie would be like being left up in the air. No bases, no nothing."

"Do you think you would seek to cry out the truth and unmask the lie you have been led to believe?"

"Surely," he said.

"See? We are more alike than you think."

Pilar had learned that there is a time for everything. In matters of patience and strategy, she had a postgraduate degree.

If capable, she would have erased her history.
A dark past full of secrets, lies, threats, and death.

"Today's conclusion: tell me what your truth is and I will tell you who you are," she said.

They both laughed. The train approached the station fast. Very fast.

Just as quickly, the time would come when the absolute truth about who Pilar was and who Arnaldo was would come to light.

CHAPTER III

MYSTERIES OF
THE KINGDOM

(1

STURP sought to prove the real existence of Jesus Christ crucified.

What its organizers never imagined was that it would also awaken the darkest of ambitions in a group of scientists.

—*Palo Alto, California.*
November, 1978.

A week after arriving on U.S. soil, Kevin Davis was analyzing and studying the piece of Shroud he had stolen.

All this was carried out in the basement of his house, where he had a small and very sophisticated laboratory.

He heard the telephone ringing. On the other end of the line, a familiar voice greeted him.

"Hello! Good evening!" said Kevin.

"Bud, this is Dr. Mullis speaking!"

"Hey, the great Dr. Mullis! Nice to speak to you again! How was your trip back?"

"Fortunately, everything was alright. I'm here in California till Saturday, so I have a couple of days left. I'd like to meet up. I want to talk to you about some important issues that may be of interest to both of us."

"Yes, of course!"

"How are your plans today? We can meet if you want," mentioned Mullis.

"That sounds excellent!" answered Kevin.

"Where are you staying? I can come to you."

"I live in Palo Alto. There's a bar named 4141 El Camino. We can meet there at eight."

"Perfect! I'll see you there!"

When Kevin arrived at the bar, Mullis was already drinking a whiskey on the rocks. They greeted each other fraternally.

They first discussed the STURP experience: the colleagues, the organization, and the unusual things that happened there. After that, Mullis went straight to the subject he was interested in.

"Kevin, I admire your intelligence, your sagacity, and your speediness. I am twenty years older than you. I'll be direct. I saw you cut off a piece of the Shroud!"

Kevin was speechless. He did not expect that. He swore no one had seen it. He really swore by it.

"It can't be! Are you crazy?" rejected Kevin.

"You've got some nerve! But don't worry. For me, unscrupulous people have a great value. They are people who go for big things. And yes, I'm crazy and I think you are too."

"What are you talking about?"

"You have something we're both interested in. I saw you. Let's cut the bullshit! What do you plan to do with what you stole?"

A brief pause, one of those between doubt and decision, interrupted the dialogue.

"Well, I simply wanted to do other studies. Evaluate without time pressure and see if I could develop some other kinds of tests."

"I don't think many days will go by without someone noticing that the Shroud is incomplete, and they will start investigating!"

Mullis knew there was more to it.

During their participation in STURP, they had become good friends. They always shared their research concerns. Their debates often became heated.

For Davis, the Shroud of Turin was the one that had covered the body of Jesus Christ. He wanted to prove it scientifically in his quest to be recognized worldwide.

For Mullis, the piece of fabric could be the bridge to a new and even more controversial project.

"I'd like to share something with you. I know you'll be interested," said Mullis.

"Well, tell me about it. I'm all ears!"

"For some time now I have wanted to carry out the most controversial experiment ever. I want us to be the first to clone a human being!"

"To clone a human being?! Are you serious?!" asked Kevin skeptically.

"Not just anyone! I want to clone Jesus Christ."

"To clone Jesus Christ?! Have you gone crazy?!"

"Don't give me moral speeches now! I am inviting you to be part of history, to change it, to write it anew."

Davis was somewhat displeased. Not because the idea seemed illogical, but because it was already on his mind. His competitive side would not let him take in that he was not the only one who had thought of cloning the Son of God.

They had an argument. Mullis's intelligence dampened Kevin's egomaniacal fury. Beyond his arrogance, the young scientist was clever and shrewd. He knew he had a golden opportunity in front of him. He had to join in to win.

"How would we do it?" asked Kevin.

"We are partners. Two mad scientists together who are going to change history. Are you in or not?"

Kevin stared at him, picked up the drink from the table, and invited Mullis to raise his.

"You're right! We are going to achieve great things together. For our society and the projects to come!"

They toasted.

An alliance had been formed. A partnership that would take them beyond science itself.

They had a great plan.

But to pull it off, they would need more than a piece of cloth.

2

There is more turbulence than can be felt inside an airplane. The experience at the Nuremberg Group convention had shaken Mikhail's principles and beliefs.

It was pouring on the Milan-Russia route. The plane was shaking hard. A sudden thunderstorm had caused the emergency lights to remain on inside the aircraft for most of the flight.

Mikhail had never liked airplanes. He always took a sedative before getting on one. He was so distressed by that report that he forgot to do it.

That shook even more.

He arrived in Russia at almost midnight, still under a torrential downpour. He took a cab home; a yellow line one. He got soaked as he took out his suitcase and ran to the entrance.

"Finally home!" he thought.

He arrived agitated, with fear. When he opened the door, he dropped his keys. He wet the entire entrance hallway. Anxiety had taken hold of him. His wife, Ivanna, was already sleeping.

Although her son Anatoly had his own apartment, he had stayed there those days to accompany his mother so she would not be alone.

Anatoly was sitting in the living room reading a book. When he heard the noise, he jumped up from the couch in shock. He turned the light on. He saw his father's disheveled face. His scared eyes. He knew something was off.

"Dad, what are you doing here? Are you okay? What happened? Weren't you coming back on the weekend?" The questions came out like a machine gun. He did not give respite.

"I don't know, son! I don't know!" answered Mikhail, confused.

He certainly did not know.

He set the briefcase and the bag aside and sat down on the cabinet. He leaned his head back as he ran his hands through his wet hair. He took a deep breath. For the first time in many hours, he felt he was safe.

"Let me get you some water. You're not okay. What's wrong with you?" Anatoly insisted.

"I prefer vodka."

"If so, I'll join you! By the way, Dad, happy birthday!"

Anatoly and his father had a very close relationship. They had truly enviable communication. That night, drinks in hand, his dad told him in detail what had happened. He told his son what they spoke about in that hall. He showed him the report.

"Dad, this is madness! No one will believe it."

"I know. That's why we can't tell anyone. Yet. We need to be careful with these people. Very careful. I'm scared."

Mikhail asked him to photocopy it and keep a copy for himself. He knew he had opened the gates of hell. After this, Dimitriv or someone from the Nuremberg Club would seek to contact him. To explain his arrival, he would tell his wife Ivanna that his participation in the event had ended earlier and that it was a birthday surprise. For both of their birthdays.

It was almost dawn. The guest room was downstairs. He decided to rest there so as not to wake his wife.

More dazed by the exhaustion of his father's confession than by the drinks, Anatoly took the briefcase. He went up to his room. He did as requested and copied the report. He kept it in a desk that had a double pocket in the drawer. He went downstairs and left the briefcase in the hallway.

He went to bed but could not sleep. He could not rest no matter how many times he turned over. He was agitated. He thought obsessively about everything his father had told him. No wonder. He heard his mom's footsteps coming down the stairs. There was no point in trying to sleep. He decided to sit up. He took a bath and headed downstairs.

The smell of freshly brewed coffee permeated the house. His mom was in the kitchen, her favorite place, still wearing her robe. She was back to him, preparing some eggs when Anatoly greeted her.

"Good morning, mom! Happy birthday!" said Anatoly with a tired voice, but trying to sound cheerful.

"Thanks, son! You haven't slept well. Look at that face! Did you stay up late studying?"

"Dad arrived last night. We stayed talking until late."

Mikhail's briefcase was still in the hallway.

She had not noticed.

"How is it that my love arrived? Where is he?" she said illusion of one who has not seen her beloved in years.

"He's sleeping in the room downstairs, mom. He didn't want to wake you up."

Ivanna ran out to find him. She was going to congratulate him. She opened the door. She approached carefully. She found him fast asleep. She smiled. She kissed him on the forehead. She returned to the kitchen.

Anatoly placed the eggs on the plate.

"They almost got burnt! I can't have breakfast with you, because I have things to do."

"Always on the run, son!"

He said goodbye as usual and left for Lubianka Square.

The previous night's rain had turned that morning into a cool autumn day. Arriving at the square, he made his way to the Federal Security Service of Moscow. A large yellow brick building where the successor executive body of the Soviet KGB had been founded two years earlier.

Vladimir, one of his best friends, worked there. He wanted Anatoly, once he graduated, to be part of the institution.

"There are lots of benefits!" he always insisted.

To become a member of this security corps, it was necessary to be at least 25 years old, have some work experience, be a graduate of an accredited university and pass the admission test.

Anatoly met part of the requirements needed. He only needed to graduate and that would be done in a matter of days.

He dialed his friend from a pay phone.

"Hi, Vladimir! It's Anatoly! Good morning!"

"Hey! Good morning! What's this? To what do I owe the pleasure of this call right now?"

Something serious had to be going on. In all the years of friendship, it was the first time he had called him during the workday.

"Sorry to bother you, do you have a few minutes?"

"What's wrong? What happened?" Vladimir asked worriedly.

"I need to talk to you in person. It's urgent."

"Right now we've just been called for a meeting. Do you mind if I call you as soon as I get free? Or we can meet at lunchtime at about two o'clock. What do you say?"

"Perfect! I'll come over and we'll look for a restaurant around here."

Vladimir had no idea that by that time it would already be too late.

The luncheon would never take place.

That is life. In a matter of seconds, everything can change.

Someone is born.

Someone dies.

~

Anatoly went for a walk in the vicinity. He needed to clear his mind. To fully exhaust himself so he could rest when he got to his parent's house. At least for a couple of hours.

The day would be longer than expected.

When he entered his house, his dad was just getting up. He was coming down the hallway and greeted him.

"I haven't stopped thinking about last night, Dad! I could hardly sleep. Those people could be dangerous, that's why I went to see Vladimir."

"What did you do? We agreed that you wouldn't say anything," Mikhail scolded him.

"I know. But I want to get advice. All this gives me a bad feeling. Anyway, for your peace of mind, I couldn't say anything to him. He was about to enter a meeting. We arranged to have lunch."

"I know he's your friend, but we should be cautious."

"Don't talk to me about caution! Look, Dad, I'm tired. I'm going to rest for a while. Besides, Mom is around. We'll talk later."

He went straight upstairs to his room.

He lay down. He fell fast asleep.

Minutes later, a black van parked outside the house. Three tall, stocky men and a slender, athletic woman got out of it. They wore long, black jackets. They rang the doorbell.

Ivanna was in the kitchen and heard the sound. She lowered the flame on the stove and reached over to open the door.

One of the men pounced on her. He covered her mouth with a white cloth. She had no time to scream.

Within seconds she was unconscious. It happened fast.

As the woman fainted, another opened her mouth. He poured a liquid that made her swallow by squeezing her throat. It was radioactive polonium 210, a metalloid that spreads rapidly throughout the system causing damage to tissues and organs. It is difficult to detect its presence. To obtain this volatile metal, you need a particle accelerator, the knowledge, and the necessary connections needed to make it.

Lethal, in the doses it was administered.

It was undoubtedly a very well-thought-out plan.

She was left lying in the entrance hallway, while the woman and the other man stealthily searched the lower part of the house.

"Who was it, my love?" the sentence was heard from the guest room.

It was the perfect sound that indicated the place where they should go.

The woman entered the room. She carried a loaded gun in her hands. It had a long barrel. It had a a silencer.

Mikhail turned around. He looked at her face.

It was the last thing he saw.

Without pause, the woman shot the scientist in the forehead.

Not once, but twice.

The wall was impregnated with that tormenting crimson red. Blood gushed onto the beige carpet and a scarlet halo formed around his head.

"You shall not betray trust," she said.

Mikhail fell to the ground slowly fading away. His eyes were still open. There was no screaming. No time. Nothing. She stared at Mikhail. Another of the men came in.

"Sometimes breaking the rules can come at a high price. We can leave now," she said.

"Shall we check for anyone else?" asked the man who had just entered.

"No, they live alone. Do you have the report?" she exclaimed firmly.

"Yes, we already got it."

The woman entered the kitchen. She saw that the pot with the *borscht* was less than half full. She took a slice of bread. She dipped it in the broth.

"Mmmm, this is good," she thought as she licked her fingers.

They left the house. They closed the door. Only the boiling of *borscht*, Mikhail's favorite tomato soup, could be heard. The one Ivanna was preparing with such fervor to celebrate their birthdays and that he was back. That unmistakable red color, bubbling thickly in the pot, was paradoxically the same color that now bordered Mikhail's head.

Can a man seal his fate?

The pungent smell of that broth made Anatoly wake up. He stretched in the bed, got up, and went to wash his face. He saw the clock. It was almost one o'clock.

"I'm late!" he said out loud.

He showered again trying to wake up. He put on a pair of jeans, a shirt, and a brown leather jacket. As he came down the stairs he shouted to his mother.

"Mom, that smells great! I can smell it from here! I agreed to have lunch with Vladimir, but please save me some for dinner!"

He walked toward the living room to leave. He saw his mother lying in the hallway. He shouted. He shouted in despair. He ran to grab her. He was still screaming.

"Mom! Mom! What's wrong with you? Mom! Dad! Dad!" he called him to come and help him.

Nobody answered. The silence was total. He left her on the floor. He ran for help. To make a phone call. The door to the guest room was open. There was his father lying in a river of blood. As he held him in his arms, he screamed louder. He was crying his eyes out, like a grief-stricken child. Despair seized Anatoly.

"No! No! Mom! Dad! No!"

Silence reigned again. He carefully placed his father on the floor. Limp and zombie-like, he approached the phone. He called emergency. He just could say:

"My parents have been murdered. Please, come quickly."

He gave his address. He threw himself to the ground. There he remained, in a fetal position.

Every moment went through his mind at once. The last conversation with his father. The damned report.

"It was them! It was them! Those bastards!" he repeated.

There, right there, he swore revenge.

There, his decision to join the Federal Security Service was made. To enlist in Russia's elite spy agency.

Had he been aware that life can turn around in a second, he would have seized the moment differently.

The guilty were going to pay.

One by one.

Dearly.

CHAPTER IV
THEFT AND BETRAYAL

$\left(1\right.$

The partnership between the two scientists had been sealed.

What Kevin did not know was Mullis's shady past.

Three months after the end of STURP, there is a new uproar.

The alarms have gone off under the Cathedral of St. John the Baptist in Turin. The Royal Chapel of the Duomo di Torino has been attacked.

The Holy Shroud was stolen.

The criminalistics unit has arrived on the scene. The area has been cordoned off and several units are searching for evidence. They take fingerprint samples. They carry out the respective interrogations. Security guards, priests, and cathedral workers have been called to testify.

There are no footprints. No clues. Nothing.

A perfect assault.

An aggravated theft due to the value of this piece.

Throughout the city, police car alarms are heard. Security forces search everywhere for the relic. They do not waste any time. The first 72 hours are decisive.

There is no doubt: those who carried out this robbery belong to a well-organized criminal network.

Within the Roman Curia, there is also great commotion. They have requested assistance from Interpol and other international bodies. The alert has been communicated to airports and borders. All of this, in order to find the whereabouts of the Shroud and to arrest the guilty.

Nothing happens.

Hours pass. Days too.

It has been more than 72 hours and they are still without a single clue.

They must take the investigation to another level. They must question anyone who has been close to the Sacred Mantle in recent months. The entire STURP team, without exception, is included in this list.

In several cities in the United States, there is a police movement.

Three vehicles surround the area near Kevin's residence in California.

They ring the doorbell.

Two uniformed men are standing by.

"Good afternoon, we are trying to locate Dr. Kevin Davis, if you would be so kind..."

"Yes, that's me."

One of the policemen pulls out his credentials. He identifies himself as part of the Interpol. Kevin's heart begins to race.

"We have an interrogation warrant for the disappearance of the Shroud of Turin. May we come in, please?"

"Of course! Come in."

They enter the house. They look around. One of them asks if he can take a look. With some trepidation but showing great self-control, Kevin accepts. Internally, he prays they do not go down to the laboratory.

"Did you notice anything strange while at STURP?"

"Not at all. The group of professionals that were there were of a high level," said Kevin.

The interrogation was also taking place simultaneously in Washington.

"After your return, with whom have you shared information about the evaluations you did?"

"Only with one of my colleagues, Dr. Davis," said Mullis.

"Only with Dr. Mullis," Davis replied to the same question.

Both were being questioned at the same time. They were asked the same questions. Different places. Different cities.

The agents withdrew.

Mullis and Davis could breathe.

It was not long before Mullis called Davis and told him what had happened. This was not just a fright. A real alarm had been set off, urging them to seek measures to safeguard the piece of the Holy Shroud. They also needed to find a "controlled and safe" space to carry out their project.

Those were days of anguish. It was not long before the Italian police found the whereabouts of the Shroud. According to the report issued, the police had received an anonymous call indicating the location of the Holy Shroud. It had been left in the basement of an abandoned building on the outskirts of Madrid.

According to the report provided by the authorities,

The Shroud was found practically "intact." It only has a small cut in one of its corners.

A note was on the Shroud.

The day is coming.

Few people understood.
The Second Advent was underway.

2

After the fright they experienced with the theft of the Shroud, Mullis and Davis put their research in the underground laboratory at Kevin's house on hold for a while. The situation could become complicated. It could even jeopardize their career and, most importantly, the cloning project. If something went wrong and they were discovered, jail could await them.

To continue, they had to change more than just strategy.

Reaching agreements in new partnerships is not easy. Conversations. Proposals. Heated debates. Multiple options. Biased opinions. Clashing egos.

Finally, they reached a solution. One that they struggled to reach: to leave the USA. What was coming required peace, calm, and concentration. They did not have it. The place: Argentina.

Mullis proposed this country because he knew it well. He had lived there before.

The conditions seemed ideal: no one would be looking for them, there would be no intruders, and it was familiar to him.

Kevin would stay in California but not without resistance. In addition, someone had to find the funds.

The police knew that someone had a piece of the Shroud. At any moment they could appear again unexpectedly. The two would probably not be as lucky next time. He had no choice but to rely on Mullis.

But for a personality as egomaniacal as Kevin's, letting go of his greatest possession was no easy task. They agreed to split the sample. Kevin would keep it in a safe, just to guarantee a copy. Simple control.

It all seemed absurd, but they had to move forward.

During their stay in Argentina, the first step would be to double check that the blood on the Holy Shroud belonged to the Son of God.

Since the investigations began, the failures were multiple and continuous. It was frustrating. They knew they were on the right track, but something was missing. They could not figure it out. In addition, one of the biggest hurdles to overcome was their finances.

Although they started with a considerable amount, they realized along the way that it was not enough. Money began to dry up quickly.

They had to get more, much more.

However, they did their best not to let their spirits drop. They met twice a year. Kevin was the one who traveled. His domineering and egomaniacal nature made arguments a routine part of every day.

There were no concrete advances. Just complaints. The atmosphere became heavier and heavier and the mood was becoming more and more irritable. Kevin was bothered by even the slightest thing about Mullis. He could not even stand the opera arias Mullis whistled while they worked. In addition to this was the issue of financing, the lack of resources. Everything was turning into a time bomb.

When Mullis moves to the southern cone, Kevin manages to get a job as a biophysicist at NASA's Biological Research Center. He needed to become steeped in space technologies to see if he could find a new way to corroborate the origin of the Sacred Shroud DNA through them and achieve cloning. Therefore, thanks to his "impeccable conduct and professionalism" he was invited to join the board of the Center of Sindonology in Rome.

Kevin felt at ease. 'Out of danger.'

If there was one thing Mullis knew about, it was leveraging resources. And for him, time was the most valuable of all.

A time that kept on passing.

In vain.

He deeply believed that there were times when it was necessary to stop in order to continue. For Kevin, it did not work that way. On one of those trips, the inevitable happened.

Once again, these two trains collided. Squarely.

"Kevin, we need to talk. I tried to evade this issue and see if we could find another way. But this is best discussed face to face while you are here. We cannot continue. We are at zero. We don't have the certainty of having the blood of Christ. And, to top it off, we have no resources."

"What do you mean we have no resources? You mean you've sucked us dry?"

"Do you think what you send is enough? I've tried to work magic with what arrives."

"Oh, really? What have you done to find more resources? So far, I'm the one who has brought in the money. I've mobilized investors, I'm the one who seeks, in every way, the income for you to stay here comfortably."

"Comfortably?"

"Yes. You spend and spend. You don't contribute! Besides, I remind you that you are here thanks to me, to my contacts. Even to the money, I have invested from my own pocket so you don't starve to death. It's very easy to receive without doing anything and complain."

"I can't believe what you're saying..."

"Your job is to work and apparently you're not doing it because we're still in the same fucking place!" criticized Kevin.

The tone was rising. The atmosphere was increasingly tense. Mullis tried to remain calm.

"Your role in this partnership was to help with resources!" Mullis pointed out.

"Where's that written? Because I really don't remember. It seems to me that you are not doing what you should be doing, to be honest."

As much as Mullis tried to be in control, it became impossible.

"It's easy to sit there comfortably with the excuse that you might be found out, waiting for me to accomplish the feat here alone! I'm sure you want to take all the credit for yourself! Let's see if you get it if I tell you slowly. We cannot carry out this project the way we are doing it," he paused at each word. "We're missing the most important thing!"

"More money, Mr. Bloodsucker?"

"Yes, more money and something else that we can't figure out. That's why I think we have to stop all this."

"Do you think we're going to get anywhere by stopping everything? What type of researcher are you? Are you telling me I wasted my time and money believing in you? I should have trusted my instincts!" Kevin scathed as he screamed in rage.

That hurt Mullis's pride. After all, the idea had been his.

"I didn't know your instincts pointed elsewhere!" said Mullis. "That's why they say that if you lie down with dogs..."

"You better shut up!" Kevin interrupted. "I think you've already got what you were looking for in the first place. I was an idiot to think you could be someone with vision, despite how decrepit you are!" he shouted as he walked toward the door.

Mullis felt like he had been stabbed in the back and checkmated.

Kevin was not thinking rationally. He was a bundle of uncontrolled impulses.

"You're not listening to me!" said Mullis trying to surpass Kevin's voice. "This childish reaction makes no sense. All I wanted to say was that..."

Mullis did not manage to finish his sentence. Kevin's outburst did not allow him to continue. The sound of a door slamming was heard. Amid the silence, he was left trying to understand the outburst of his "partner." He saw himself in the middle of that improvised laboratory in Argentina. He thought about the time invested. About the project they had on their hands. It was absurd. Very absurd.

"He'll think it through later and it will pass," he murmured.

Knowing how to recognize the perfect time to say or do things is something to aspire to. Fortunately, Mullis had it.

Kevin is more the type of person who does not give in. He is convinced that there is only one way of doing things: his own.

If he bends his character and learns from his mistakes is it possible that then, and only then, will he win the battle.

Kevin is about to learn that.

3

Two pieces of the Shroud of Turin.
Two totally different people.
The same intention.
The result?
Two versions of the same thing or a clash between enemies.

Mullis knew that in order for the cloning of Jesus Christ to be successful, he needed to corroborate that the DNA actually belonged to Jesus. Moreover, he urgently needed to find a different view of the events. One that would allow him to abstract and rethink the idea from another dynamic.

However, not everything he did while he was in the Southern Cone was in vain. One way or another, Mullis had made progress in the investigations. Hence his desire to seek new knowledge that would allow him to find the missing piece.

He really had part of what he needed to make that dream come true.

He decided to close the laboratory.

He has thought it through. It is time to return to the United States.

Since his arrival on U.S. soil, he has tried to get in touch with Kevin many times. It has been impossible. He does not answer him. If Kevin did not want to be on the project, he would do it on his own. The partnership had broken down.

He joined the Institute of Genetic Medicine at Johns Hopkins University in Baltimore. After a couple of years of research, he presented his studies in nuclear transfer in 1993. That same year he was invited to join a biotech company called PPL Therapeutics, which had founded the Roslin Institute in Scotland.

Mullis became part of the team carrying out a cloning project. A sheep would be cloned with adult cells during nuclear transfer. For many, doing this would be an experimental aberration. An identical reproduction of mammary cells.

In everything that meant transgression, Mullis felt fully at home.

This topic not only generated controversy but also marked an important scientific advance for humanity. For an unscrupulous man like Mullis, it meant crossing a red line, something that could turn the world upside down. And so it would be. No one imagined that what he had been making on the sly in Edinburgh would challenge scientific dogma.

He had managed to corroborate that the blood on that small piece of cloth corresponded to the man who had conquered death. Mullis held in his hands the DNA of Jesus Christ himself.

He was in the right place, validating his theories and absorbing everything; and then doing something that bioethics did not necessarily consider "wrong."

The moment of achieving the cloning of the first mammal was near. Mullis knew it. If so, also close was the possibility that the plans he had previously had with Kevin would come to fruition; the cloning of the first man. Not just anyone. The Son of God himself.

Kevin was still working in biotechnology at NASA and had founded, in 1994, a group on the nascent *deep web*. The formless place of cyberspace, where everything of a dubious legal nature is found.

Despite their differences, Mullis knew of Kevin's talent and ambitions. That is why, after seeing the progress being made at Roslin, he endeavored to recruit him to the team.

To do this, the first step was to break down the pride of his former colleague.

Mullis understood that the strategy was to put his pride aside.

It was time to tear down the walls that divided them.

4

—Tuesday.
October 13th, 1995.
For some, it was a day of bad luck.

The story goes that Judas Iscariot was the 13th participant in the Last Supper.
It was also the day of the Roman deity Mars, the god of war.
Others are of the complete opposite opinion.
For Pythagoras, the number 13 represented immortality.
It signified a time of harvests and achievements.

Kevin believes that Tuesday the 13th is a lucky day. He identifies more with Pythagoras than with Judas.

He got up early as usual. He sipped his coffee and went out to check the mail. There he found a large yellow envelope from Edinburgh. It had the Roslin Institute's seal.

Inside were two letters.

The first, with a job offer inviting him to join the research group of the cloning project. The juicy financial proposal quadrupled the amount he got for his work at NASA. He was excited. Undoubtedly, luck was on his side.

The second letter quickly brought him back to reality.

It was a note from Mullis.

Friend. Colleague.

First of all, I want to apologize for what happened. I am not a man of many friends or affection, but I consider you my friend. Everything that has gone on between us is absurd.

I miss our endless conversations and discussions in pursuit of the lofty dreams that unite us. Yes, in the present tense. I know that they continue to unite us.

Upon my return from Argentina, I tried to contact you, but it was impossible. Life went on so I stopped insisting. I am currently working at the Roslin Institute. Everything points to the fact that very soon we will be able to clone a mammal by nuclear transfer. You'd really enjoy this!

The progress I see in this field only makes me think about how close we are to making our project a reality.

Cloning the first man is still my dream. I'm sure it is yours too. I insist we are one step away from achieving it. Our goal is so close that we can both almost taste it. I want us to change history together. I hope you accept the offer.

P.S.: By the way, we verified that the blood on the Sacred Mantle belongs to Jesus Christ. 100 % confirmed.

Kevin had followed in Mullis's footsteps. He knew every detail of what he had done during all that time when their friendship had been frozen.

He took the phone and made a call. He arranged some paperwork.

He read the letter again. He made another call.

"Hello, old decrepit man! I hope you'll be the one looking for me at the airport. I just booked everything. I land in your city the day after tomorrow, at three o'clock in the afternoon."

A strange feeling of joy came over them.

There are absurd quarrels, and vain discussions, which stop the natural process of events. Empty spaces that cannot be filled no matter how hard you try. They will remain inert until the wheel of destiny turns. Until it meshes. And everything goes back to the beginning.

What is meant to be will always find a way to manifest itself and cross paths again.

This was about to happen with Mullis and Kevin.

~

Edinburgh Airport was a mere 7.4 miles from the city. That day it was very crowded, as usual. It is not one of the busiest in the United Kingdom for nothing.

The sound of the screens announced the arrival of flight A2110 from California.

For Mullis, it was one of those moments when joy is mixed with uncertainty.

What would the reunion with his old friend be like?

They greeted each other with a warm hug. They were joyful. There was no doubt about that. The apartment was very close to the Roslin Institute. Kevin could walk to his new job.

On the drive from the airport, they chatted non-stop. They apologized to each other, laughed about the moments they remembered together. Upon arriving at Kevin's apartment, they opened a bottle of whiskey.

"You did it, you old fool! You managed to corroborate that the blood does indeed belong to Christ. I find it hard to accept, but I congratulate you," said Kevin.

"And I want to congratulate you. You were the cheeky one who stole the piece of the Holy Shroud! Besides, we are the only ones who know that secret," pointed Mullis.

"What? That I stole the piece of fabric?"

"Yes. And we're also the only ones who know that this blood is of the Son of God! Kevin, we have the DNA! Jesus' DNA! We're doing it!"

"You were right; we are two mad scientists about to change history. Cheers!"

Apparently, the storm had passed.

The lobbying that Mullis had done at the institute was of such magnitude that everyone seemed to have known Kevin forever. As part of the welcome protocol, Mullis and the general manager showed him around the facilities.

Within days, Kevin knew the internal dynamics inside out. His extroverted nature meant that he adapted quickly. "He had everyone in his pocket."

Mullis was one of the directors. His successful proposals made him stand out in the group. He stood out for his genius and hunger for knowledge. This is how he gained power. That is why he was able to easily bring Kevin into the project.

The developments inside Roslin were impressive. Moments of euphoria in which everything pointed to the immediate achievement of the cloning of the first mammal.

Suddenly, the smallest variable changed, and the adjustments began again.

Such is the process of science: trial and error.

Everyone sensed that, at any moment, the cloning would end up happening successfully.

Soon after, a new scientist joined the team. His stay would be brief. He was directly endorsed by the center's CEO. He had excellent references.

To everyone's surprise, the scientist was also a priest.

"A priest joined the team today," Mullis told Kevin.

"A priest? Why?"

"They realized that this place needs an exorcism," Mullis joked.

"You can't be serious, can you?" said Kevin in surprise.

"Yes." He said seriously. "But I am concerned about you."

"About me?"

"I'm afraid when they pour holy water on you, you'll be a wreck." He began to laugh out loud.

It was one of the few times Mullis brought out his dark humor.

"I hope you're not around then, lest you get splashed by the water and get it worse, you old fool!"

"Ha ha ha, it was a joke. But a priest really did join. Apparently, this priest is also a scientist. He has been doing research in genetics for several years and could be of great help," said Mullis.

"Sounds interesting."

A few hours later, Mullis and the CEO entered the laboratory with a man wearing a clerical collar and dressed in black. They all turned around.

Kevin came over to greet and welcome him.

"Glad to meet you! I am Dr. Kevin Davis. From your attire, there is no doubt that you are the priest joining the team."

"Yes. The pleasure's mine. I am Father Arnaldo. Arnaldo Romero."

Kevin extended his hand to the priest's companions as well.

"Dr. Aguilar, Dr. Mullis, nice to meet you too! When I heard that a priest had joined I thought it was strange, but certainly interesting. I heard that you are a scientist and have several papers in genetics. Is that right?"

"You've been well informed," said Arnaldo, smiling.

"I hope we can have time to talk soon!"

"We will!"

Mullis, Aguilar, and Arnaldo said goodbye to continue the tour. From that day on, Kevin and Arnaldo bumped into each other on multiple occasions in the hallways. They greeted each other, exchanged a few impressions, and went about their business.

On one of those afternoons, they met at the café. Kevin went forward and sat at the table where Arnaldo was sitting.

"May I?" He asked Arnaldo.

"Sure! Go ahead! Take a seat."

"How has it been?" continued Kevin.

"Good. Everything is interesting."

"May I ask what a priest is doing in a research center like this?"

"Sure! Everyone asks the same! I am also a scientist. I have done some research where religion and science come together. Eventually, we are assigned as part of research support groups."

"How's that?"

"They are multidisciplinary groups that contribute to a project from their respective fields. For the time being, I will only be here for three months."

"But isn't it weird to have the Church involved in science?" Kevin insisted.

"The Church has not been a hindrance to science. On the contrary, many priests have contributed to humanity with their scientific contributions. "Nature, the world and God are related." As Pope John Paul II said, "Science too is a way to truth; for God's gift of reason, which according to its nature is destined not for error, but for the truth of knowledge, is developed in it."

"The thing is that I am not given to the Church, or to prayers, or to God. However, let me tell you that I had the opportunity to be on the team that evaluated the Shroud, and it was interesting."

"I find it fascinating to be able to meet one of the few men who has had that privilege. What an honor that we can work together!" commented Arnaldo.

"As of today, you'll be able to say you know two. Dr. Mullis was also there. In fact, we met at STURP."

"Double fortune for me! I understand that the results did not yield the expected information. But, from what I've seen and read, everything points to the fact that it could be real. It's a debate."

Kevin pauses. He smiles.

"You never know when science can surprise," he said sarcastically. "However, with the Church involved, everything will be a debate."

"Why do you say that Dr. Kevin?"

"Now, Father Arnaldo. If as scientists we seek to create a better version of, say, a glass of milk, couldn't we at some point think of creating an even better version of the Son of God?" Kevin inferred.

"That'd be impossible! God cannot surpass himself."

"And how do you know that God cannot surpass Himself? Can God create a stone so big that He Himself cannot move it?"

"This is a game. A semantic trap, dear doctor."

"Or a debate."

"I insist, it seems like a game."

"So, my dear Father, let's stop the game and ask you seriously: if we could clone Jesus and make "adjustments" for his perfection, would you do it or not? Would you participate or not?"

Arnaldo remained thoughtful, searching for the right answer. He knew that this type of conversation does not always end well.

"Would you participate or not?" insisted Kevin.

"I feel it is an empty debate. First, everything has an order. Even in the midst of what today may be chaos, there is an order established by God. Not a leaf moves without His will."

"It means, if I can figure out a way to clone Jesus, that's God's will, isn't it? Because if I do, it was already pre-established by God Himself."

"We would enter into a debate on ethics and freedom, of free will. If we talk about it in terms of science, there is an ethical principle that tells us that human beings are not aims for themselves. Nor can we, at the scientific level, use them for other purposes, even though they may be very laudable."

"When is anything important ever achieved by following the rules, Father?"

This would not be the only debate they would have. From then on, all of their conversations ended in heated discussions. Fiery. Controversial. All on the same topic.

Mullis joined them, making this trio explosive. It sounded contradictory, but they enjoyed those moments where science and faith intersected.

The three months passed quickly. It was time for Arnaldo to return to his parish. The team had more than 250 cloning attempts, with nearly a dozen female surrogate sheep.

Arnaldo entered the laboratory to say goodbye. At the back was a woman meeting with one of the research groups. He had seen her several times before. He did not have the opportunity to meet her personally. Her name was Angelika Schnieke, a notable professor and scientist.

She was suggesting using cells she had grown from adult sheep to produce a new animal from scratch. Arnaldo also found this interesting, but it was time to leave.

Had he stayed, he would have gone down in history. It was this woman's idea that achieved the great feat 148 days later. That would be attempt 277.

The one that would give life to Dolly the sheep.

The level of excitement and buzz at Roslin that day was unparalleled. The credit went to biologists Wilmut and Campbell. However, the vast majority of researchers at the center, including Kevin and Mullis, gave the credit to that reddish-haired woman. She was considered Dolly's real mother.

For science, it would be the beginning of many things.

For Kevin and Mullis, it was the turning point they had been waiting for. They already had the missing piece. The gateway to the most controversial of all experiments.

The idea of cloning Jesus Christ was getting closer and closer to being achieved.

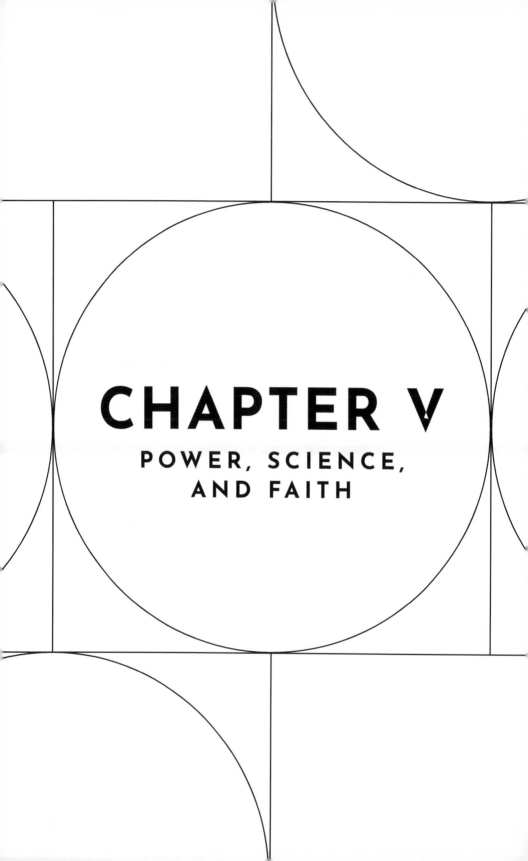

CHAPTER V

POWER, SCIENCE, AND FAITH

S ince ancient times, in all cultures and religions, man has aspired to perfection.

Their quest has inspired the most sublime and beautiful acts. Also, the darkest and most horrific.

For Hitler, it was the consolidation of his *Lebensborn* program, which sought the development of a "superior Aryan race." His obsession.

In German, *Lebensborn* means 'source of life'. A project is suitable only for the racially pure. They were breeding grounds of supermen where anything less than "perfect" was purged.

To carry it out, he had allies such as the Nazi doctor Josef Mengele, who, curiously enough, was raised in a Catholic family and performed sadistic experiments on humans to achieve the superiority they desired.

For others, "perfection" is the Holy Grail expressed in detail, in excellence, in the rigorousness of work. That is the case with the great men who have made their contribution to art, music, sports, or science.

One of these men is the Spanish microbiologist, Juan Martínez Mojica, from the University of Alicante. Thanks to him, the first studies of CRISPR-Cas9 sequences were carried out in 1993. A revolutionary technology that makes it possible to manipulate cells and edit DNA genes.

This technique and the success of Dolly's cloning became the bastions Mullis and Davis needed to finalize the details for their controversial and ambitious crusade: the cloning of Jesus Christ.

NELSON BUSTAMANTE & CARMEN VICTORIA PARDO

They have decided to continue for some years more at the Roslin Institute. They need the advances from the relationships they will be able to build, and it is also the perfect place to stand out on merit.

Here they have met a very influential man, vital to their plans. A scientist is very well linked to high spheres of power. The face behind the financial support in the research that has been carried out at the Institute. His name is Dimitriv Basov. A Russian with hundreds of research studies conducted in conjunction with the most renowned men and women of science in the United States. He also had great connections and the money they need for their purposes.

Kevin's astuteness and keen nose have led him to detect the *"homo perfectus."* They have created a close bond with him. His warmth, intelligence, and camaraderie have earned his trust, affection, and admiration. He has not been afraid to share his ideals about the next big step in science with him. In fact, he has spoken about it on multiple occasions. Dimitriv has been greatly impressed. Kevin has shown him ultimate perfection.

Dimitriv, as part of the board of a club, that was about to take place; so, he considered it ideal to apply for a permit to bring a guest. This was not a frequent occurrence, but he had license to do it. He felt that Kevin's presence could be invaluable.

Breaking their own rules, Nuremberg's management agreed.

It cannot be otherwise if in the end they write, rewrite, and change them whenever they feel like it.

Surprisingly, when Dimitriv extended the invitation to Kevin, he declined.

How could such an intelligent man not be willing to change his plans to gain access to a space where only the elite gathered? Why did he turn down this invitation from which he could benefit so much?

Kevin was conducting research that would have a major impact on the scientific community and required his presence. He could not be absent. He excused himself to Dimitriv.

He knew of Kevin's ambitions and ideals. What he did not know was that these projects had taken on a new dimension after some revelations that changed the course of events.

That is why Dimitriv's curiosity was exacerbated. An opportunity such as the one he was giving him could only be passed up by someone who has what is at hand beyond imagination. He would soon find out what it was all about.

Dimitriv was a man of vision. Sharp, clever. An old hand.

He had been closely following the career of a friend, whom he had not seen in a long time. This man, named Mikhail Stuling, was in charge of several secret scientific investigations of the Russian government. Dimitriv wanted to know what they were planning.

He did not waste the opportunity the club had given him to bring a guest, and he extended it to that forward-thinking, loyal, honest, brilliant man of science, for whom he had great esteem and respect.

He had long wanted to add him to his team.

He did not know how.

The Club of Rome was the way to lure the prey to the bait.

2

—Saturday, 7 p.m.
August 17th, 2013.

As usual, Kevin had gone to Darnell Mullis's apartment to meet, have a drink, talk about the Institute and review the research.

Their lives revolved around work. Around science. Just that.

"You know what, Kevin? Maybe I never told you this, but I really appreciate all these years of friendship. We have shared many things together. However, I have not been fully transparent. There are things you don't know about me. I want to show you something."

The years bring death closer and make human beings vulnerable.

Darnell stood up from his chair. He walked over to a shelf full of books and dust.

"It's my way of telling you that I believe in you and in what we have in front of us. It's time to tell you who I am."

He bent down. From one of the lower drawers, he extracted several old, yellowed notebooks, which had been looked through many times. He carefully placed them on the table.

"What is all this?" Asked Kevin.

"Just read."

Darnell had thought about it a hundred times before taking this step. He spent many sleepless nights analyzing whether it was right to share that. A well-kept secret. A story that lay underground. A window full of dark possibilities. Past and future. Of significant relevance. Transcendent.

Kevin started reading.

The silence was total.

"Is this real? How do you have this?"

"It is the original. Hand-written. A jewel. Pour yourself another drink."

That man decided to open Pandora's box.

"When I was barely twenty years old, I went to Argentina in search of what I thought was the love of my life. At the time, I was a sophomore science major in college. But I chose to venture out and run after the woman who captivated me. For that love, I left everything. I lived in a boarding house on Paraguay Street, in Palermo, and had started working in a nearby store. At the beginning of the relationship everything was going well. It was intense. With time I understood that it was also fleeting and painful. Very painful. Little by little everything cooled down."

What did that story have to do with what he now held in his hands?
Kevin did not understand.

~

Darnell worked ten hours every day. There was no rest. One afternoon, the owner of the business where he worked had a family emergency. He preferred to close. He gave everyone the afternoon off. For Mullis, it was the ideal moment to treat himself to a different kind of time with the woman he loved. Perhaps, rekindle the passion. He bought flowers.

The apartment where they lived was small. A single room. He went in. There she was. In the bed. Half-naked.

Certainly, there was passion.

But with another man.

His mind became clouded. He leaped on her. With his hand, he pressed on her neck. He was choking her. The man grabbed his clothes and ran away. She managed to break free and escape, still half naked.

That was the last time he saw her.

He was devastated.

He drank non-stop, and he did not eat. He cried like a child. Days passed like this.

Still sleepless with broken heart, dark circles under his eyes and the foul odor emitting from his body, he decided to go out in search of more alcohol. He needed to keep drowning his sorrow. He was wasted. Inside and out.

Near the boarding house was the Montecarlo bar. He decided to go in.

He sat at the counter and ordered a double scotch. Next to him was a man with a foreign appearance. He was about 40 years old.

He kept looking at him.

"What's the matter, young man? Lovesickness?" he asked.

"How do you know?"

"I have a postgraduate degree in suffering. If I told you I enjoy it, would you believe me?"

"Are you a masochist?" asked Mullis.

"No, I am a physician, and I have always been interested in the study of and resistance to trauma and pain. First of all, let me introduce myself, my name is Helmut Gregor.

"Nice to meet you, I am Darnell Mullis."

They talked all night long. Darnell told him how he had given up his science career for that love.

"I don't know if it's best to go back. Maybe I should never have come."

"Or perhaps this encounter is not coincidental. I am here because I needed to do some paperwork. The reality is that I am opening my practice and I am looking for an assistant. Would you like to work with me? That would reconnect you with your career."

It was tempting.

"Why not?" he thought.

"The problem is that you'd have to move. The consultation is located in Villa Devoto, about nine hours from here. It is gynecological. I'd pay you well so that you can live peacefully."

If Darnell needed anything, it was a change of scenery.

In every sense.

He did not think long about it. He took him at his word.

That night would mark the beginning of an obscure professional relationship.

Gregor had a Ph.D. in Anthropology and Medicine, in addition to a degree at the Institute for Hereditary Biology and Racial Hygiene in Frankfurt.

They did very well together and made a great team.

Just like Helmut's fortunes, Darnell's were rising too.

As time went by, Dr. Gregor managed to open another practice in the upper part of La Ópera coffee shop, in Corrientes, and Callao. He also acquired a house in Arenales 2640, in the province of Buenos Aires, just seven minutes from his work.

Helmut used to whistle opera arias while attending to his patients and performing his experiments.

~

For the first time in all that time, Darnell was putting all the cards on the table in front of Kevin. He poured himself another drink before continuing.

"Helmut Gregor was an influential man. Once I accompanied him to a ranch where President Perón was staying. It was called *Quinta de Olivos*. I couldn't believe I was in the same place as the president. You can't imagine how Perón was entertained by stories about Helmut's scientific discoveries. He was a true Master of Public speaking and a specialist in genetics. From him, I learned the love for this branch of science, his passion for experiments."

Kevin listened carefully. He was trying to make sense of it all and find the connection with the document he had in his hands. He was anxious to get to the end of the story. To know who the man who had become his research partner over the course of twenty years was.

Mullis continued his story.

"Helmut always told me 'Your mind must operate as men of science do. While you concentrate on your studies and do your experiments, feelings are left aside! No regrets. No regrets!'"

Darnell was an excellent apprentice. Boy, did he become well trained!

He spent almost six years at Helmut's side. His practices were obscure and the experiments in which he accompanied him, in many cases, were appalling to him. However, it was all "for science."

He always remembered his professor's phrase:

"No regrets. No regrets!"

In 1956, Helmut had been preparing some paperwork at the German embassy to apply for his passport. A few days later, Darnell received the envelope containing that identity document. He opened it.

He was surprised to see the real name of the man who had a fascination with pain. "Josef Mengele." Better known as "The Monster of Auschwitz."

Josef Mengele was a man without scruples. The SS captain was the one who decided who was to die in the gas chambers, who were to be used as slaves, and which bodies were to be dissected or handed over to Nazi science for evaluation.

He had at his fingertips a human reserve that gave free rein to his ambitions. All of them "more ideological and racist than scientific."

In Auschwitz, ethical boundaries did not exist. It was an ideal space for someone like him.

Like Hitler, Mengele was a man obsessed with eugenics. Although this political and ideological movement that sought to improve the human race was associated with the Nazis, it actually had its origins in 1890 in the United States, shortly after Charles Darwin published his Theory of Evolution.

Darnell confessed to Kevin how he had worked with someone who had not only entertained the idea of human cloning but had produced 94 children with Hitler's genes. Darnell was the right-hand man, the assistant to the "Angel of Death" himself.

Every time Mengele did an experiment or research, he took notes which he then kept inside a brown briefcase. There were all the observations of the studies carried out in Germany while he was an SS doctor.

One afternoon, Mengele had gone for a walk to get some fresh air. Taking advantage of his absence, Mullis entered the office. He did it just as the Angel of Death had taught him: with "no regrets." From the bottom of an old closet, he took out that precious suitcase. He marveled at what was there.

He had enough money.

He had learned what was necessary.

In his hands, he held a priceless treasure.

He simply took it and left.

"Casually" sometime later an extradition request was presented by the German Embassy in Argentina. But, it was already too late. The death angel had already disappeared. Once again.

As Kevin listened to Darnell's confession, his guts opened up. His inner demons were unleashed. An uncontrollable sadism awoke in him.

That research was the yellowed books Kevin held in his hands.

"I would like to peruse these reports! They are pure gold! They're a goldmine!"

"You'll read them, my friend, you'll read them! That's why I'm telling you all this. I don't know how many years I have left to live. You are brilliant, and in your hands, this information can be used to great ends."

There is no doubt. The proximity to death brings down some walls.

Everything has its own time.

That of endings.

That of new beginnings.

For this reason, Kevin had not accepted Dimitriv's invitation to join the Club of Rome. After perusing those Mengele notebooks, he was headlong into the investigations.

Popular wisdom says that what is meant for you will come, no matter what.

Two weeks after the Nuremberg meeting, Dimitriv called Kevin to meet. They needed to do it in private and away from the Institute.

Dimitriv was a straightforward man.

He got to the point.

"Tell me everything about the project you have been working on. I can help you if you tell me what it's about."

Dimitriv resembled Kevin. An unscrupulous egomaniac with a deep desire to make history. When an idea was fixed in his head, he would move towards it without being stopped.

Kevin knew it.

He told him about his idea of achieving perfection. He aspired to absolute power. Through science.

What better way than to clone Jesus?

This was perfectly in line with what Dimitriv also wanted.

"What do you need?"

"A little more time and a lot of money."

Neither condition was a problem for Dimitriv.

A new partnership had emerged.

One that would destroy the foundations of everything imagined.

3

We all keep secrets.
Who does not?
Science says that we hide at least thirteen of them
throughout our lives.
Facts we dare not confess.
That we prefer to keep quiet.
Actions from our past that fill us with shame.
Sometimes, with fear.
Kevin is keeping his own secrets.

His restless temperament and effervescent temper do not allow him to sit still. During the time he broke off relations with Mullis, he created an online community. One where only "thinkers" like him can connect. It has gained many followers. He meets with them five days a week. They call it *CC, 'Code Christ'.* It is on the dark web.

Hidden from search engines Untraceable. However, he is able to see who is surfing on it.

The majority of those who participate in this community are men following the transhumanist trend, an intellectual movement that arose in 1923 thanks to the British geneticist J. B. S. Haldane, and which today continues to gain followers. They use technology to transcend permissible human limits.

Code Christ has a clear interest in the development of eugenics, ectogenesis, and improving human characteristics through the application of genetics.

Some of the men in this group are scientists. Like Dr. Davis, they are mostly biohackers. Others are intelligent people but without any kind of prejudice. They seek to "improve" and modify the human body in order to eliminate defects or create more intelligent beings.

Just as a computer-literate person can hack a system in order to add new functions to it (even if it is not designed to do so), "biohackers" do the same by using their own or other peoples' bodies as walking laboratories. *Made in Home. Do it yourself.* They have no problem with it. They want to perfect themselves.

In the grand tradition of Machiavelli, "the end justifies the means."

Undercover, *Code Christ* has been working from the shadows for more than eighteen years. Although it was born earlier. Much earlier.

In its beginnings, it was just a brand that united the "bad" gangs of a neighborhood. Being in it generated *status quo*. Having its seal was a symbol of power. As time went by, it took on a different hue. A darker one.

Code Christ was born with Rik, one of Kevin's closest collaborators. They studied together. A well-connected man. He was a grinder. An extremist. He used his own body to perform risky operations and to see if they had any side effects.

The first time he tried something on his body was when he was sixteen years old. His grandmother had died, and the ashes had just been given to him. His love for her was immense. His parents had abandoned him, and she was the one who took charge of his upbringing.

That pain and that love made him mix his grandmother's ashes with ink and tattoo himself with them. That way, she would be impregnated in him. This act generated in him a degree of unconscious belonging. He repeated it with his friends. Mixing the ink with the blood of both. Their DNA was there. They became blood brothers. Rik was not alone anymore. He had a family.

Since then, his body became a laboratory.

In *Code Christ*, they are united by the search for the transcendence of man over man. Of man over God himself. They live in a cult where they promote, with enthusiasm and unbridled passion, the imminent change that humanity will bring about through the use of science.

Science is within everyone's reach.

Through shared ideals of greatness and transcendence, their top leaders manipulate their members. The most powerful tool they use is the word. If there is one thing Kevin and Rik are good at, it is just that. In the manipulative power of the word.

Perfect speeches, full of emotion, that know how to communicate what others want to hear. With impeccable mastery, they move primitive forces within each man. They set hearts on fire by tuning frustration into burning desire.

Those who listen to them feel very special. Understood.

Code Christ is a sect that is growing by leaps and bounds.

The heads have taken advantage of the lack of direction of some, the anxiety of others, or, simply, the inert desire of the human being to belong to something that surpasses him. Their speech promotes "commitment to a cause bigger than themselves." They are controversial. Radical. Disruptive. Emotionally manipulative.

Transgressing limits is part of their unconscious philosophy.

Their creators have something in common: they wish to make their names eternal. Kevin has asked them to bring back to life the one who, it is said, defeated death.

Jesus Himself.

The Son of God.

His followers applaud the idea.

He has told them that they are the "chosen ones" and are part of the plan of the world's salvation.

When he decided to tell his followers about his intentions to bring him back using CRISPR-Cas9 breakthroughs, the focus shifted to him. This greatly annoyed Rik. He lost prominence. He felt left out. He was disturbed by the excessive devotion shown towards Kevin. The cult. The odes. The respect.

He became a zero to the left.

He awakened the monster that dwelled within him.

It was time to resume his leading role. To be in control again. This he would achieve at all costs.

4

Christianity would not be the same without its betrayer Judas Iscariot.

Neither is the Catholic Church without the Eucharist.

So, without Judas and the Eucharist, the story would be different.

This sacrament, introduced by Jesus at the Last Supper, reveals His deep love for us. A love that appears when Christ Himself becomes incarnate every time the priest consecrates a piece of bread and wine on the altar, where the miracle of transubstantiation takes place. This is Jesus who is alive and desires to love us so much that he becomes small, goes unnoticed, and enters to dwell in us. The simplest and clearest form of love.

Therefore, to speak of the Eucharist is to speak of God's love; and to speak of Eucharistic miracles is to bring to life the value of this sacrament.

If anyone is supposed to know this sacrament well, it is a priest.

Especially Father Arnaldo, who has investigated them from both a scientific rather than a faith-based perspective. Even a priest may become Judas at some point. Even if Christ Himself appears in front of his eyes and the graces given to him far exceed his calling.

Arnaldo had not only witnessed these miracles in Betania, Venezuela when he accompanied his professor to be part of that research; but also, with the authorization of Rome, he was given the task of analyzing one of the most famous events of the 8th century: the miracle of Lanciano in Italy.

A host started to bleed twelve centuries ago when a priest, doubting the presence of Jesus, saw that host transformed into flesh and blood before his eyes during the consecration.

Arnaldo was asked to evaluate this case once more. He conducted a number of analyses.

They continued to conclude that the flesh was indeed flesh.

Flesh belonging to a heart.

The blood was indeed blood. With the proteins present in fresh blood. With minerals. AB blood type.

It was no coincidence. Arnaldo had a lot in common with that Basilian monk. He had been doubtful of that living presence as well. He still was.

But God never gives up. He continued talking to him.

Just before leaving for the Institute of Trieste, he was sent on a special assignment in Argentina.

A new Eucharist miracle occurred in Santa María's Church in Buenos Aires. Not once, not twice, but three times.

On this occasion, the host had fallen to the ground during communion and was placed, as usual in such cases, in a container with water to be dissolved and purified. Ten days after, the water had turned to blood, the host had become a piece of flesh and its size had increased considerably. Just like in Legnica.

In the middle of his crisis of faith, Arnaldo had no choice but to accept the new assignment.

The fourteen-hour flight from Rome to Argentina was eternal. He was constantly wondering why he was there. He tried to get some sleep, but every time he did, that dream that had accompanied him since he was a child appeared again. He woke up worried in the middle of that "don't let me down." He felt he was failing Him and that tormented Arnaldo.

After leaving all his things in the rectory where he was staying, he decided not to lose time. He wanted to get out of this whole situation as fast as possible. To speed up the days. These would be a bit long, and tedious, but it would be better to hurry.

He headed once and for all to his destination: the parish of Santa María's Church.

The cab he had taken could not leave him in front of the church. The street was under construction. He had to walk about a city block.

"There you can see it, Father! On the corner. The slightly red one" said the cab driver.

Certainly, its walls were covered with facing bricks. It had a predominant Neo-Romanesque style.

As he was walking, he was wondering if this was something he really wanted to do. He was worried to the core. Everything was part of his feeling of unease.

When he reached the front of the church, he decided to take a break.

"Calm down, Arnaldo," he said to himself, "you can't go in like this!"

He breathed deeply. He stood in front of the stairway. He blessed himself. He tried to calm his inner demons. He continued.

It was his first time on Argentine soil. To his astonishment, "she" was there. The patron saint of the Mexico that took him back to his homeland: the Empress of America watching over the left side aisle.

Seeing that picture of Our Lady of Guadalupe filled him with calm. On the right side was the statue of Saint Juan Diego with the cape of roses.

"I don't know what's wrong with me! Forgive me, Lord! There is no doubt that you are with me. Thank you, my beloved virgin!" He said in his thoughts.

In his head, he heard that phrase that the lady of Tepeyac said to the Mexican Indian.

"Don't be afraid... Am I not here who am your Mother?"

For the first time in a long time, Arnaldo felt some peace.

The main parish priest welcomed him with joy. He told him how everything had happened that day of Our Lady of Luján.

On the back of the church, he had created an improvised sanctuary. He took him in front of the sample of that piece of living flesh. There was a platen with blood as well. There they stood, illuminated in a small wake.

In order to verify a Eucharist miracle, a notary must be present to certify the entire procedure and the investigation team must evaluate two phases.

All the studies are issued as if they belonged to a private individual. The name of the researcher in charge does not appear. Nor the name of the church. When samples are taken, it is never stated where they are taken from.

The first phase consisted of verifying the credibility of the witnesses. Therefore, Arnaldo conducted interviews with priests and people who were present at the moment of the transubstantiation.

In order to corroborate this phase, he also used as evidence the notes in a spiritual notebook, which one of the fathers had been keeping daily for ten years. What happened that day was described there is detail.

The second phase concerned the analysis of the sample.

As procedure dictated, Arnaldo used some reagents that change their color in the presence of hemoglobin. As soon as it came into contact, the color changed. Clearly, it was blood, though it looked more like a piece of flesh.

He took a piece. He placed it in a small transparent container which he put in a sealed envelope. The tissue would be sent to a laboratory in the USA.

Once everything was certified by a notary, he asked to be alone with the Lord for a while. He wanted to talk with Him. In the presence of the supernatural sign, he questioned his priesthood. He felt overwhelmed. Devastated. Lost.

On his knees, with his hand on his chest and his head lowered, he prostrated himself before the host turned into flesh and before the statue of a small Christ hanging on the wall. He started praying with fervor. With his soul torn. The silence echoed so loudly that it was deafening.

"Abba, Father! Abba! Forgive me, God of mercy! Even in the presence of all this, I do doubt if you are really there. How can I say I am sorry? I did let you down!"

He started crying. It was the cry of a lost child. A child who felt abandoned, alone.

"Where are you, my Lord? How do I deal with this emptiness inside me? I don't understand what you want from me! I can't hear you. I did let you down...! I keep letting you down!"

"Why don't you come once and for all?"

He looked up. He talked to him openly. More than talking to him, he was reproaching him.

"Why didn't you leave me in peace in Santa Magdalena? Why did you go so far away that I can't find you?"

Once more, he heard that "don't let me down."

He put his hands on his head.

"Get out of here! Get out of here! If you don't tell me clearly what you want from me, how can I do your will? What will?"

He had a lump in his throat.

"If you are so powerful and you love me, why don't you make me breathe your spirit? I say! If you do exist, come! Come and blow away my weakness. Renew me if you are really there. Tell me, how can I serve you if I doubt you?"

"Take me with you!" he heard.

Who did the voice belong to?

Him?

God?

The devil himself?

NELSON BUSTAMANTE & CARMEN VICTORIA PARDO

He started talking with that voice.

"Who are you?" Arnaldo questioned.

"I am your beloved." He heard it inside his head.

"How do I know you are real?"

"What other truth do you need if I am here alive in front of you? I have revealed myself to you again and you don't want to believe!"

"Get out of here, Satan! Get out of my head! What do you want?"

"Why do you refuse to believe?... I just don't want you to let me down!"

There was a long silence. A strong smell of roses permeated the place.

Suddenly, he felt an unexpected impulse. He was not the one in control. He could not stop it.

He put his hands to his chest, where was the cross that always wore around his neck. He opened the hidden compartment.

How do we recognize the voices of the spirit?
There are impulses and temptations that might be an open window for the devil to sneak in. His astuteness always urges dialogue with our dark thoughts. With our suppressed weakness.
If we cannot recognize it with wisdom, the dialogue becomes the doorway to hell.
Defeating Satan is the proof itself.
If the Son of God was tempted, how could we not think that Arnaldo would be?
Does not Genesis begin with temptation?

He moved closer to that portion of miraculous bread. He took an instrument from his bag.

"I won't let you down! I won't do it again. You're coming with me!" he thought.

Indeed. He decided to take a tiny piece of that living host in the secret compartment of his crucifix. Pure sacrilege.

Just as Judas betrayed with a kiss, Arnaldo did it by stealing the body of Christ. Both followers, key pieces in the strange way in which God writes history. Different in time and appearance. Essential to assemble the puzzle of humanity.

It would not be long before Arnaldo discovers whose voice was talking to him that day.

5

The results of the analysis of the so-called Eucharistic miracle of Santa Maria, in Buenos Aires, took some time to arrive. So much that, even among the many obligations he had upon his return to Rome, Arnaldo had forgotten that he would receive them.

This is how time goes by. The seasons pass by. Most of the time, we do not even notice them.
As in nature, there are seasons in the life of man. Splendid summers. Falls where everything falls down. Winters that freeze us. Springs that make us bloom.

From the winter in which Arnaldo found himself, it now seemed a glimmer of bloom was peeking out again.

The journey to Argentina had a sedative effect on him. Little by little, he started to recover his serenity. Paradoxically, keeping Christ, pulsing and alive, in his chest instilled him with a state of relative peace. Highly relative. Only a glimmer. But peace after all.

It did not last long. It did not take long for him to scold himself for what he had done. The anxiety came back again.

He woke up every night frightened. He even thought about confessing, but he was stopped by the fear of being judged. He preferred internal jail to the freedom given by the liberating sacrament of confession. He knew that what he had done was grounds for ex-communication. He had profaned the Eucharist.

How could he explain what happened?

He decided to bear his cross in silence.

Regularly, Hilda, his secretary, placed the mail on a tray on his desk. Next to it, is a cup of black coffee.

A few months had passed since the journey to Argentina. That day, as usual, he first took a sip of his drink and then got ready to check the mail. A big yellow envelope stood out clearly. It came from the American laboratory where the sample of the bleeding wafer had been sent to.

He opened it. He started reading.

Results of the analysis:
The material examined belongs to a fragment of the heart muscle. Specifically, to the wall of the left ventricle.

Purified blood comes from the left ventricle. Jesus is the one who purifies His parishes of its sins. In the Eucharist, He makes himself present, once again, to continue to do so.

"God and his stuff! Left ventricle!" he said out loud.

That supernatural thing apologetically made a lot of sense.

The analysis continued:

> *The heart muscle shows an inflammatory condition and a large number of white blood cells. This indicates that the heart was still alive at the moment the sample was taken. It is a living tissue of a person who has suffered. The tissue comes from a person of around thirty years old. The blood type is AB.*

He immediately brought his hands to his chest. He held the cross where a piece of that bleeding heart was kept. He squeezed it tightly as he closed his eyes. He remembered that phrase he heard when he was a child. "Arnaldo, son, my bleeding heart waits for you. Don't let me down."

"It's you!" he said. "It's you!"

He remembered that time he experienced that manifestation.

A sublime moment, incomprehensible to the eyes of man. Intimate. That instant next to the beloved. Of the love of loves.

He went into ecstasy.

He melted into the pain of Jesus himself. The minutes seemed like hours to him. A loving, but bleeding intimacy.

Suddenly, shaken, he opened his eyes. Conflicted because he felt he had betrayed him.

He took a breath.

This new confirmation of Jesus alive in mystical and supernatural manifestations made him feel miserable remembering the times he had doubted his presence.

Those analyses coincided with those of the blood of the Holy Shroud of Turin, the Holy Shroud of Oviedo, Bethany and also the bleeding host of the miracle of Lanciano.

Paradoxically, days before he had conducted studies on the blood that had flowed from some statues of the Virgin Mary. This was as well as AB blood type. Mother and son had the same blood type.

> *How many more times would God need to reconfirm to him that He was present?*
>
> *How many winters would he need to live through?*
>
> *Hopefully, the one he experiences will not be the winter of death. "Our Sister Death", as Saint Francis of Assisi would say.*
>
> *If so, it is likely that just before that final winter, Arnaldo will review his life.*
>
> *He will review the times that, like Peter, he denied Jesus.*
>
> *He should assess everything.*
>
> *Hopefully, at his last crossroads, before death catches up with him, he will repent.*

CHAPTER VI

THE UNSEEN

1

"For there is nothing hid, save that it should be manifested; neither was anything made secret, but that it should come to light."

Mark, 4:22

After meeting for the promised coffee, little by little, Arnaldo and Giacomo struck up a very good friendship.

Whenever there was a chance, they went out and talked about their lives, their past, and topics that were not always explained within the world of logic. Faith. Daily life. Controversial topics.

This is why their talks were pleasant and generally long.

Arnaldo's curiosity found support in someone who not only managed the largest library in the world but who was also a walking source of knowledge. The prefect of the Vatican Archive. His friend.

—Saturday.
October 29th, 2005.

As usual, these two good friends are gathered.
This day will mark the beginning of many things.
However, they do not know it yet.

Arnaldo and Giacomo are shocked by the triple attack that took place that day in New Delhi. Sixty one casualties. One hundred eighty eight injured. A little-known Islamic group has claimed responsibility.

They are talking about it. They remember the attack on Pope John Paul II. The issue of his predecessor arises.

"Do you think the hypothesis of the 'poisoning' of John Paul I is true? I know we are both part of the Church, but the reality is that the doubt was sown when the result of the autopsy was not disclosed," Arnaldo asked.

"You're right! The truth is that John Paul I sought to end corruption. He considered making a series of changes among the cardinals and bishops who had greater power. In this way, the situation could be handled better. At least, that's what he thought."

"In other words, to put it bluntly, the Pope was certainly a threat to some people."

"Exactly!" Giacomo agreed.

"And there are no declassified documents in the archives where the information about this pope's death is kept?"

"The papal archives are in the library. When a pope dies, his archives are kept sealed for seventy years. Only his close family can have access to them."

"In other words, we are some forty years away from having access to them and knowing the truth."

They talked with ease, but also with respect.

Certainly, some secrets might cost dearly.

"Aren't you curious to go through them? What do you think?" Arnaldo insisted.

"Of course! But no! There are rumors of financial scandals involving the Vatican Bank and, of course, they tarnish the Church. Remember that we had come from the long period under Paul VI, in which quite illegitimate business was done. Besides, apparently, there was a relationship between the Vatican Bank and the Italian mafia. The power inside the power.

Fourteen years later, that conversation would no longer be speculation. An Italian hitman named Anthony Luciano Raimondi would confess his participation in the assassination ordered by organized crime.

"What other things are kept in the archives that caught your attention?" Arnaldo continued researching.

"Do you really want to know?"

"Of course!"

"Well, inside there is a covert collection held by the Vatican Archive known as the Apostolic Archive. The chronovisor can be found there."

"What's that?"

"It's said to be a machine capable of obtaining images and sounds from the past. The moment of Jesus's crucifixion was registered there," Giacomo mentioned.

As director of the Vatican Archives, he had been in front of the chronovisor. He did not know if it worked or not. But it was real.

It was there.

The device was developed by the Benedictine Father Marcello Pellegrino Ernetti, together with two scientists: the former Nazi Von Braun, whose work at NASA took the United States to the Moon, and Fermi, who won the Nobel Prize in Physics in 1938.

Arnaldo found it fascinating.

Giacomo did not stop talking. Arnaldo listened to him carefully.

The basis of that time machine was linked to the principle of classical physics which states that 'energy can neither be created nor destroyed; rather, it can only be transformed from one form to another.

"In the field of science, that makes sense," reflected Arnaldo. "Condensed energy, both sound, and visual waves are governed by these same physical laws of matter. Hmmm... It's weird, but it might be true! At least, it makes sense!"

"Can you imagine being able to travel back in time and have Christ in front of you?" Giacomo speculated.

"If I told you that I already traveled to the past and I had him in front of me, would you believe me?" Arnaldo said.

"Now I truly believe you have a screw loose. I had thought about it before, but now, I'm sure. Let's see, how is it that you traveled back in time and saw him? Maybe you were dreaming..."

"In other words, I have to blindly believe in the chronovisor but you don't believe that I was with Christ in the past," replied Arnaldo while laughing.

"Alright, tell me the story so I can believe you."

"Yes, it's a dream. You're right about that, but it's been repeating again and again ever since I was a kid, when I was about nine or ten. It became recurrent. I know it sounds crazy. Have you ever had a dream that feels so real that you question if you were actually there?"

"I believe everybody has felt that way sometimes."

"Even awake?"

"How is that possible, Arnaldo?"

From the look on Arnaldo's face, Giacomo knew he was serious.

"I don't know. I felt I was there," replied Arnaldo, sorrowful.

"Tell me the dream. It really seems like something that touches and worries you."

"I'm worried about letting down the Lord!"

"Well, tell me about it..."

Arnaldo started to tell him the dream. Once he did, he seemed to be transported back to that instant. He described everything in detail.

"In my dream I was seven years old. I was accompanying Jesus on the Via Dolorosa. Walking next to Him. There were a lot of people, a lot of commotion. I was trying to keep an eye on Him. I clearly heard those who were mocking Him. He carried the cross on His back. His skin was shredded. The crown was tearing His head. There was a lot of blood, Giacomo, a lot of blood! I could feel his pain in my body. It was weird! I was even hurt by the people's insults and rejection."

As in his dream, Arnaldo could feel everything again. In the flesh, in the present. As if he was back in that place.

"I see how He falls down for the first time. The ground is soil and stones. He hurts his knees. I see the suffering in His face. I try to get through the crowd to get closer, but the soldiers won't let me. I feel like every step He takes is his last. Like He will definitely fall down there. Next to me is Mary, his mother. She is calling out for Him. It is heartbreaking to see her suffer so much. The pain was overwhelming. All of a sudden, a woman makes her way among the soldiers. She removes her veil. She wipes the sweat and blood from Jesus' face. It's Veronica. While this is happening, I ask myself 'what should I do?'"

Arnaldo stopped talking. He looked Giacomo in the eyes.

"What should I do, Giacomo? What should I do?"

He repeats that question as one who seeks to find an answer today.

Silence takes over the room. His eyes well up. Giacomo is moved, wrapped in the special halo of this dream.

As Arnaldo continued to narrate his sleeping thoughts, he felt that he was also there with him, in the flesh, in the present.

Arnaldo wipes away his tears. He continues.

"In the middle of that scene, I can see the second fall of Jesus. The pain is overwhelming. I can feel it. I start crying. My eyes are locked on him. I want to go with him. The torment, the helplessness, invades me more. I see Him there with that heavy cross. A few steps from Golgotha. And then, His third fall... He falls looking down at the ground. He can't take it anymore. Simon of Cyrene does not arrive... he never does. At that moment, it is just me. Only me! When I realized this it filled me with courage. I make my way among the crowd. I run up to Him. I fall to my knees beside Him. I reach out my hand, which touches His. Amid His pain, He lifts His face. For the first time, I feel He's looking at me in the eyes... I wanted Him to look at me so much and now that He does, I don't feel worthy! Right there, when I look down, He calls my name. He takes my hand and says: "Arnaldo, son, my bleeding heart waits for you. Don't let me down!." He calls my name. He tells me: 'don't let me down... Don't let me down!'"

Arnaldo repeats that phrase like an echo, like a mantra. His tears are flowing in torrents. Giacomo can feel that his pain is profound.

"I feel like I've let Him down and that I'm still doing so by trying but failing to understand what he wants! My friend, it is the exact same dream. Repeated thousands of times. So real. Thousands of times..."

"Why do you think so? I'm sure you haven't let Him down."

Giacomo also wipes away his tears. He gives him a fraternal hug. Arnaldo does not dare reveal his secret, the reason why he feels like a traitor.

Though he listened carefully to the story, Giacomo feels somehow disappointed at being unable to do anything. Curiously, he felt what Arnaldo experienced in his dream. He does not comment on anything, but he tries to comfort him.

"I must remind you it is just a dream!"

The minutes went by.

Little by little, Arnaldo starts to calm down. To return to reality. It was a strange experience. For both of them. Giacomo wanted to improve the mournful feeling that was in the atmosphere. He wanted to bring him out of that sordid state. Adding a little humor to the conversation.

"If we turn on the chronovisor and you travel back in time, would he clarify your doubts? After all, you are a scientist! You might make it work!"

Arnaldo smiled. The idea worked.

As for the chronovisor proposal, it sounded hare-brained but tempting.

"I'll take your word for it!"

"Are you serious? We have nothing to lose. What if it really works?" said Giacomo.

"I hope you're the one who isn't being serious!"

Both of them laughed.

"I prefer to imagine having Jesus in front of me, but in the future," replied Arnaldo.

"If you were, what would you say to him?"

Arnaldo thought about the answer.

"I would say: I hope I didn't let you down!"

"I'm sure you didn't," replied his friend.

"In fact, instead of using science to fix the chronovisor, why don't we speed up His return to see if He sorts this out?"

They both smiled again.

A strange idea was beginning to grow unconsciously in Arnaldo's mind.

Soon enough he would have the perfect excuse to execute it.

2

Who should be feared the most?

A man who speaks his mind or one who does not and whose thoughts are always a mystery?

Jun Lee is a brilliant man, a genius. He goes beyond the rational in many aspects. During the STURP days, a phobia of social contact had been activated again. Sharing with so many people around him, being noticed, and being judged, even made him nauseous.

As soon as he could, he slipped away to the bathroom to breathe. His heart was beating in an exacerbated manner. His mind was blank, as he made little contact with the people present there. He tried not to say anything so he wouldn't be exposed.

That is why he did not say goodbye.

He just wanted to get home again.

After STURP, the symptoms worsened. In his childhood was the root of that social anxiety disorder that was getting worse.

He began to drink to evade his surroundings. It was all part of his childhood memories.

And they were not happy memories.

When he was seven years old, the monsters that lived in his head appeared one night in his room. It was pouring down, even thundering. After lightning lit his room, the deafening sound of thunder followed. The shadows of the night wandered into his room. Lee was scared to death.

That is why he wet his bed.

Although his father had forbidden him to sleep with them at night, he ran to protect himself in his mother's room. The corridor was long and narrow. With every step his tiny feet took, the old wooden floor creaked more. The cold seeped through the walls. The lightning and thunder continued doing as they pleased.

Finally, he felt safe. He reached his parent's room.

The door was half-open.

He tried to come in. He could not.

He wanted to shout. He could not.

He wanted to move. He could not.

The fear had paralyzed him. He just watched.

In front of his innocent eyes, that grotesque picture would be engraved forever. A cruel, vulgar Dantesque spectacle, where his father, drunk as usual, raping his mother.

Colossal claps of thunder drowned out the woman's desperate screams; they drowned out the beating her husband was giving her.

Jun Lee was there. Once again, he was wetting himself.

He wanted to save her, but he did not have the courage.

He was not that brave!

He ran away. He preferred the monsters that had been left in his small, dark room.

However, monsters do not forgive.

The creaking of the floor triggered the ears of his violent, drunken parent.

Minutes later, that disgusting and sordid man came into the little boy's room. He lifted him by his hair.

Now he was the one being beaten up. The one who was abused.

When the nightmare was over, poor Jun was left curled up in a corner, squatting, with his underwear around his thighs. Scared to death.

His mother did not know anything.

She was on the floor too, beaten up. Powerless.

Hours later, when that now-sober man realized what he had done, he went to the closet. He took the gun. He headed back to his son's room.

In front of his child, he asked for forgiveness. He placed the gun in his mouth. He pulled the trigger. He took his own life.

Lee could only see his father covered in blood on the floor. He listened to his mother's heartbreaking cries.

That day, that child, without realizing it, decided to face something for the first time.

He had accounts receivable.

Where was this famous Jesus who never appeared?

The one his mother always told him about. That kind and good God who carried his cross with her.

How would a good God allow all that?

If heaven existed, he hoped one day to meet this Jesus face to face. He would do it.

Since then, he has counted down the days until this moment.

(3

Everything that had happened to Lee in his childhood made him a hermit. That is why he avoided contact. He shut himself away in his books and science.

After STURP, going to the MIT research center became a real sacrifice. His social anxiety grew. More and more. That is why he avoided bumping into any colleagues. He started to work at night. He rested during the day. Not always successfully.

The debt he had been seeking to reclaim since he was young and that invitation from STURP has sparked the idea of reproductive cloning in his head. Since then, he has been focused on that.

It was not until 2004 that a news item published in the journal *Science* revolutionized the scientific world and opened up new options for Lee. South Korean Hwang Woo-suk, a former professor at Seoul National University, claims to have cloned human embryos for the first time.

This caused an inner stir in Lee. Although he was a man of few words, his ego had led him to believe that he would be the first man to achieve human cloning.

He made several inquiries until he found the number of his counterpart. He tried to call him. He did not know him, but he was looking forward to talking to him. It was not successful.

There are twists of fate that can turn into a stroke of luck. It is simply a matter of knowing how to wait for the moment in the future in order to be able to connect the events.

On October 26th, that colleague was sentenced to prison in the Seoul Central District Court. He was convicted of bioethical violations and embezzlement. Acquitted of fraud.

This incident presented three points for Lee to contemplate.

First, in order to continue with his project, he had to be even more careful. He could not be discovered, nor suffer the same fate.

Second, he could no longer use MIT funds and divert them to pursue his plans. He had to find financial backers for his project.

Third, if the South Korean had been acquitted of fraud, does not this indicate that taken at face value, the cloning had been successful?

In North Korea, where Lee was born, nothing that happens to its citizens is hidden. The press and mass organizations are under surveillance. It is governed by the principles of *Juche* ideology. It is the Korean version of socialism, in which each citizen has responsibility for the fate of the collective. Whether they reside in the country or not, its citizens are monitored. Lee was in the eye of the hurricane.

But that also has its upside.

Days after the incident with Hwang Woo-suk, Lee was contacted by a government representative to fund his investigations. They knew exactly what he was working on.

They told him that they had followed his career closely and that they wanted to support him. He was an honorable, outstanding, and blameless scientist. They would share Woo-suk's progress. The only detail is that he had to set up his private laboratory in California, one of the American states with the most permissive legislation on cloning.

Lee did not see anything wrong with this; he only suggested that he would like to work with the DNA from the Shroud of Jesus Christ. The people who contacted him assured him that they had no problem fulfilling his request.

Some millionaires seeking "preservation" have also contributed large sums of money. Exorbitant amounts.

And so he begins to work obsessively with stem cells derived from adult cells. He uses some of the variables that his colleague Hwang Woo-suk was supposed to have used.

Two years later, Seoul National University issued a condemnatory report concluding that the scientist's entire research had been based on fraudulent data.

Lee starts the whole process all over again, now from his own perspective. He receives an important notification: he has won the Nobel Prize in Science. He celebrates the good fortune that accompanies him.

It is the long-awaited moment for any researcher.

When he calls his mother to share the news, the world comes down on him. He is told that she has just passed away. For this reason, he could not go to receive the award personally.

The death of the most important woman in his life reawakened in him that thirst for revenge that had been growing in him since he was a child. He had many questions to ask "that Jesus" and a debt to recover from him. Face to face.

He immersed himself in books, research, and tests to get away from the world.

He has even learned that a religious movement, which was born in France in 1972 and supports human cloning, has made a comeback. A Canadian sect called *Raelians*. An atheist religion that defends science and technology and claims to be in contact with extraterrestrials.

They have appeared in the middle of this wave of "scientific successes", also announcing that they have achieved the birth of the first cloned baby. The baby's name is Eva. She is a replica of her mother, a thirty-one-year-old American.

He found that the American researcher of Argentine origin named José Cibelli had also made a first attempt at human cloning.

Just one attempt. But progress. Nineteen oocytes did not survive the first divisions of the embryo.

Lee feels that his toes are being stepped on.

He understands that he is not alone in this dizzy race, and he wants to speed up human cloning.

"They can try anything they want. I'm going further!" he says to himself. "That bastard's going to pay for it!"

As at MIT, in his current lab, Lee used to arrive at six o'clock in the evening, just when everyone else was finishing their workday. It was the perfect system. He did not see anyone. The night shifts were ideal for his research. No pressure of any kind. He usually finished at six o'clock in the morning. Before dawn.

The laboratory did not have many windows. It was large, with white walls and long folding metal counters. Divided by sliding glass doors, on which Lee wrote the formulas.

Few could understand them.

A very well-equipped center. High-definition microscopes. State-of-the-art computers. Special instruments to study sequences. In the central part, there were two giant transparent incubators, shaped like nuclei.

He began experimenting with nuclear transfer technology. He was obsessed with finding a way to transfer the nucleus of a cell into an artificial egg without a nucleus. He used large cloning rings.

Lee is a genius who, in the laboratory, has created sperm cells and artificial eggs that have the ideal chromosomal content. He has, in addition, a fictitious reproductive cell, previously emptied, where he has placed all the DNA. A device that replaces a surrogate mother.

From the outside, he can open this transparent incubator with windows and panels. This allows him to manipulate the interior.

The main mission of his study is to get the genes belonging to the embryo to grow.

It has been an arduous task.

There have been many attempts. He does not lose heart.

Suddenly, a flash. Eureka! He thinks he has the answer. He realizes it requires creating a cocktail of proteins and nutrients. He tries it. He tries it again. He needs help. He cannot do it alone. He has no choice but to gather allies, to look for other scientists and assistants to work with him.

A small group of men and women of science join the project. He tries to be careful about the experiments.

"What do you want to achieve, Dr. Lee?" asked his colleagues.

They all believed the studies were for genetic progress and therapeutic cloning. The use of transgenic cells for the production of embryonic stem cells.

But nothing is hidden between heaven and earth.

Legally and ethically, this man, winner of a Nobel Prize and, until now, upright and blameless in the eyes of many, was breaking what has been agreed in the

Universal Declaration on the Genome and Human Rights. What was presented in the Oviedo Convention, where attempts at human cloning are forbidden.

He did not care. This game has another purpose, and the way to achieve it is through science.

Although he may have says otherwise, the ethical and criminal implications of being discovered caused him more anxiety.

And with his anxiety grew his intolerance.

And with the intolerance, clashes with his colleagues.

He does not know how to deal with them, he does not interact, and he has almost established selective mutism. He protects himself from everybody else. He is on the defensive.

In this way, without realizing it, Lee begins to have more enemies than acolytes within his own team.

He uses the night to monitor the egg, which he hopes can grow with the "borrowed" genome.

He shocks it with electrical impulses; with several shots using syringes.

Over two hundred tests have been carried out.

Several attempts seem successful, but after a few minutes, like a house of cards, everything falls down.

He must start from scratch. He is close to achieving it. He knows it.

He does not give up. He perseveres.

But still nothing.

The eggs are obtained from altruistic donors, who do not appear in any legal document. There is no trace of them. In other words, they are donors who lend themselves to make their contribution to science from the most perfect anonymity.

Ariel is the one who is in charge of getting the donors, but he believes it is for another purpose. He is the son of one of the directors of another large research center in California. This young man, full of principles, has a special passion for genetics. He joined the center three months ago and he is a scientific ethicist.

Sharp. Lively. Cutting. Talkative. This is precisely what makes Lee not like him very much. However, Ariel has made a great attempt to adapt. He considers what he has been given to be a "golden" opportunity, although he dislikes the cold and silent environment.

The laboratory is a space where basic human contact is non-existent.

At first, he found it fascinating to do the interviews and track down the whereabouts of human beings seeking to contribute to science. But, little by little, he begins to see things he does not like. They disgust him. He understands that there are other, questionable interests at play.

When he arrived, this young man with rounded glasses believed that the research being conducted there was a banner that would show the world the benefits of therapeutic cloning. The thought of finding the key to eradicating genetic diseases, defeating infertility, and improving conditions, in general, was something he obsessed over.

But the hidden scandal behind Lee's experiments is of unimaginable dimensions and Ariel has discovered it.

After finding some of Dr. Lee's notes, he feels bad about himself. He believes his work to be illegal. Not at all ethical.

Out of bounds.

The limits of humanity have also been broken. On a daily basis, the laboratory has become a living hell. Lee discredits the work of his team. Every day he is more and more intolerant of human contact. A very common pathology in people who have suffered abuse. He does not seem to know that patience has its limits.

Ariel's patience has reached its peak.

Ariel wants to shut down what is being conducted at the center. He has evidence of improper egg retrieval. He decides to leave the project, but not before informing the authorities and the press.

He confesses being part of it, but he did so without knowing the reality of what was taking place there.

One of the principles of the law states that ignorance of the law does not exempt compliance with it.

He has not considered an important detail: behind Lee, there are people with a lot of power. The press and the authorities that Ariel made contact with have been silenced.

There is too much money involved.

Ariel has two options: to pay the price for having taken part, or accept the bribe and hand over the evidence, disappear for good and never open his mouth again.

Even the most upright man has a price.
Ariel chose to keep quiet.
How long would this silence last?

4

In the municipality of Temixco, couples always find a hiding place to unleash the fury of their desires. The vertigo they feel when escaping surpasses that caused by the height of some viewpoints where they usually meet.

The teenagers do it again. In an old white and beige Volkswagen Kombi, they promise each other a furtive encounter. They take the road to the state of Morelos, along the federal highway. This time they go to the Viewpoint of Cuernavaca. They love to escape and dream together of their lives when they grow up.

Arnaldo drives. Margarita has let him. The car is not his. It belongs to Margarita's father. Once again, that beautiful young woman, full of the vitality of an eighteen-year-old, has stolen the car. If the car could talk, it would have many stories to tell. Inside the vehicle, as if there were no tomorrow, Arnaldo and Margarita have finished exhausted with pleasure hundreds of times. During the day and the night.

As he drives, he turns to enjoy her black hair waving in the wind. Margarita has a sweet, oval face. Thick eyebrows. Her full lips stand out.

From the viewpoint, against the light, they can see the city in its entirety. It is December. It gets dark early. If they had arrived earlier, they would have been able to see as far as the volcanoes. This spot was, in general, the hiding place where they had their endless get-togethers, where they drank, smoked weed and talked about everything.

They were great friends. Friends with all the benefits of lovers.

But just that, friends. Great friends.

This would be a different night. The following day, Arnaldo would turn twenty years old. The two arrived eager to talk. Eager to share a great secret. Each was keeping one. Arnaldo, as a proper gentleman should, asked Margarita to talk first.

"I'll listen to you," she said.

"No, Marga, you go first. I want to know your secret."

"And I want to know yours."

"And I want to know yours."

"And I want to know yours."

They spent a few minutes in a game of giving up first place in the confession. They decided to to leave it to luck.

"A coin?" Margarita asked.

"A coin it is," replied Arnaldo.

"Heads or tails?"

"Heads," he said. "Because I always face things head-on!"

They laughed.

Margarita flipped the coin. It slipped between the Beetle's seats and fell right underneath her.

"Ah, it can't be! We don't know what it was," said Arnaldo as he bent down to try to grab it.

In this uncomfortable position, his face was close to Margarita's. She leaned over and kissed him on the lips. That kiss was different.

"What was that?" asked Arnaldo.

"Nothing, I just felt like it."

Arnaldo grabbed the coin without knowing what luck had brought them. Neither of them would ever know that the coin had landed on tails. She would have had to tell her secret before he did.

But we already know that life is not about what could have been.

Now Arnaldo had to flip the coin. He caught it in mid-air, turned it around, and placed it in the palm of his left hand. He closed his hand immediately.

"What do you think it is?" he asked his friend.

"Ah, c'mon! Put us out of our misery, we are getting old."

Arnaldo opened his hand. The head on the coin shone and seemed to be smiling at him. Destiny, sometimes, is written in an indecipherable way.

"You cheeeeeated, Arni!"

"How's that possible? I'm right in front of you."

"I don't know, but you cheated. Well, dear Arnaldo, your secret will be mine now!."

There was a pause.

"I'm so excited, Marga! You know that for some time I have been thinking about the possibility of joining the seminary. To serve God."

"Yes!"

"I've made my mind up. I'm going to join."

"What do you mean you're going to join? When? How? Why?"

"You already know why. I've wanted this with all my heart. The _how_ is just by turning up. I walk through the door and join the seminary," only he laughed at this comment. "And the _when_ is... are you ready..."

"Oh, c'mon!"

"On Monday!" he said excitedly.

"On Monday? Which Monday?"

"This Monday," replied Arnaldo.

"This Monday?" Margarita was surprised.

"What's up? Aren't you happy for me?"

"Of course, I'm happy!" Margarita lied.

In reality, Arnaldo's secret had hit her like a bucket of ice water.

Like a storm of ice water.

Like a hurricane of ice water.

"Congratulations, Arnaldo! I'm sure you'll be an extraordinary priest!"

She hugged him warmly and kissed him on the forehead.

"And your secret?" Arnaldo asked.

Margarita hesitated for a moment.

"My secret. Yes, sure, my secret!"

She reached into her pocket and pulled out a crucifix. A beautiful piece of goldwork, carved in silver.

"What's this?"

"This means a lot to my family. It belonged to my grandmother. She gave it to me to protect me. Now I want you to have it."

"I don't believe you. For my birthday?"

"No. I just wanted to give it to you. I had it before."

"And you're giving it to me today? Just when I tell you that in three days I'm going to join the seminary! What a coincidence! God and his stuff!"

"Yes, God and his stuff!" repeated Margarita while lowering her eyes. "But this is not everything. The crucifix is special. First, because it belongs to my grandmother.

But also because of this. Look. Surpriiise!" Margarita said, forcing a joy she didn't feel.

"Wait... what?!"

Margarita gently pushed with her index finger on one side of the crucifix. A secret compartment was opened from the cross. A kind of mini-safe.

"What is this? That's crazy! It's so beautiful!" said Arnaldo. "How do you open it? How does it work?"

"Let me explain it to you later. But look what's inside."

Margarita had placed inside the cross a small note with the message: "don't let me down."

"I don't believe you, you're perfect! You're amazing! No, I won't let God down. What a miracle having you in my life. You're just amazing!"

She forced a smile as Arnaldo hugged her.

"We need to celebrate this! A tequila and a toast."

"No, Arnaldo, I don't feel like drinking tequila today. I don't feel well. I'll drive you home."

Arnaldo never suspected that, just as life and luck can change at any moment, that woman changed the secret she wanted to tell him. She made up that the cross was the secret.

Yes, she had it on her for him.

Yes, the message was for him.

But she thought that maybe he would understand that the note was not from God.

However, this remained a secret.
A secret that would change Arnaldo's life, and perhaps that of humanity.

CHAPTER VII

THE OTHER SIDE
OF THE COIN

1

Friday, September 8th, 2006.
The Catholic saints' calendar celebrates the Nativity of
Mary.
Ten o'clock in the morning. The phone rings in the office of
the new director of the Pontifical Academy of Sciences. His
secretary had requested that day off. The previous director,
Dr. Arner, had died of a heart attack two months earlier.

"Good morning, the peace of the Lord be with you."

"Good morning," replied a sweet voice on the other end of the line. "Would you be so kind as to put me through to Father Arnaldo Romero?"

"Arnaldo speaking."

After taking a deep breath, the broken voice of a woman trying to keep her composure was heard. Her heart was on the verge of bursting with nerves.

"Arnaldo, it's Margarita."

There was a long silence. It came to his mind, in a fraction of a second, his whole past. He did not know whether to cry or burst with joy.

"Margarita?! How joyful! I don't know what to say. I didn't expect this phone call, but it makes me so happy to hear from you. How are you? What a surprise! How is everything?"

"Good, Arnaldo, or I don't know if I should say, Father Arnaldo."

Both of them were nervous.

"Wow, how many years? Twenty?" said Arnaldo.

"Yes, twenty. How time flies, right?"

"And to what do I owe this surprise?"

"I'm in Rome. I need to see you."

"Are you here? That's great! Sure, let's meet up! What about lunch?"

"Excellent," she said without hesitating.

"There is a very convenient café that I usually go to. They serve lunch, their pizza is the best and the coffee is incredible. It is in Via della Conciliazione. The name of the café is Caffe Giacomelli. See you at noon?"

"I'll be there!"

The morning passed slowly. Very slowly. The unexpectedness of her call kept Arnaldo from concentrating. He was looking at his watch constantly. He was excited to see his friend again.

Margarita's anxiety was killing her. She walked around all the nearby streets. She felt like she was running out of breath.

The truth is that she was really losing it.

They were more punctual than they used to be when they went on their clandestine dates in their youth. If time was valuable then, it was much more valuable now.

When they saw each other, they approached each other tenderly. They did not say a word. They gave each other a long, eternal hug. The kind of hug that your memory and your soul store away for you to remember during hard times. During the winters of life; those that inexorably come.

There, immersed in that hug, Margarita felt the crucifix on his chest, which brought back so many memories.

After sighing, she stepped back only slightly.

"The cross," she said.

"Yes, the cross."

"Can I touch it?"

"Of course."

Margarita held that cross in her hands again. Silently she asked the man who was crucified to fill her with the strength of his spirit because she felt that she was fading away.

Arnaldo sighed as well. He looked at her tenderly. He stepped back slowly. They sat down. He could not stop looking at her.

That woman, around her forties, was prettier than ever. Thin. Really thin, but beautiful. It was then that he noticed the baby carriage next to her. A beautiful little black-haired girl, about three or four months old.

He tried to hide it, but it certainly made him shiver. They had often dreamed of a life together. It was logical to think that this woman would have a daughter.

"Wow. What a pretty girl! Just like you! Your daughter?"

"No, Arnaldo, look closer," she replied with fear. Trying to find strength where there was none. "She's just like you. She's your granddaughter. Her name is Guadalupe."

2

Arnaldo thought about how life can change in a second.

Just as in the Genesis, he felt that his life had suddenly become disordered and empty earth and he was staring into a dark abyss.

He instinctively touched the cross. He held it tightly in his icy hands while his heart beat rapidly. He could hear the rhythm of his own breathing. He was overcome with fear and confusion. This could not be happening.

"I don't understand, what are you talking about?" he asked.

Finally, twenty years later, that coin had landed on "tails" for Margarita. Without the need to be flipped.

Because life is circular. Because God always moves His cards so that everything that was chaotic at the beginning resumes its natural order.
Perhaps to fulfill his designs.

Taking a breath of air, she told him the secret she could never tell him that night at the viewpoint of Cuernavaca.

That she was pregnant.

That she would have his child.

That night at the viewpoint, she decided to remain silent while he told her that he wanted to be a priest, just because she loved him.

"Why didn't you tell me anything before?" Arnaldo reproached her with restrained fury; trying to control himself.

"You always told me about this calling you felt. I knew you were in discernment, but when we were together, I felt what we had was real. I didn't want to interfere with your calling," she said with tears in her eyes.

"Then, why are you telling me this now?"

Margarita burst into tears.

Like someone who could not take it anymore and needed to let go of the weight of the cross she had been carrying on her shoulders, she blurted out the truth in a breathy voice.

"Our daughter died in childbirth, Arnaldo. We were in town visiting my mother and Myriam went into labor early. That was her name, Myriam. The outpatient clinic is still just that, an outpatient clinic. There were a lot of complications. They only managed to save Guadalupe."

Now it was he who felt what she had experienced years before.

A bucket of ice water.

A storm of ice water.

A hurricane of ice water.

As a poet would say, life is full of surprises.

"She never knew who her father was. Nobody knows. Those were very hard times with my family, but time goes by and heals wounds. I'm here to ask you a favor. I don't want you to change your whole life; I just want you to help me."

A lump formed in his throat. She was overwhelmed with tears and the mix of feelings that overcame her.

"Arnaldo, I have cancer. Metastasis. The doctors say that I have not got long to live. That's why I came. I don't know who I should leave Guadalupe with. I have no one. I don't know what to do."

He didn't know either.

The child's cry brought them out of the silence that had suddenly surrounded them.

Margarita wiped her tears. She breathed one more time. She approached the baby carriage. She held her as she calmed her with a lullaby.

"She must be hungry."

With the girl in her arms, she tried to get a bottle and some milk from the baby bag and prepare a bottle.

"Do you need help?" he said, seeing her struggling.

"Can you hold her one second, please?"

Clumsily and fearfully, Arnaldo took her in his arms. He had never experienced anything like it before. It was inexplicable. An indescribable love. That fragile and innocent baby stopped crying as soon as he held her. Time stood still. Tears began to flow from his eyes.

> *What would his life have been like if Margarita had told him her secret first?*
>
> *What would it have been like spending time with his daughter whom he never knew, and whom he would never know much about?*

The bottle was ready. She took the little girl in her arms again.

"I can't leave Rome, but we can take the child to my parents in town in Mexico. I'll work out what I'm going to say to them. I know they will take care of her. I don't

PLAYING GOD

have the nerve to ask you for a favor, but you would need to take her there. That's the only thing I can think of," said Arnaldo.

"Don't let me down", she replied.

Only then did Arnaldo understand the note inside the crucifix she gave him.

"Don't let me down," he heard deep inside.

Arnaldo was no longer sure where the voice was coming from.

He thought it was her talking.

Eventually, he would understand that it was once again the voice of God.

He could not let her down twice.

Not either of them.

Not any of the three of them.

From that day on, Guadalupe was part of the equation.

3

Guilt and lies end up like a pressure cooker that is ready to burst at any moment.

After Margarita's confession, Arnaldo decided to gather his courage. He has requested a meeting in Rome with several prominent prelates.

Once and for all, he needed to let go of the heavy load on his back.

173

NELSON BUSTAMANTE & CARMEN VICTORIA PARDO

In the days prior to the meeting, he could hardly sleep. The dark circles under his eyes, his tiredness, and his very high tendency to get distracted were clearly visible.

Arnaldo knew that this confession could change his whole life. It would surely mean his expulsion. For this reason, the demons within him were struggling. He prayed the rosary fervently day and night. He barely talked.

Until the day came.

That morning, just before leaving, he knelt in front of the cross of his room. He prayed with more devotion than ever. He prayed with a repentant heart, begging for mercy.

"Father, Father! Who am I to ask you to see me? How many times have I sinned? I only want to ask you, Lord, to be present on this day. Let it be your will and not mine!"

This could be his last day in Rome.

The meeting was with the cardinal and some auxiliary bishops.

The moment of truth was approaching.

He left. He continued to cry out for God in silence. He entered the Episcopal Palace. Finally, he arrived at the meeting room. Cardinal Ismael Domínguez was waiting for him there. He was easily distinguished by his impeccable buttoned cassock and his amaranth-red sash, trim, and calotte. Bishops Monsignor Cavalli and Monsignor Gabriel Oropeza also accompanied him. They were dressed in purple as usual. The color of piety. What Arnaldo needed so much.

The atmosphere was one of majesty and sovereignty.

"Good morning, Eminence!" Arnaldo said as he bowed to Cardinal Dominguez. "Bishops!"

They greeted him with the affection they professed for him. At least the bishops.

The cardinal went straight to the point. No holds barred.

"Let's see, Arnaldo, what is this important thing you have to tell us to gather us here?" He said laconically.

"Your Eminence, Monsignors. I have something to confess. A truth that accompanies me and that I can no longer hide."

"Go ahead, Father Arnaldo, we are listening!" said the red prelate.

"Before I joined the seminary, I used to visit a young friend with whom I always went out. Like every adolescent boy, we were often more than just friends. Three days before I joined the seminary, we had a date. I wanted to tell her the news! I was so excited! She wanted to tell me something too. We flipped a coin. I spoke first. I told her that I had made my decision and that I would begin my career in the Church. She never told me her secret."

Everyone was staring at him. Trying to guess where that story would lead them.

"She, Margarita, appeared a few days ago. We met up here in Rome," continued Arnaldo.

The cardinal interrupted him arrogantly.

"If what you came to tell us is that you are now confused, and that after having seen her you are thinking of her as a woman, or that you have been considering leaving, I must tell you that you are only going through a spiritual crisis. We've all been there at one time or another. Believe me, it's temporary. Was that everything?" he said as he stood up from the high-backed chair where he was sitting.

"No, Your Eminence. It's not that."

The cardinal tried to hide that he was annoyed at himself for that impetuous comment. An interruption that gave no room for dialogue and that clearly showed the differences he had with Father Arnaldo.

"Go on then," he said with arrogance.

"At that time, she was pregnant. She was going to have my child. A daughter to be more specific. That's what she wanted to tell me, but I never knew. I only found out about this when we saw each other three days ago. My daughter died giving birth to a baby, my granddaughter. Margarita has terminal cancer and that is why she came to contact me, to tell me the truth. To go in peace and to ask for help."

A deep silence invaded the place.

Long.

The cardinal stood up from his seat. He walked until he was in front of Arnaldo. He looked him in the eyes and said:

"Arnaldo, did you really not know about this?"

"Believe me. If I had known, maybe everything would have been different in my life. This is the result of a somewhat messy youth, but I know that it affects my investiture in the Church."

"Thank goodness you are aware! Unfortunately, you are the result of the least common of transgressions. But it is a transgression and, as such, has consequences."

Arnaldo was wondering what the sanctions would be. Would he be expelled?

The cardinal turned around and in a low voice asked one of the Monsignors for something. The man left the room. The prelate took a seat.

The atmosphere was tense.

"What do you want to do Arnaldo? What have you thought?"

"The truth is that I can only tell you that I am aware of my responsibility. I want to support Margarita and, of course, my granddaughter."

"How?" asked the cardinal.

"I will talk to my parents in Mexico who can help me with the child, although they are old. In that respect, everything is solved."

"You haven't done that yet? Why? How irresponsible! You think you're going to solve this just like that!"

"I must confess that I have not had the courage. But I will do it. As for me, I would not want to leave here. I wish to continue practicing my priesthood."

"I believe it's unfortunate, but that's not going to be possible. Ethically and canonically what you should do is resign. You shouldn't be here anymore."

The cardinal's tone was quite blunt.

At that moment, the auxiliary bishop came in with some documents in his hands.

"Give it to Father Arnaldo, please," said his Eminence.

Arnaldo viewed the documents with fear.

What was there?

Could they dismiss him from his position?

His world had truly been turned upside down.

Deep inside, he felt a deep urge to cry, but he contained himself.

As he tried to hold himself together in silence, his voice cried out, crying out for God to not forsake him.

"These are the Vatican's guidelines on how to deal with priests who have children."

The bishop gave him the documents.

On the outside, "Children of the Ordained" could easily be read.

"I did not know about the existence of this document, cardinal," Arnaldo said.

"It has existed for longer than you can imagine. You are not the only case of the ordained with children," he replied. "Do you know Rodrigo Borgia?"

"Do you mean Pope Alexander VI?"

"Exactly. Pope Alexander VI had four children when he was a priest. All of them with his lover. One of the excesses that motivated Martin Luther to create his Protestant Reformation. The Church has "everything" planned, Arnaldo. There is no room for mistakes. These are in-house documents. Confidential. You cannot keep them. You will have enough time to read them, but you will do it here. You must return them afterward. If you have any enquiry please do let me know."

A new silence reigned in the place.

"We appreciate you very much, Arnaldo, but your duty is no longer here! You have a new responsibility now, with your family. You already let the Church down; don't let the child down now."

"Your Eminence, with all due respect, I know my responsibility, but I do not consider it fair to say that I have let the Church down. This happened when I was just a boy, and I had not even joined the seminary at the time. My dedication to the Church has been one of total service. Had I known this news earlier, I would not be standing in front of you right now."

"You should have told us earlier!"

"How could I do that if I just found out?"

"That is the damage that secrets can cause."

"I told you, I didn't know!" he said, annoyed.

"May I remind you of your vows of obedience. Take your time and read the documents. I believe it is clear what you have to do. However, my duty is to show you what you have in your hands. When you have read it, let us know on the in-house phone and we will be back. I have other matters to take care of. May God be with you in your decision!"

Everybody left the room. That meeting was cold. Fast. Without the mercy he needed.

Arnaldo fell to his knees. He cried.

"My time is running out!" he thought.

He stayed there for a long time. Then he stood up. He dried his tears.

He took the document and started reading it.

It was clear that the responsibility in these cases required the priest to abandon his habits and devote himself to his family

The bishop was right. However, it was not fair.

"If Pope Alexander VI had four children and a lover, even knowing that he had such an investiture, why should I have to leave the Church?"

He closed his eyes looking for guidance.

He prayed like never before.

"Show me your designs, Lord, let not my will but yours be done! May my obedience be to you and not to men!" he said out loud, holding tightly the crucifix in his hands with his head leaning.

He took a breath. The one he felt he was missing.

At the end of the document there was a paragraph stating what might be a small light amid the darkness.

"It is impossible to impose renunciation of the priesthood. Only the priest can request it."

The decision was in his hands.

He took one of the phones in the room.

"Good morning," said a female voice on the other end of the line.

"Elena, it's Arnaldo."

Elena was one of his very best friends. A single mother with two teenage children. A warrior in every aspect. He had not talked to her for a long time. She was a lawyer in Rome. One of the best. If anyone knew canon law, it was her.

They talked for a very long time. Arnaldo told her the reason he was calling. He mentioned that "confidential" document they gave him to read it. Of course, she knew it very well. It was not her first case.

Despite his confusion, the only thing Arnaldo knew was that he did not want to waste any time.

"What would you like to do, Arnaldo?" she asked after listening to the whole story.

"I don't want to leave, Elena! The Church is my passion. I only know how to serve the Lord. The cardinal emphasized that I must leave and be with my family. I know it would be the correct thing to do, but this case is different. I don't want this to be misunderstood, but my place is here. I will not evade my responsibility for what happened. I will take legal, financial, moral, and personal responsibility, but my place is here!"

There was silence.

"We have several options. If you want to fight, we will fight. This is not a canonical crime! Legally, there is no reason for termination. They can't fire you, although they may try to get you to leave. You know well this is a scandal for the Church and they will try to silence you."

"It can't be! It wouldn't be fair! I didn't break my vows. Everything happened previously and I didn't know anything about it."

"Remember that you are within the ecclesiastical institution. The main principle in these cases is the protection of children. However, to be honest, this is a different situation. That's the reason why I'm saying that if you want to fight, we will fight," Elena repeated.

Arnaldo breathed. There was a way out. A light at the end of that unexpected tunnel.

Even if he has to fight with the Pope himself, no one will take him out of Rome.

At least, that was what he thought.

4

The cardinal was dealing with other matters. However, he was still waiting for Arnaldo to finish reviewing the documents about "Children of the Ordained."

"I think Father Arnaldo has had enough time to read the whole document!" he said to one of the bishops. "He can't expect to keep me here all day. Call him! Tell him we are ready, waiting for his answer."

At that instant, the phone in the room rang.

It was Arnaldo. They did not have to call him.

The time to talk came.

Without wasting time, they came back to the room where the Mexican priest was waiting anxiously.

"Arnaldo, are you ready? Did you read everything? You had enough time!" indicated Cardinal Ismael.

"Yes, cardinal."

"What did you decide?"

"I will continue serving," said Arnaldo with a firm tone.

"I was hoping you would act nobly. I am afraid that this will not be possible."

"This is not a canonical crime. Legally, there is no reason for termination. You cannot dismiss me."

"Yes, we can!"

"With all due respect, I must tell you that if you try it, I intend to submit the matter to an ecclesiastical court. I will appeal it. I would rather hope for your common sense. I have already spoken to a canon lawyer friend."

The cardinal got angry.

He tried to control himself, but his anger could be seen in his eyes.

"A friend? It seems you have too many girlfriends, Arnaldo. Besides, your tone is disrespectful. May I remind you that there is a hierarchy that you must respect," he exclaimed, his eyes alight with fury.

"I'm merely telling you that I'm appealing to my right to remain in the institution. I'm not leaving!" he replied raising his voice.

"We will see!" said the cardinal, leaving the premises and slamming the door.

The bishops were left behind. They did not have time to leave. Realizing the situation, they speeded up their pace.

A fight to the death had begun.
A power struggle, where God's twisted designs would initiate the path that would fulfill his word.
The new Babylon was coming.

5

Cardinal Ismael Domínguez had heard about Father Arnaldo before Arnaldo was transferred to Rome.

He knew about him because the deceased Supreme Pontiff held him in high esteem. It could not have been any other way. The Pope was a friend of Father José Luis, who filled Arnaldo's heart with his love for the

Eucharist. The same man of faith who took his life in Santa Magdalena de Jicotlán when Arnaldo was nine years old; just an altar boy.

The friendship between the Pope and Father José Luis lasted many years. They studied together in the seminary, creating an intimate brotherhood that was never lost, not even when the Supreme Pontiff occupied the chair of St. Peter. They would always talk with each other. About everything.

Father José Luis even told him about that special and smart boy who was his altar boy. He used to say his spirit resembled that of the prelate of Rome when he was young. They both laughed while remembering everything.

He felt a special affection for that little boy. He was clever, full of talents. With a deep love for the Eucharist. He looked forward to receiving communion, and he even stole the unconsecrated hosts, while pretending he was at Mass. That Mexican little boy, lover of the Virgin, who never revealed the secret he kept in his heart.

Before taking his life, Father José Luis not only left a letter for his parishioners. He wrote one as well to the Pope. To his friend.

Dear Holy Father.
Dear friend,

I am writing to you from the depths of my misery, as the coward who does not deserve to be in the Church of Christ. I do not deserve your mercy, the brotherhood professed, nor the friendship that has united us for years. Far less do I deserve to receive communion.

I have desecrated the Holy Eucharist. It is indeed just as you read it.
Sometimes I wonder why I did it, but I cannot get an answer. Even though we are God's instruments to absolve blame and restore peace to others, I do not feel able to ask for it for myself. I do not deserve it. I cannot restore peace because I do not have it. The guilt is consuming me.

This will be the last time we communicate in any way. I have no one except my old friend, and I really want to tell him why I decided to take my life.

A few months ago, in the middle of the consecration, the host was full of blood. When I saw the body of our Lord in my hands dyed red, my heart could not stop beating with emotion.
I yelled "Miracle! Miracle!" ...I thought it was a miracle! I was thrilled to see the grace that had been conferred to me.
Yes, to me! I felt like the chosen one: special, different from the rest, even you! A kind of spiritual pride took hold of me.

For fractions of a second, I felt powerful.
Almost omnipotent in front of that sublime manifestation

that was happening to me!
Seconds of glory that felt eternal.
They were not. It was not a miracle. It was not.
I immediately saw the blood flowing from my finger and that is why the consecrated host was stained red.
In the face of the clamor of the congregation and their euphoria, I did not dare to deny what had happened. There, with the Lord in my hands, I lied and continued with the lie.
I did not want to take away their happiness. There was great jubilation in the church that Sunday. A call that affirmed faith and hope for the members of my congregation.

How could I tell Mrs. Hilda, who now seemed to be praying more fervently, that everything was a lie?
How could I take away from Arnaldo, my altar boy? How could I tell the special little boy I always told him about, whose passion and love for the Eucharist had been awakened in him even more?
From that moment forward, the church began to fill up with more and more people, who seemed to multiply like the loaves and the offering. From one day to the next, I found myself with more resources to help than I had in my entire career as a priest. I was overwhelmed with greed. Spiritual greed.

I appeared to be fulfilled on the outside. But the reality? I was empty inside. Empty deep inside!
How can I lead the flock given to me if my hands and soul are dirty?

I feel like Judas. An apostate. A sinner who deserves no mercy.

I know that ex-communication is the punishment. I deserve that severe consequence. However, I cannot think of my life without being able to give the Eucharist. Even less can I think of not being able to receive the Eucharist. That is why, if I could still ask for anything, I would ask for your forgiveness and your prayer for my soul, even though I do not deserve it.

That confession had broken the Supreme Pontiff's soul.

As he was reading the letter, he could imagine the unhappy ending. Once he finished reading it, the first thing he did was grab the phone.

He called the sacristy in Mexico where his old friend was, with the unbroken hope of listening to his voice.

Arnaldo's mother was there. She always went to clean the Father's office. She never stopped doing it, even though there wasn't a priest, Mass, or as many parishioners as before. When the phone rang, she hurried up to answer the call.

"Good afternoon, Church of Santa Magdalena de Jicotlán," said Mrs. Ana.

"Good afternoon!" said a sweet voice on the other end of the line. A voice with a foreign accent, but very clear. "Excuse me, is Father José Luis there?"

She remained in silence. For a moment, she remembered her parish priest.

"Don't you know the news? Father José Luis passed away almost a month ago."

Those are the things nobody wants to hear.

NELSON BUSTAMANTE & CARMEN VICTORIA PARDO

Just as Jesus with his friend Lazarus, the Pope loved his seminary colleague and longtime friend. That was the news he was imagining, but he wished it were a lie. Despite his faith, he could not at that moment tell him to "come out of there" as Jesus had done before. The cave of death had trapped him.

"With whom do I have the pleasure of speaking?" she said kindly.

With a sad and broken voice, he answered:

"It is the Holy Father, from Rome. Father José Luis and I were good friends."

For Mrs. Ana, that moment of pain became a moment of glory almost at the snap of her fingers.

No one in that dusty town would believe that she was talking to the very successor of Peter.

"I am Ana, Arnaldo's mother!" she said, hastening to speak and tell the story. "My son was the altar boy in the church. It was he who found Father José Luis. Oh, my poor son loved him so much, as did everyone in town! He was a man of God! I must even say, Holy Father, that he experienced a beautiful Eucharistic manifestation. This town was different. I believe God was preparing him. That man was a saint! My son Arnaldo loved him as his own uncle."

The Pope, with his characteristic gentleness, could only say to her:

"Yes, my friend was very special! Certainly, I had already heard about your son, as Father José Luis always mentioned him. I would love to meet him someday."

"Did you know about my son?... Oh, Father, such a blessing! Forgive me the intrusion, but please Holy Father, can you give us a blessing and, of course for my

Arnaldo too. Hopefully, he will follow the steps of Father José Luis and become a saint like him."

In the most beautiful Latin, the Pope anointed that woman and her son with his blessing. As he did so, Ana's skin bristled. She could feel the presence of a strange force, the Holy Spirit Himself descending at that instant.

"Well, Mrs. Ana, I just wanted to confirm if the news that had reached me were true. May God have mercy on the soul of Father José Luis, forgive his sins and rest his soul."

Hearing her name from the mouth of the Supreme Pontiff ended up caused her to rejoice, full of great joy.

"Amen, Holy Father! Amen!"

"May the spirit of God descend upon you!"

The Vicar of Christ hung up the phone. Ana fell into a state of spiritual ecstasy.

"Nobody is going to believe me!" she said excitedly, as she clenched her fists and jumped with excitement. "Nobody is going to believe me!"

As usual, within minutes the whole town knew that the Pope himself had spoken with Ana. In the streets, amazed, they talked about the news.

"Can you believe Ana talks now with the Pope?"

"Oh, right! She is so lucky! I heard he even knows her name."

"As I was told, he had given his blessing to Arnaldo directly from Rome, who, he hoped, would also become a saint like Father José Luis."

"A saint like Father José Luis? That sounds like a canonization is around the corner! Who would have thought that? There will be a saint from Santa Magdalena of Jicotlán!"

After all, in that small town, everything was news. The fervor caused by the good tidings began to spread.

The faith of the people, although without a priest to say Mass, remained intact.

Fortunately, Arnaldo had torn up that letter. The one that Father José Luis had left to his parishioners telling them the truth.

Arnaldo was keeping that secret.

Happiness, undoubtedly, depends on the lens through which one looks at everything.

6

Many years after that phone call, people in Rome began to hear of a priest who was committed to his people and who loved science. This man became part of the team in charge of evaluating Eucharistic manifestations and miracles. He was even called upon to participate in important researchs, including those of The Roslin Institute.

Once again, the name of Arnaldo Romero reached the Holy Father's ear. A priest from Santa Magdalena of Jicotlán.

It couldn't be a coincidence. It had to be the same one his old friend, Father José Luis, told him about.

That is why they say that we have six degrees of separation from others and that it's a small world after all.

The Holy Father wanted to fulfill the promise given to Ana years ago by telephone. Besides, he felt a certain commitment to the boy, because of the love he had for his old friend.

That is the reason why Arnaldo was invited to Rome.

In order to coordinate it, the Pope spoke with Dr. Arner, director of the Vatican Academy of Sciences, and Cardinal Vitesse, director of Communications. He told them that he wanted to have that Mexican priest among those close to him.

That is the world. Small. Interconnected. Perfect. Full of "Godincidences."

When Arnaldo received the invitation from the Vatican, he could not believe it.

The first thing he did was to inform his mother.

He called her and, between screams, Ana said that all this was triggered by the blessing that the Holy Pope had given her in that phone call.

"Look, son! It wasn't a coincidence that I was cleaning the sacristy that exact day. It wasn't! Please, son, when you see the Holy Father, send him my greetings. Tell him I'm your mother, I'm Ana. I'm sure he will remember me!" she said with a mix of pride and happiness. Now, who will bear it when I tell the girls that you were called to work in Rome! My son in Rome! The day you were born I said: 'This boy is going to do great things! He's going to be somebody important!' May you be a saint like Father José Luis will be at some point, my son! Oh, by the way, tell the Holy Father not to forget about that, about the canonization of his friend!"

Arnaldo listened to her carefully.

Ana had repeated the canonization of Father José Luis so many times that she really thought she had heard that he would be canonized. He did not say a word. It made no sense to put an end to his mother's happiness. That must be why they say that a lie repeated a thousand times ends up becoming the truth.

There was much to celebrate.

But there is news that, for some, generates joy; while for others it produces total unhappiness. In life, everything has two sides.

That was the case with Cardinal Ismael. A man close to the Pope and adviser of the Pontiff. A traditionalist within the heart of the Church.

He would have liked the successor of Peter to be as attentive to him as he was to that young, recently ordained priest. That perfect stranger named Arnaldo Romero, whom he had heard so much about lately.

No one had noticed, but even before Arnaldo set foot in Rome, an internal rebellion was brewing. One that would grow over time. One that would develop in silence.

Yes, even if he would not admit it, he was envious of him. For free.

Cardinals are also known as "Princes of the Church."

In Ismael's case, he was not only a prince of that institution. He had no siblings. He was the favorite; very spoiled. Since he was a child, he had the power to do whatever he wanted. He always sought to stand out and to be the center of attention. For his mother, he was the "prince" of the house.

When he did not get what he wanted, hell would break loose.

There are some things that do not change over the years. Nor did anything change with Ismael when he joined the ecclesiastical system.

That is why he tried to stop the young Mexican priest's transfer to Rome. His promotion as well.

The cardinal was very skillful. He did everything to defend his thesis of keeping that Mexican priest out of the Vatican.

Now, Arnaldo had given him the perfect excuse: a woman from the past, a daughter, and now a granddaughter.

Too scandalous for a priest living within the bosom of the Church.

The perfect justification for him to lose the clerical state.

For Cardinal Dominguez, Arnaldo was a pebble in his shoe, and he would remove him at any cost. He believed he held all the cards, playing in his favor.

However, he did not expect Arnaldo to have an ace up his sleeve. The last ace.

CHAPTER VIII

THE THEFT

1

—*July, 2010.*
There is a small Bulgarian monastery on the small St.
Ivan Island, located in the waters of the Black Sea. There,
among the ruins of a church, a group of archaeologists
led by Kazimir Popkonstantinov has found some human
bones.

Protected inside a small marble coffin, there is an ulna, a bone of the forearm and one of the hands, a rib, a tooth, and part of the skull.

The bones are said to belong to John the Baptist, Jesus' cousin. The one who baptized him in the Jordan River. The precursor of the Messiah. A figure not only venerated in Christianity but also in Islam.

The one who announced the arrival of Jesus. The one who was beheaded by order of ruler Herod Antipas.

On the cover of that small coffin it was written in Greek: "God, save your servant Thomas. For St. John. June, 24th."

The date coincides with the birth of St. John.

The news of this discovery has generated a great commotion in the Church and the scientific community.

For the former, having a relic of such magnitude is highly significant. If it is real, this would be what is known as a first-class relic. These relics create a deeper experience with the saint.

Within the Ecclesiastical Body, relics are a means through which God performs his miracles. Venerating them is a practice that dates back to the first centuries of the Church.

As for science, it is a way of confirming history. Even of approaching it to try to repeat it.

For scientists, having the DNA of Jesus' cousin means also having the DNA of the main figure of Christianity, Jesus himself.

With all those bones found there is a complete genome.

In order to verify its legitimacy, DNA and carbon dating tests have been performed. The same tests that were carried out with the Shroud of Turin. The results are shocking as they validate the hypothesis.

There is no doubt. After analyzing the genetic code, they are sure this is the man who baptized the Messiah.

The news has gone public and the Church has decided that the reliquary of John the Baptist will be displayed in a church of Sozopol, Sofia, the Bulgarian capital.

From that moment on, the number of devotees visiting increases greatly, like the miracle of the Feeding of the 5,000. Stoically, believers stand in long lines to see the reliquary. They do not mind waiting.

They hold small pieces of paper with requests. They place them in a basket next to the flowers, just below the reliquary. Part of the ritual includes lighting the candles for the saint to intercede for them and perform the miracle.

In just one week there has been an impressive number of visitors. The church in Sozopol is overwhelmed. They did not expect so many people. They have to put measures in place. The law enforcement authorities together with the Church have decided to set a timetable.

It would be open to the public between 8 a.m. and 6 p.m. Outside the opening times, only members of the clergy may have access.

However, the world's smallest and oldest army, the Swiss Guard, will be there around the clock to guard the precious treasure. This military corps, in charge of the security of the Pope and the Holy See, has been sent directly from the Vatican for this purpose.

Formed in 1506, was made up of the best guards, those who had a reputation of being fierce warriors. The blue, yellow, and red colors of their uniforms were characteristic of the Medici family, synonymous with power.

The changing of guards takes place every five hours in perfect military formation. The sentries who finish their day leave from the right, while the new members of this elite security corps come in from the left. A perfectly coordinated dance.

6 a.m.

The alarm is ringing in the Sozopol church.

The security cameras were deactivated.

No one has heard anything.

What once was perfect order is now in total disarray.

Barriers, police, and all kinds of army vehicles surround the area. Everything has been cordoned off.

The Swiss Guards lie dead on the floor.

It is the first time this has happened. These men have been trained in terrorist tactics and the use of modern weapons.

What happened?
Nobody can explain it.
The reality is that inside the Sozopol chapel, the base that supported the reliquary is empty.
John the Baptist is no longer there.

2

—September 10ᵗʰ, 2010.
In Bulgaria, the remains of John the Baptist have been stolen. Chaos has erupted.
There is uproar in Rome.
Pilar, the deputy director of communications, is missing.
The director of this department is on vacation, out of the country. It's an atypical day. Excessively active.

The communications group is relatively new. They have called Pilar's cell phone several times, but she is not answering. They do not know the communication line that the church wants to handle this type of case and they feel without direction. Lost.

Looking for other ways to approach the news, one of the journalists from Pilar's team decided to learn about the repercussions of John the Baptist's bones in the scientific field. He wants to know how this theft could affect the ecclesiastical institution in one way or another. He decides to interview the main spokesman of the Pontifical Academy of Sciences, Father Arnaldo Romero.

"Good morning, Mrs. Hilda. I don't know if you remember me, I'm Frank, from the communications department. Would it be possible to talk to Father Arnaldo for a few minutes?"

"Hello, Frank! Good morning! Unfortunately, Father Arnaldo isn't here. He's on some out-of-office assignments. He's always in and out."

That was a lie. Hilda has tried calling him hundreds of times, but it goes to voicemail. She knows about the commotion happening on the Vatican radio and in Bulgaria.

She suspects something happened. Father almost always comes in early, or he calls her if he has something unexpected. She saw Father Arnaldo and Pilar leaving the compound together the night before. It was very curious that none of them showed up.

She knows about their friendship. They share similar ideals and values. What she does not know is that they do not only have long gatherings in the vicinity of the Vatican. They can often be found in a café or restaurant. Sometimes, in Pilar's apartment as well.

They are early meetings. They never last until late. Arnaldo is one of those who goes back to his room, at the latest, at ten o'clock at night. He is usually already in his residence, sleeping soundly at that time.

But despite their good relationship, Hilda doesn't like the deputy director at all. She doesn't have a good feeling about her. She feels she cannot be trusted. She is not the only one who thinks so. Many others also feel that they don't know what to expect from Pilar. They all agree that, there is something in her eyes, that they cannot decipher.

Pilar sees things differently since she was young. Her eyes keep a lot of secrets. Probably, that's what they see in her. Or what they fail to see.

However, Arnaldo is convinced that his friend is impeccable. She has shown to be loyal and enjoys her company very much. They always have deep and interesting topics of conversation.

Hilda is alone in the office. Worried. For both of them. The morning is almost over. They haven't appeared yet.

Otherwise, Arnaldo would have at least given her a call.

She spoke out loud while walking in a zig-zag.

"Did something happen to them?" she wonders. "Here crime is the daily bread. I don't know why I didn't listen to Juan when he said to go to his town, who is at ease knowing that they live in the place with the highest crime rate? Oh my goodness, may they be well!"

At that moment all I could think about was what I had seen the night before. Would it be related to all of this?

Chaos had not really started that day in Bulgaria and Rome.

No.

It had started a day earlier.

Only no one knew about it.

—6:30 p.m. Thursday.
Arnaldo and Pilar leave their offices.

That day Hilda regretted not trusting her hunch. She was behind them, although they did not notice. She remembers seeing them walking and chatting placidly until they reach the Aurelai/Bonifacio VIII terminal. There they were waiting for the bus.

Hilda was "catching" them.

She found such closeness to be suspicious. She wanted to know if these two were on some strange wanderings.

"When has it ever been seen that a priest goes around so much with a woman? For heaven's sake! One of these days, with all due respect, I'm going to tell Father Arnaldo that he'd better watch out for evil tongues" she said.

She was hiding, spying on them, so they wouldn't discover her. She noticed that on the other side of the street there was a tall man who was also staring at Pilar and Arnaldo. He was robust, with a dark complexion. His hands were inside his brown jacket.

Hilda remembers seeing a certain nervousness in Pilar.

Again, she searched with her eyes for that suspicious man.

From that moment on, everything happened very quickly.

At that moment, the passing of a couple of buses and a truck made her lose sight of them. All three of them. In a matter of seconds, Pilar and Arnaldo were no longer there. Neither was the stranger.

She was worried. She tried to look for them.

She had no choice but to return the same way.

Without intending to, the search for answers led her to new questions.

The mystery surrounding the disappearance of Arnaldo and Pilar could be linked to the man who stared at them.

Hilda was not so far from the truth.

3)

Since the night before, the remains of John the Baptist were stolen, the events began to accelerate.

That day Pilar was once again in the spotlight.

She knew it immediately. The past had found her. There, in the station when she was with Arnaldo.

He never noticed. It was impossible for him to do it.

Yes, Hilda was right. Behind Pilar's eyes there were many things hidden.

If only we were aware of how events repeat themselves to give us signals. If only we could look beyond and see events as a whole!

—*September 10th, 2012.*

And without suspecting it, everything was about to change.

Pilar had asked Arnaldo to meet her that day. It could not be any later. For Arnaldo, that invitation was strange. It was only Monday. After the weekend, she was determined to do it.

Intrigued by Pilar's insistence, Arnaldo suggested going to a nearby restaurant. The restaurant closed at 9:30 p.m., which guaranteed they would both go home early.

Pilar's plan, however, was different. A plan that would perhaps take all night.

Proximity creates bonds. It breaks the mold. Skips the processes. And life, which does not ask questions, makes unexpected turns to modify the course of events. That happened with her.

They walked to the station to take the bus to the restaurant. They talked as usual. Pilar had had an intense day. She suffered from migraines. Her head began to ache. She needed to get away from the noise and street lights. She wanted to talk to Arnaldo. At least that's what she told him.

How could she not have that pressure, if she knew "that" would be the day?

Plans and the bus route were changed. So, they ended up at Pilar's apartment.

The building was old and historical. Her apartment was small but cozy. The white walls of the place contrasted with the ceiling of old dark wooden strips.

The atmosphere was warm and intimate. There was a pair of comfortable armchairs under a dim lamp. A few steps away, the solid mahogany dining table. On it, there was a computer. It was closed.

Pilar took a painkiller. She breathed as she tried to lower the revolutions of her agitated brain. She poured Arnaldo a glass of red wine. They talked about the day as her discomfort faded.

She finally got up the courage.

"There's something I need to tell you." "But first, give me a few minutes. I'll be right back!" she told him as she got up and went to her room.

"Sure, take your time!"

Arnaldo approached the balcony. The view of the Vatican at night looked breathtaking.

The room was not very big. The queen-size bed was neatly made. Two bedside tables and a small closet were next to it.

Pilar walked towards the closet.

She stood there for a few seconds.

It's amazing how just one decision can change our lives.

Coldly, she opened the closet. From the bottom, she pulled out a safe. It was hidden behind her clothes. She entered a code. She opened the compartment.

She pulled out a small pistol. She walked out with the gun in her hand.

As she walked back to the living room, she was taking a good look at it. "Am I really doing the right thing?" she wondered. "You never know who might betray your trust", an inner voice was telling her.

She decided to ignore it.

Arnaldo was enjoying that majestic view of the city. Hearing the footsteps, he turned around. She hid the gun in the pocket of the red jacket that she was wearing. Her face turned pale.

"Is everything alright?" he asked her.

"Yes," she replied with serenity, but at the same time with fear.

She was breathing deeply. She took courage.

She approached him. She stood very close to him. Arnold felt the depth of Chanel No. 5 that wrapped Pilar. He shuddered.

On more than one occasion, Pilar caught him, admiring her figure.

It was the gaze of a man. Not the gaze of a priest. At least for her.

He stayed at that distance for some seconds. For Arnaldo, it seemed like an eternity.

"Come closer, Arnaldo."

"I can't."

"Just a little bit more."

"I shouldn't."

"Come just a little bit closer."

They remained within the distance of a kiss.

"I'm not what you think. I respect your priesthood, but tonight I need the man."

It had been years since Arnaldo has been moved by a woman's perfume.

He remained immobile. He couldn't understand what was going on.

Who would control his impulses?
The priest?
The man?

4

After the death of his parents, Anatoly could only think obsessively about one thing: finding the whereabouts of the murderers.

In the face of grief, he remembered hundreds of times the last conversation with his father about that damn report.

His friend Vladimir had tried to contact him, but Anatoly was not answering the phone. Seeing that several days had passed without hearing from him, he decided to look for him at his parents' house. So, he liaised with a colleague from the FSB, and they decided to go there first.

He felt guilty for not having been able to meet him when he called that morning.

How could he not have anticipated that something serious was going on?

Everything seemed normal outside. He knocked on the door several times. When there was no answer, he decided to force his way in. He checked every corner until he reached the guest room. There he was stunned by the river of dried blood on the floor that still remained as evidence of the crime scene. He could not say anything in the face of the dark red that was splattered against the walls.

His eyes filled with tears.

"I still can't believe this!" he repeated to himself in despair as he put his hands on his head.

Those dear people had become his family. There was no trace of his friend.

He had to find him.

Anatoly was a talkative and outgoing man, but in difficult times he preferred to shut himself away from his surroundings. That is why Vladimir did not have to think twice. The next stop would be his friend's apartment.

Anatoly's car was in the parking lot. Vladimir felt a mix of sadness and fear.

He quickly went up the stairs of the building. He knocked incessantly on the door. Nobody answered.

"Shall we knock it down?" said Vladimir's colleague.

"No holding back," he replied.

With a single blow the door opened wide. The apartment was small, it had only one room and no light was coming in from anywhere. All the curtains were closed.

Vladimir's heart skipped a beat. Anatoly was there. He could see his shadow on that piece of furniture. Without reacting.

Is he dead?

On the table, there were several bottles of medicine lying around. They were painkillers. There were empty bottles of vodka everywhere. He ran to grab him and found his brother, his gift by fate, all dirty, smelly and almost senseless. He was in deep depression. He grabbed him by the shoulders. He shook him to wake him up. Anatoly opened his eyes.

On the one hand, he was glad to find him alive. On the other hand, he felt a great indignation to see him like that. He started crying.

"Forgive me for not answering your call that day, brother."

They hugged each other. Anatoly did not say anything. He was absorbed. In another world. Although his crying was deep, no tears came out anymore. He was dry deep inside.

"Come on, my friend, get up. What are you doing here?" Vladimir said. "How much have you drunk?" he asked when he saw the bottles of medicine and liquor.

He did not answer.

He lifted him up with the help of the man who was with him.

They opened the windows. While the man cleaned up everything, Vladimir took him to the bathroom.

"Come on, take a shower. We have work to do. I will help you find who's responsible."

These words became the driving force for that destroyed man. Anatoly stared at him. He finally heard his voice.

He only said:

"Thank you."

He went into the bath, still with a strange feeling that everything in his head was spinning.

Slowly.

Full of pain, hatred, and revenge.

The intense smell of alcohol that floated through Anatoly's body could be perceived from miles away. It was clear that he had ingested nothing but drugs and liquor.

Vladimir took him to lunch and then to the Federal Security Service in Moscow. Anatoly hardly spoke at all.

"What's wrong with you? What would your father think if he saw you like this? I told you we will find the people responsible for this. I need us to use that rage and that helplessness. Come on, between the two of us we can do it! Think again about joining the Federal Security Service. Finish your degree. You're almost there! I'll help you find who's responsible," he repeated.

His story was marked by that day.
The life that would begin from the pit he was currently in.
Usually, life always bounces back when you think you cannot sink any lower.

Vladimir decided to take him home for a while. He did not want to leave him alone. Anatoly had two things that were needed to become an agent: the wisdom found in the streets and the necessary interpersonal skills. And so, he turned his pain into revenge, and revenge became the focus.

As part of the protocol for joining the Russian security corps, a detailed background check is conducted. Polygraph tests and several interviews with psychological overtones must be passed. All to determine if a person is suitable for the elite spy agency.

He passed the tests. He decided to take fate into his own hands and wring its neck.

Once he felt a bit better, he showed Vladimir a copy of the document his father had left him. He tried to remember every detail of the story. They already had a clue about the person responsible in their hands.

Vladimir stayed overtime to investigate the case. He could not tell him what he had found. He needed to be very sure before telling him. Had it been corroborated; he would share it.

Anatoly learned to operate in secret. He studied and worked hard day and night.

He thought everything was getting back on track, but life always has surprises in store and once again, it would shake him to the core.

5)

It took almost a year after the murder of his parents for Anatoly to open up to the world again. During that time, he shut himself up in his studies and work. He refrained from socializing. The only one he talked to was Vladimir.

That began to worry his friend. He wanted Anatoly to reconnect with other things. That is why, despite his constant refusals, he kept inviting him to any event he had. Finally, one day he said "yes." That day everything changed.

It was a private party at a renowned nightclub. It was organized by a friend of Vladimir's. The atmosphere was excellent. Full of good music, liquor, and beautiful women. So that they could dance better, and more people would fit, there were only high cocktail tables to place the drinks. When they arrived at the place, the party was not yet at its peak. So many were just chatting.

Anatoly felt awkward when he arrived. He did not know if it was a good idea to accept the invitation. Vladimir encouraged him as he introduced him to the friends he came across. He felt a little intimidated. Bad for being there celebrating. After a few minutes he decided to walk around the place.

"I'm going to get something to drink," Anatoly said to Vladimir. "Be back in a moment!"

"Sure, buddy! Enjoy, I'll be around."

He walked over to the bar. The show the bartenders were putting on when serving each drink caught his eye. He stood in the corner watching, waiting his turn to be served and order something.

He was amazed at how uninhibited everyone was.

Suddenly, his eyes met those of a woman who was chatting at one of the nearby tables.

He found her stunning.

She wore black leather pants and a shirt that exposed her defined shoulders. A woman of great bearing. He was enchanted by her intense gaze.

Who said love at first sight does not exist?
Love is sometimes like that.
It appears unexpectedly. Without warning.
Before they knew it, love had come to snatch both of their lives.

Surprisingly, it was that woman who took the reins and broke the ice. With total impertinence and without hesitation, she approached him.

"Hello! Do I know you from somewhere?" she said as she cracked a smile.

An unusual vertigo overcame him. The only way to subdue it was to take a step forward.

211

"I don't think so, but nice to meet you! My name is Anatoly," he said as he held out his hand.

"I'm Helena," she replied with mischievousness in her eyes.

"Because of your beauty, no doubt your father must be Zeus."

He felt ashamed of himself for that cheesy comment. They both smiled. Their worlds had changed.

"Can I buy you a drink?" she asked.

"Of course! I was here waiting for my turn."

"Waiting your turn? You'll be here all night 'waiting for your turn' like that. Look, just leave it to me. I'll explain how this works. Give me some room, please."

She gave a sign to the bartender. He quickly approached.

"Two 'midnight ecstasies', please!"

The drinks arrived instantly. She raised her glass and said to him:

"If we're going to start this relationship, we have to do it the right way! You already know, whenever you want something fast and well done, I'll take care of it."

They laughed, toasted, and talked as if they had known each other all their lives.

That first drink was followed by so many more. Enough to lose count. To them, the world seemed to have stopped that night. They did not remember their sorrows, nor the tormenting past they each carried on their backs. The whole universe had conspired to create that moment.

Vladimir went to look for him on a couple of occasions. When he saw him so happy, he decided not to approach him. He was happy to see his friend back.

From the euphoria of that encounter, and the multiplying sum of drinks, the ecstasy extended beyond. It was a long, passionate night. Those perfect strangers ended up entwined under the warm sheets of Anatoly's small apartment. That night they became accomplices. They wanted to perpetuate laughter and happiness. Without realizing it, unconsciously, their pains sealed a pact that would keep them together for the whole year to come. An intense year, in every sense.

A year full of passion. Full of secrets. Full of conflicts. Full of fire.

A fire that burns.

Wow, how it burns!

For Anatoly, life began to make sense. They became teenagers again. Their hormones exploded uncontrollably at every moment. They made love a rite that they fulfilled day and night. It was in this unforeseen way that Anatoly's small apartment gave shelter to a life together.

With a daily routine in place, they tried to make the most out of every second they had the opportunity to share, as their schedule was quite irregular. They worked and studied. They opened books and closed deals. They exposed their bodies, but not their souls. Despite how close they became, "the truth" in their lives was only half known.

It often happens that spies families do not know what they do for a living. It is a prudent career that forces discretion as part of the confidentiality agreements they sign.

That is why Anatoly did not talk much about himself. He only ever mentioned that his parents had passed away. He avoided the subject of family and work as much as possible.

Like all women, Helena always talked constantly. The truth is that her imagination was vivid. She was very good at inventing stories. She would go into a trance telling her childhood stories and she always mentioned how special her mother was. Her father had abandoned them when she was months old.

A year together passed by in the blink of an eye.

The date of their anniversary was approaching, so to celebrate it Anatoly decided to surprise her a little earlier. They would go out for dinner at one of the best restaurants in the city: Moskovsky Bar.

It was located in the luxurious Four Seasons Hotel, very close to Moscow's Red Square, the Kremlin, and the State Duma.

The place was a modern-day version of the bars of the 1930s. It was well known for its extravagant cocktails. As such, she was quick to order one. When in Rome, do as the Romans do,' goes the proverb.

He preferred the traditional options. A vodka.

With one drink came the next. And another. And another. Once again, they lost count.

That was a very special day. A very sensitive date for Anatoly.

That night he was not so talkative. He was feeling emotionally troubled. If they were alive, his parents would be celebrating their birthdays. They were both born on the same day.

Ironically, on the same date they were born, they were murdered.

That is why he drank everything as if it was water.

"Love, are you all right? Is everything all right?" asked Helena. "I've never seen you like that before. I don't know what's wrong."

"Yes, beauty," he said, already tongue-tied from the effect of the liquor.

"Let's ask for the bill and go home, shall we?"

"Yes, ask for the bill, but I want you to go with me to a place first."

"Where? Wouldn't you prefer to leave it for another day?"

"No. I'd love to go with you today. I'd already planned on it."

They left the bar and Anatoly took the car. He headed to the north, about fifteen minutes driving. He tried to keep his eyes on the road. With that amount of liquor in his body, keeping the vehicle aligned was not easy.

When they arrived, he parked. Helena did not understand what was going on.

"What are we doing here?" she asked.

"It was my parents' house. Both of them would be celebrating their birthdays today. I know they would have loved to meet you. I want them to meet you, as crazy as all this may sound. Their essence is here, I brought you because I love you."

Helena was speechless. It turned her life upside down.

She knew that place well.

She had been there before.

If there is one thing God has, it is a strange sense of humor.

Sometimes too hard to understand.

6

Anatoly got out of the car. She remained inside, immobile. She did not know what to do. He approached and in a gentlemanly gesture, opened the door for her.

Helena got out. Her legs were shaking. She wanted to run away, to escape.

This was a practical joke; life was playing with her.

Anatoly held her hand as they approached the house and opened the door. He entered. Dizzy from the liquor, he walked down the entrance hall.

"I know they're here! Their birthdays would be today. We'd be celebrating it."

Helena wanted to cry. She couldn't talk. None of this could not be happening. She wanted to disappear.

She wanted to wake up from that nightmare.

As Anatoly went through every corner of the house, he talked to her about his parents, about his childhood. About the nostalgia that overwhelmed his soul. For the first time he spoke openly about them. About himself.

"My mother was the best cook in the world. Her food would've made you lick your fingers!"

He stopped in the guest room. Between sobs he told her the sad and atrocious way his parents had died. How they were vilely murdered. With each and every second, she felt more and more miserable.

"Let's go upstairs, I want to show you my room! There's something I want to share with you there."

They went upstairs. When they got to his room, Anatoly stopped. He turned around and looked at her straight in the eyes.

"Do you have something to tell me?" asked Anatoly.

"What do you want me to tell you?" Helena answered very nervously.

"I don't know. You haven't said a word. I wanted to bring you here because I love you. I would have loved them to meet you. I know they're here somehow. That's why I brought you."

Damn time, never forgiving and always returning inexorably to expose our miseries bare in front of us.

"I want to tell you something I haven't told you before," Anatoly opened his heart. Helena looked at him with tears in her eyes. "I'm studying at the Russian Security Agency. I'm doing my best to become a spy. We're not supposed to talk about it, but I don't want secrets between us, because I love you."

Helena was still speechless. She was not processing what he was saying.

She wanted to ask for forgiveness. Tell him the truth. She could not dare.

Run. She wanted to run away.

She was immobile.

Anatoly walked over to the desk. From the bottom drawer he pulled out the report his father had given him the night before his death. The one he had looked through so many times searching for a clue that would lead him to decipher more about the person responsible of that cruel and scathing act.

"They murdered him because of this," he said as he handed her the manuscript.

She wanted to scream. She could not.

She wanted to turn back time, to make it run backwards like one old watch her mother had given her. That was not possible either. Time does not run backwards. Only defective clocks do that.

With trembling hands, she took the document. She glanced at the cover. She looked down.

"Look at it later... It's yours! Today I need to release all this hell inside me . I don't want to keep secrets with the woman I want to be the mother of my children," he said, sobbing.

He reached into his pocket. He pulled out a ring. Tongue-tied from the alcohol and trying to keep his balance, he knelt.

"In front of my parents, because I know they are here, I want to ask you to be my wife. Will you marry me?"

There was a long silence. Eternal. Infinite.

The individuals, who a year earlier seemed to be together forever, realized at that moment that the most unlikely stories are intertwined so that truth prevails.

Certainly, nothing is hidden between heaven and Earth.

The report slipped from Helena's hand and fell to the floor.

She covered her face with her hands.

She started crying. Bitterly. In pain. Tearing apart.

"I'm not worthy of a man like you!" she told him.

She turned around.

Finally, she could run away.

He did not understand what was happening. He couldn't stop her. He tried, but he could only lean against the wall to keep his balance. A little stunned, he tried to sit up.

He heard the sound of the door.

The excess of alcohol had won the battle.

As one who is destined to live on memories, he stayed there once again, in his room. Face down. Alone.

Just when he thought life was smiling at him, life itself came to bring him to his knees again.

What he did not know was that life would keep knocking him down until he was finally defeated.

7

Helena's disappearance left Anatoly in a new and unfathomable void. A pervasive sorrow that eroded his soul.

Beyond the pain that accompanied him, he was left waiting for answers that never came. He did not understand what had happened.

It was not easy. It took him a while to shake off that feeling of abandonment and sadness. He tried not to sink back into the depressive state that he hated so much for being a part of himself. He needed to stop thinking about the woman he loved so much.

Therefore, he connected with that desire wich before had lifted him off the floor. He resumed his focus with more determination. He wanted to find the whereabouts of those responsible for the death of his parents. He focused again on taking justice into his own hands.

He longed for the "eye for an eye and tooth for a tooth" from the Book of Exodus.

The legal principle of justice in the law of retribution.

Collecting outstanding debt.

His unquenchable thirst for revenge remained intact.

Although he was obsessed and in love with Helena, love did not blind him while they were together. During that year he did not stop researching about the Nuremberg Group for a single day. He continued to take any opportunity to collect and corroborate as much information as possible, to allow him to remove the sacred veil that existed around these "untouchable" men.

The group's communication line seemed impeccable. Well-managed. Seen from the outside, they were men and women concerned about curbing the issues that afflict us as citizens of the world. Elite and powerful people in search of alternatives to improve our lives. However, in the document his father had given him and in everything he was investigating, the backdrop was something very different.

The documents he was compiling not only corroborated the dark and crazy plans they had executed and hoped to implement, but also included the list of men and women who over the decades had endorsed all that. Some of them were even responsible for some of the world's truly dark chapters, as was Dimitriv Basov.

In the reports, his name and money were associated with men of science whose experiments escaped the rational, similar to those performed by surgeons such as Vladimir Demikhov, a Russian and pioneer in organ transplantation beyond acceptable limits. Sidney Gottlieb, a biochemist, American military psychiatrist, and director of the chemical division of CIA, who carried out the MK Ultra mind control project. Also, men like the renowned American neurosurgeon Robert Joseph White, adviser of Pope John Paul II on Ethical Medicine, and obsessed with head transplant experiments.

Anatoly had to be careful how he approached Dimitriv. He knew that, after what happened to his parents, his own life was also in danger.

He focused so much of his energy on work that he spent hours without thinking about that woman.

His mailbox was usually full of envelopes. He used to check it once a week. Everything was accumulated there, from unpaid bills to local bargain promotions. It had been a while since he had last checked it, so he decided to stop by and pick them up.

He grabbed everything there. As he walked home, he checked the envelopes. To his surprise, one of them was from Helena. As soon as he read her name, his heart began to race.

All you have to do is stop looking for something and life will bring it to you.

His hands became cold and sweaty. He sped up his pace, he wanted to get home already and read what was written there.

He threw everything else on the table. He opened the letter.

My beloved and sweet Anatoly:
What more would I have wanted than to shout "yes" from the rooftops that night at your parents' house. Ever since I met you, I have wanted nothing more than that, to be your wife.

You changed my life. You transformed what I was. You gave me new wings. However, sometimes life gives us low blows, those that we can't recover from. Just as you, I also have a past that burdens. You can't imagine how much.

I would like to bare my soul to you, but I cannot today. You, better than anyone, know the value of a secret. Thank you for telling me yours.

I am writing to you from a hotel room far from Moscow. I left Russia and decided to look for a new horizon, as I feel that my soul needs to find a way to redemption and forgiveness. If there is one thing I long for, it is to find peace. The peace I lost long ago.

I know the thirst for revenge you have for your parents. I know that. I know how it feels. I've been there at one point too. I only pray that, if God exists, he may guide me at some point. I hope I have the strength to seek you out in the future so we can talk. So you can listen to me. So I can

tell you, looking in your eyes, everything that I can't today.
I want you to know that I love you too. Like no one else.

For now, I only ask you to take the key and look at what I
left for you in the little box you kept that belonged to your
mother, the one I placed next to your bed. I think it is the
only way I can ask for your forgiveness and contribute to
your finding peace. I hope you find there everything you
are looking for.

I hope someday you can forgive me for what I have done
to you.
You are the best thing that ever happened to me.
Please don't ever doubt that.

Yours,
Helena

Inside the envelope was a small silver key. He took it out. He did not understand anything. He went straight to his room. The small old metal box was there. Inside there was a USB drive.

He looked for the computer. He plugged in the device. He read what was on that drive. Everything made sense. His father's report was just the tip of the iceberg. Controversial murders of recent times. Beginnings and endings of wars. Undercover videos. Strategies they followed to carry out everything, from stock market crashes to world conflicts and even to biochemical wars. Nuremberg was behind it.

No mind, not even in its most twisted facet, could imagine the plan these people had in motion. It was like something out of a movie.

Some very well-known names from his country were also on the list. Now more than ever he had to be cautious. The evidence he had in his hands compromised high places.

How did Helena have all this?

Who was that woman really?

Would Anatoly ever get an answer to these questions?

The documentation also addressed specific objectives to be reached in the future and, step by step, the ways to achieve them. One of the paragraphs stated:

> *The stated goals include:*
> *Elimination of 75 % of the world's population in the next thirty years.*
> *Creation of a single currency.*
> *Creation of a single world government.*
> *Creation of a single religion.*

It is one thing to read these purposes and quite another to know that they will be or are being executed.

What was the best way out of this situation?

Anatoly had to be strategic.

He paced trying to think and put everything in order.

With this conclusive evidence and the report his father had given him, revealing what was behind it was only a matter of time.

At the same time, losing such a precious resource as time was not an option.

In the book *The Art of War*, written more than 2,500 years ago, it is said that in combat the one who knows when to fight and when not to fight wins. Additionally, the army whose officers and soldiers are better trained will be the victor. It is a real treatise on military practice and war strategies.

Anatoly had to think that way.

The key was to be among the best trained. He was.

He picked up the phone. He made a call.

"Vladimir, it's Anatoly! I think I have evidence of the ones responsible for my parents' death. I need to see you. Everything seems to indicate that the time has come, but I need your expertise."

Indeed, the time had come.
Life wanted to see Anatoly defeated.
He would rise to strike back with full force.
Someone would definitely be knocked out in the ring.

8

Arnaldo was standing in front of Pilar. Within the distance of a kiss. He didn't understand what was happening.

"Pilar, I can't play this game."

"It's not what you think, Arnaldo. Can you keep a secret?"

"I live on secrets."

"Arnaldo, I'm not whom you think I am," she said.

She pulled the small pistol out of her pocket. She pointed the gun at him. He got up startled.

"What's that, Pilar? Why do you have that gun?"

Pilar stared at him. She was spinning the gun around.

"Surprise, Arnaldo! Do you remember that I told you that not everything is what it seems? This is me!"

"What are you talking about? I don't understand anything," he said nervously.

"Don't be scared! Calm down. Please, sit down."

"What do you want from me?"

Arnaldo did not know what to do. He decided to comply with what Pilar told him.

His legs were trembling.

"What is all this about?" he thought.

"Arnaldo, our lives are in danger. I've already lost the people I loved most. I don't want to lose you too. I thought I'd never trust anyone again and I consider you my friend."

"Why do you say our lives are in danger?"

"Let me explain everything and you'll be able to understand it better."

Arnaldo was trying to put it all together. The fear that overwhelmed him increased more and more.

"Do you remember when I told you that I'd give my life for what I considered to be the truth?"

"Of course, I remember."

"So, for many years, I was one of the security agents for a select group of men of power. Of much, much power. They were my Gods. I'd have given my life for them. The truth they professed was 'my truth'."

"Who are you talking about? Who are they?"

"I'm talking about a group called Nuremberg. They're the masters of the world. They want to establish a new world order. A new church. And they've everything to do so. What I am telling you is real, and it is serious. I collaborated with them."

"Have you gone crazy or what?"

Pilar had thought about telling this to Arnaldo many times, but she was waiting for the right moment.

However, they had been following her for some time. That man had come to eliminate Pilar.

But in life, some angels clear the way.
Pilar did not imagine who was taking care of her.

She knew well the modus operandi of her former bosses, so every night she went to bed waiting for that fateful moment to arrive.

There is always a day.

Once again, the old clock began to turn backward. If there was one thing that Pilar did not have at that moment, it was time. That is why she decided to tell Arnaldo the truth. They were after her. They were also after him.

She had changed her name hundreds of times, and for a long time, she had come to believe that she has escaped from the Nuremberg people.

But to them, no one escapes.

"Do you remember the story I told you about my mother?" Pilar asked him.

"Yes, I remember."

"That day I didn't dare to tell you everything. My mom was one of Nuremberg's agents. I grew up with them. I felt protected, so I protected them too. I was part of their pack."

"And then, what happened?"

"The day my mother was no longer useful to them, they killed her."

NELSON BUSTAMANTE & CARMEN VICTORIA PARDO

When she said that, she felt the sound of her voice like a bomb exploding inside her. Again.

Her face changed. For a moment she was no longer the woman, she was the girl who waited alone and anxiously for her mother's arrival. A little girl full of sadness. Also full of much anger.

"How did they kill her?" Arnaldo asked her.

"Cold-blooded. In a vile manner. Without mercy. The same way we were taught how to do it."

"How come you were taught to do it?"

"I told you I'd have given my life for them. My hands are dirty. I didn't kill one. There were several."

Arnaldo was speechless.

Probably those people in the halls, who said she was not to be trusted, were right. Perhaps they saw what he did not.

But Arnaldo was a man of God. At that moment not only was the friend, the man, but also the priest.

"Pilar, if this was so many years ago, why now?"

"Because with them, debts are not pending. Eventually, they'll be settled. They already found my whereabouts and are looking for me. They know we talk. I need you to walk away."

"I don't understand, why?"

"Because you're in danger," she replied staring into his eyes. "My mom knew more than she should have. I don't know how. That will remain a mystery. What's certain is that she became a danger to the interests of the group. She was brilliant. Overly intelligent, Arnaldo. The night before her murder I was lying in bed when she arrived. At that moment I'd just turned off the light on the bedside table when she came into my room. She was carrying a gift for me. "Here you have my love, a little present I brought you, this will help you to wake up", she told me. It was a simple wristwatch. I never switched on the light. I remember she told me to set the alarm for the next day. Then she told me, "I have to do something tonight. I'm going out again. I came to give you this little gift and to see how you were." Finally, she came closer and whispered to me «I love you». I thanked her. We hugged each other. She left. I never saw her again."

Pilar started to cry. Arnaldo holds her hands. He hugged her compassionately.

"How do you know it was them?"

"We had a pact. None of us stopped coming home. When I woke up, and I couldn't find her, I knew something had happened. My partner was also a member of that group. He called to tell me the news and confess the truth. I went crazy. I wanted to kill them all. I felt like my world was falling apart."

"What did you do?"

"I walked around every corner of the house. I touched every one of her belongings. I was a wandering soul. It was then when I saw a note she'd left the night before on the refrigerator chalkboard, *"Remember, time is gold, with love, mom."* I went upstairs to get the watch she'd given me. It was the thing I had with her scent. As I put it on, I noticed that the needles were running in the opposite direction. Suddenly, like a puzzle in my head, everything sta}rted to come together. It was no coincidence. That was just what I needed to do. To go against the clock. She wanted to tell me something. They were clues. Wiping away my tears, my heart started beating fast. I remembered my mother's words:

"this will help you wake up." I opened it and there it was. There was a brilliantly embedded chip. They were the evidence of the atrocities that the Nuremberg group planned to do. Absolute power. The extermination of a part of the population, the total control of the world, and the destruction of the church. Just to name a few of them."

Arnaldo could not get over his shock.

As a confessor and part of it.

He did not know what to do.

His heart was beating fast.

"What am I doing here?" he wondered.

Pilar knew that, at any moment, they could enter through the door. There was a pause. She stood up. She picked up the computer that was on the dining room table. She opened it. On the screen was the classic card game Solitaire. She took the gun out of her jacket. She handed it over to Arnaldo.

"Pilar, why are you giving me this?"

"Calm down Arnaldo. I know that talking about trust is difficult, but I need you to trust me. Please take the gun and point it at my left eye."

"No!" he said. He put it on the table. He got up nervous. His hands were sweaty. "Are you crazy?"

"It's not what it seems." She insisted.

She took the gun. Aimed it at her eye. To the right one. She pulled the trigger.

Silence.

Nothing happened.

"Please trust me. Once again, I know it's difficult, but I need to show you something."

Pilar returned the weapon to Arnaldo.

"I'm going to open my eye. If you look at the bottom, you'll see a tiny spot. If you'd a magnifying glass you'd realize that it's a code. Aim there and pull the trigger. The gun isn't real. It's a digital decoding technology. It doesn't have bullets. But it's the only way you can understand everything."

With trembling hands and without knowing why Arnaldo followed her instructions. He aimed at Pilar's left eye.

He pulled the trigger.

Silence.

Apparently, nothing had happened.

However, that deck of cards that was on the computer began to activate. Inside each of those fifty-two cards, different documents began to load.

Arnaldo did not understand what was happening.

"When I found this confidential information, the message my mother left me made more sense. I knew they were coming for these files. They were coming for me. I had to do something. I couldn't waste time. I was going against the clock. Before I share it with you, I want to tell you how I hid it. I want you to be ready. To open your mind. When I started working with my mom, I accompanied her to a convention in Amsterdam in 1991. One of the 'cousins' of the Nuremberg Group is the Rome group. Let's say they oversee the area of science and breakthroughs. We went incognito to see what was being discussed there. At the time I just didn't know it. It was called Wetware Convention. At that convention, I heard this word for the first time. It is like the software or hardware of a computer, but this time, installed or connected to a person. There I met some men of science

NELSON BUSTAMANTE & CARMEN VICTORIA PARDO

who were experimenting with their bodies. Biohackers. They broke every rule. They broke the boundary between science, biomedical security, and even the security we use in espionage. My options weren't many, so knowing that time was against me, I contacted them again. They helped me create this device with brain technology and biological engineering, which not only stores the data, documents, and evidence that my mom had extracted but also allows me to feed it with more information."

The more Arnaldo listened, the more he shuddered. That was unusual.

"I imagine it's like some kind of Rfid card that stores more data than a simple bar code," he said.

"Exactly."

"I've heard of it before. I know how it works."

"The CRISPR-Cas9 technology devices that allow gene editing were also wetware. The way to add new functions or capabilities to DNA."

"You're saying that in addition to the information you've fed back and incorporated new evidence? How's that?"

"They had the idea. They decided to increase the functionality of the wetware by adding to the program a small antenna that reads brain waves and records sounds. This card implanted in my eye has a built-in chip that I program at my disposal. When I hear or see something, when I make a slight eye movement, it activates and records. I send the data to my computer via radio frequency. On the other hand, they created three advanced Rfid mini cards. Before I disappeared and became 'Pilar', I managed to install these mini-devices at key points in the Nuremberg offices. Whenever there's movement, they pick up the signal, extract the information and also send it to the system I've to process that data."

"What was that information your mom had?"

"I want you to see this."

They approached the computer. Arnaldo could not believe what he was seeing. The documents that were there. The evidence stored there. He spent the whole night reading it all. There was a file called ROME.

"Pilar, this seems unbelievable, it's bizarre. What are they looking for?"

"They want to establish a new world order. A new Church, Arnaldo."

"Are you sure about what you're saying?"

"I was one of them."

Silence took over the environment.

"How do I know you are no longer one of them?"

"I've shown you everything, and you still doubt it? I feel like my days are numbered. I needed to share this. Who better to share it with than a person like you who genuinely loves the Church. I had to be smart like my mom. And so, the gun, the device, the information behind a computer game."

"Your eye..."

"Yes. A secret agent has to be armed. A spy will always look for an external device. They'll never imagine that the information is 'installed' in my body."

The pieces of the puzzle began to fit together for Arnaldo.

"Who else has seen or knows about this?"

"My partner from years ago. But he was also silenced. Just like my mom. Now you know it. That's why you're in danger."

"Well, if they're looking for you and now for me as well, we should think of someone else. If something happens to us, this can't stay hidden."

Pilar never imagined that the famous "an eye for an eye" would be the price she would have to pay. Literally.

9)

Kevin decided to disassociate himself from *Code Christ* once and for all. He dedicated himself to only one thing: to carry out all the experiments with Mullis, trying to find new ways to achieve his goal.

But a turning point in science, an unexpected discovery opened up new opportunities.

—2012.
A new method for editing the human genome has been discovered.
"We have a tool that can be used to control human evolution," said Jennifer Doudna.
Science has made a new quantum leap.

French microbiologist and biochemist, Emmanuelle Charpentier, at the University of Umea, together with the American biochemist, Jennifer Doudna, at the University of California at Berkeley, discovered "molecular scissors" that allow DNA to be edited, corrected, inserted, deleted, or modified.

In short, these scissors give the option to cut out what is "not right."

Their discovery makes it possible to address, up to the nucleus, the genes that have been modified and insert them in the correct place in the DNA. All in a very precise, easy, and fast way.

The possibilities of this discovery are infinite: from biomedicine, through research into the development of cancer therapies, to modifying the genomes of human embryos.

Genetics has been revolutionized.
While these women and men of science are working tirelessly on clinical trials to cure diseases, a different thought has arisen in the minds of others. Light also contains darkness.

With these CRISPR-Cas9 breakthroughs, Kevin and Mullis have close at hand a tool that allows them to create "the perfect human being."

"Hitler and Mengele would be happy," Mullis says while celebrating it.

That breakthrough brings a new element to their cloning project.

"We won't just clone Jesus! We can create him perfect, in our own way!"

As participants in the search for perfection, ethically what they plan to do is insane. It infringes on the principles of autonomy, identity and freedom.

However, they have no scruples.

And they are not the only ones.

NELSON BUSTAMANTE & CARMEN VICTORIA PARDO

The moment they will have to cross the line is getting closer and closer; a moment which could change the course of history. The Church knows this and needs to stop them at all costs.

10

—*September 10ᵗʰ, 2010.*
12 m. Rome.

Finally, Arnaldo appeared. He looks more troubled than usual. His mind wanders. He is worried. Since yesterday he has had a strange premonition.

"Father Arnaldo!" says Hilda, the secretary, exalted. "How are you? Is everything all right? "I called you many times and you didn't answer. You've never disappeared for that long without letting me know before"

"Yes, everything all right, Hilda! I didn't get any rest last night and I fell asleep this morning at almost seven o'clock. I didn't charge my cell phone and its battery ran out. I heard the news about the theft of the relics of John the Baptist. What a madness!"

"Yes! Totally! The morning was quite busy. By the way, one of the communications reporters was looking for you earlier, he wanted to interview you. I told him you were out on some assignments, and I didn't know when you'd be back. A harmless lie to save you," she commented mischievously.

"Hilda, Hilda! The truth, woman! Remember, always the truth. Thank you for justifying my absence, but you get the same confession and penance," he said with humor.

At the Vatican Radio, the deputy director of communications, finally, appears too.

"Thank God you're here, Pilar! We've called you a thousand times," said Antonio, one of her younger colleagues. A mix between geek and nerd.

"A thousand apologies! I had a bad night and went to sleep this morning. I suffer from migraines. It has been a long night, as the painkillers didn't help much. I didn't hear the phone. When I woke up and saw so many missed calls, I knew something had happened. Tomás told me about the theft."

Pilar hurried to put her purse and briefcase on the desk.

She turned on the computer. The inbox began to fill up. One hundred twenty seven unread messages.

"Did you already do an official communication?" she asked as she looked over the mail.

"No. Our biggest concern is that we don't know how the Church wants to communicate this. We didn't dare call Cardinal Vitesse. But the press release is ready and waiting for your approval so we can send it."

"Show me what you have. Do you have any information on who might be behind this? Any suspects? Have the police said anything?" she asked.

"Nothing. At least not officially."

Pilar's phone rang.

"Excuse me," she said to Antonio as the phone continued ringing. "I must answer it! Please send me what you have. I'll check it and give you my feedback immediately to spread the official press notice."

"Sure, don't worry, I'll send it to you," he said and left the office.

That day will be a long one.

Just as it was the night before. A night of secrets. Of revelations. Where their bodies were so docile.

How casual was it that they were both late?

—*September 11th, 2012.*

Everything that had happened the night before was going around in Arnaldo's head. He could not finish processing all of it.

What could he do? Should he explain the gravity of what was coming? Was silence the best option?

Concentrating on that day was hard.

Today he broke the mold. He had eight cigars and the worst thing is that the hour of divine mercy had not yet arrived.

It was the first time Pilar was seen in jeans and without heels. Her hair was up. She wasn't dressed up like she always used to be.

When she arrives, Antonio, her colleague, greets and berates her.

"Hello, boss! Good morning! How awesome. Just today it's been two years since the theft of the remains of John the Baptist. I remember that day you couldn't arrive early either."

She preferred to ignore the comment.

Yes. Sometimes life repeats itself.

"I have something to tell you. Just yesterday I was listening to a group of scientists who have a web community called *Code Christ*, they announced that they were going to shake the Church," said Antonio.

She knew what and who she was talking about. She preferred not to comment anything about it. To find out a little more.

"What are you talking about?" asked Pilar. "Where did you find that information? As journalists, we've to look for trustful sources."

"Don't say that! They are serious people. They said that they have the remains of John the Baptist and with that they could obtain the remaining eleven percent of the genetic information of Jesus Christ. What they need to clone him."

"Clone him? Who do they want to clone? Jesus Christ? John the Baptist? What madness is that? I don't understand anything..."

"Jesus Christ, boss! Jesus Christ himself! I know it sounds crazy, but it doesn't seem what it is! I believe they are related to this issue. One of the people responsible is Doctor KD. I've searched for him on the Internet and he knows about it. He constantly says that science can create an even better version of the son of God. With CRISPR-Cas9 developments they can make 'adjustments' for perfection."

"What's CRISPR...?" asked Pilar.

"CRISPR-Cas9 is a genomic editing technique to improve the species. Think about it! If they have all that, why not do it? I think we're on the doorstep of a new era for the Church and humanity" interrupted Antonio.

"Be careful what you say, don't forget that you work for the Vatican! If anyone else hears you, you can get into trouble. Tell me, where do you hear all those things?"

"It's on the deep web. They meet five days a week. They have the necessary financial resources. There are people with a lot of power behind all this."

"Stop listening to crazy people! What you're talking about is very delicate"

People with power and resources. There was no doubt about that. Those were them.

The time when everything would detonate was closer.

Pilar's cell phone rang. It was Arnaldo.

"A thousand apologies!"

"Never mind, boss. But I don't think we should let these people out of our sight!" he said as he left the office.

Pilar took the call.

"Ciao"

"Hello! Did you rest?" asked Arnaldo.

"Very little, to be honest."

"Same here. I just arrived. I still can't process what you told me last night."

She interrupted him abruptly. Trying to stop any further comments regarding what she had shared hours before.

"Let's do something. I have a lot of work, shall we meet in the gardens around four o'clock? We can talk there."

"Of course, at four o'clock."

"Perfect. I'll see you there"

Each of them took care of their duties. However, it wasn't easy. Arnaldo needed to talk with Pilar once again.

Finally, the clock struck four o'clock. He went out to the meeting place.

Arnaldo paced as he waited for her.

He needed to talk about the night before.

What he was about to hear would shake his world.

She arrived a bit agitated. She hurried to greet him.

"What an unproductive day! I couldn't concentrate" Arnaldo commented as he responded to the two kisses on the cheek.

"Do you want to know the worst part?"

"Is there a worst part?"

"There might always be one!" she said. "Anyway, the day is not over yet."

They both looked at each other knowingly. They both smiled. It was a smile full of tiredness. But complicit at last.

"Arnaldo, have you ever heard of something called *Code Christ?*"

"What's that?"

"I thought you'd know. It's linked to a group of scientists. Men of science who are looking to clone Jesus. They've been with this project for several years and a couple of days ago they came out saying they'd shake the Church to its core."

"Where did you hear that?" asked Arnaldo.

"They're financed by Nuremberg. What stands out to me is that Antonio, one of the guys on my team, told me about it. That means we are running out of time."

"Do you know who the scientists behind it are?"

"Dr. K.D. is the leader. They are convinced that science can create an even better version of the Son of God. With the developments, they can make adjustments for his perfection and achieve one of their goals: the creation of a new Church."

Arnaldo had already heard that years ago.

With almost the same words.

"The truth is that some time ago I heard someone saying something similar. I remember because that comment had a huge impact on me. At that time, I thought it was impossible."

"Antonio told me that they are connected covertly. That they have the remains of John the Baptist in their possession. They themselves stole the remains two years ago. With that, they can obtain the other eleven percent of the genetic information they need to clone Jesus. By now if that's the case, they've got it."

"And where do they get the other eighty-nine percent?"

"They also have Son of God's blood."

Once again, everything seemed to make sense.

He remembered the Roslin scientist when he came to suggest the same thing to him.

The man who was in STURP.

Instinctively, he put his hands on his cross.

"What's the name of the guy who's leading the investigation?"

"He calls himself Dr. K.D."

"K.D.," thought Arnaldo. "K.D...," he repeated to himself internally. "Bingo!"

"Kevin Davis!" he said.

"Do you know him?" asked Pilar, surprised.

"Yes, we worked together a few years ago. It has to be him! He was the one who outlined the idea to me at that time, but I didn't pay attention to it. As I told you, I thought it was impossible."

That was no longer ridiculous.

"If this is true, there's a plan in motion and it could break out very, very soon. We've to do something about it," considered Arnaldo, worried.

However, Arnaldo did not suspect that in a few moments another piece of news would burst in his face. Straight in front of him.

"Arnaldo. There's no 'we have'. I'm leaving."

"Why?"

"I need to get out of here. I told you, they've already tracked my whereabouts."

"How do you know?"

"Fortunately, I still have whistleblowers. After you left this morning, I spoke to one of them. One of the few I'm in contact with."

"I don't know much about this, but what if you get a haircut or something like that..."

"Arnaldo, I've changed my identity and my style several times. I've had several names, depending on the moment. Alessandra, Helena, Valeria, Sara, Pilar, in short... I wouldn't forgive myself if something bad happened to you."

Arnaldo did not know what to say. On the one hand, he knew it was for the best. But on the other, he was overcome by a deep emptiness.

Pilar took out a key from her pocket. She handed it to him.

"It's a pen drive. If you hold the top and open it, you're going to be able to pull it out. Here's everything I showed you yesterday. Do whatever you think you'd do with that information. I trust you."

He remained in silence.

"Please, take care..." she said as she hugged him. "Could you give me your blessing?"

And so he did.

Arnaldo raised his right hand and placed it on her head. He made the sign of the cross. He blessed her. For the first time, Pilar felt a little bit of peace.

With tears in her eyes, she turned away and left.

This would be the last time they would be face to face.

What happened with Pilar has moved Arnaldo. He doesn't know what to do with the information he has. Three days have already passed without her appearing on Vatican Radio. He has tried to reach her, but she doesn't answer his calls.

He keeps the key she gave him in his pants pocket. Every time he touches it, he remembers what is inside. He prays. He asks for divine guidance. He cannot find the way. However, he has not sat back and done nothing. Through his uncertainty, he has tried to find out more about *Code Christ*. With Nuremberg in the way, he must proceed with caution. Quickly, too.

The Church is in danger.

He has gone to the communications offices to see if Pilar has contacted any of them. Nothing. He has also decided to be closer to Antonio to learn more about his closeness to *Code Christ.*

It has just turned half past ten in the morning.

He comes in with two cups of coffee. Antonio is the only one in the room.

"Would you like a coffee?" he asked him.

"Sure! How kind of you, Father Arnaldo! Good to see you!

"Good to see you too. Have you heard from Pilar? I've called her, but I can't reach her."

"She left a note three days ago saying she'll be away. I guess something came up. As far as I understand Cardinal Vitesse returns tomorrow."

Arnaldo wants to find out more about the group of scientists Pilar told him about. He doesn't want to ask directly. Takes a sip of coffee.

"Hey, by the way, Antonio, since you're always up to date on everything, I heard about something called Codex Christ... I think that's what it's called..."

"Could it be *Code Christ?*"

"Yes, I think it is!"

"Have you heard of them, Father? They are scientists like you."

"I've heard of them, but I don't know where to find them. I don't see much on the web."

"It's because their page is private. It's untraceable. That's why. You have to connect through the deep web."

"Deep web? This youth is into something else!" says Arnaldo, trying to play down the importance of the matter. "And do you know how I could also connect there?"

"You'll have to request access, since it's a private group. If you want, once I finish some things here, I'll make you a manual and share it with you by email. Or I'll help you!

"I would love to! I appreciate it very much."

People who wish to join *Code Christ* must not only know how to get to the part of the web that is not accessible through search engines, but they must also, once inside, fill out an application, send a resume and attach, among other things, a copy of their ID.

Once all these steps have been completed, a detailed check of the applicant is carried out. A thorough procedure. This ensures that there are no other interests that could jeopardize the activities of this group.

However, to Antonio's surprise, Father Arnaldo's application was accepted almost immediately.

"You're lucky, Father! They take their time. You're in! I'll leave you so you can continue on your own. I have a few things to finish before Cardinal Vitesse arrives."

He left the office.

Arnaldo decided to review everything on the *Code Christ* page and joined the meeting for that day. He turned on his camera and microphone. He corroborated his theory. He was astonished in front of the computer. It was, without a doubt, Kevin Davis. There was the same man he had met years before.

Arnaldo took in the whole scene. At the back of the laboratory where Kevin was, there was a symbol on the wall. A cross. Two thick, solid lines. Two letters were inscribed on the horizontal line across it: the symbols for Alpha and Omega. The name God gives himself in the Book of Revelation. Beginning and end of all things. It represents the eternity of Christ as the Son of the Most High.

That emblem was not alone. In the upper right and lower left quadrant was the letter *C*.

The law, the norm.

What must be.

At the sight of it, Arnaldo's skin bristles. Trembling, he slowly pulls up the sleeve of his shirt. He looks at his wrist. A very similar mark is tattooed there.

How is that possible?

A divine sign or cursed mark?

For a few moments, his mind wanders to the past. He vividly remembers that night.

He was with several friends. Among them, Alma, the girl he liked, and Ricardo, better known as "The Pest." Because that is what that boy had inside: a real pest.

They were all drinking wildly. They laughed. There were also several girls there. Alma was a little drunk. Ricardo knew that Arnaldo liked her. He could see them exchanging glances. He approached her. He told her in her ear that it was time to seal his manly pact: to penetrate that girl. To baptize her with his semen. To say goodbye to her virginity.

"Do it, do it!" he insisted.

That was not what he wanted. He liked Alma. Indeed, but not for just one night. He knew that if he did not do it, "The Pest" would convince someone else to baptize her. He had to rescue her somehow.

He went up to her. Gave her a kiss. He would not do anything else. He did not want to. He started to lead her away from the place just to try to sneak away from Ricardo's perversity. Pretended he was trying to grope her. She began to struggle. Juan, Alma's brother, came up to Arnaldo and gave him a good punch. Literally, with one blow, he fell to the ground.

It was so hard that he did not get up. He was knocked unconscious.

In his memory everything stopped.

During the *Code Christ* broadcast, Kevin was performing a test live where he was inserting a magnetic implant into a girl's abdomen that would allow her to have orgasms whenever she wanted. It was clear that the girl was excited and nervous. In the background, a voice could be heard insisting her to continue. It was Rik, his partner.

"Do it, do it!" Rik insisted.

That voice was familiar to Arnaldo.

It was the same voice that had told him with identical words many years before: "Do it, do it!"

Past or present?
It's a small world.

Once again, his mind wandered.

It was Ricardo, now better known as Rik.

Arnaldo relives the story again. He remembers being told how, after falling to the ground that night, Ricardo took the opportunity to tattoo his wrist. Blood and ink.

He tattooed him there. He felt no pain. The alcohol that ran through his veins had numbed him.

"You're part of the pack. You're sealed. My blood is your blood," Ricardo told him.

The cross was already there, calling him and sealing his life.

While that was happening, someone else baptized Alma.

That is why Arnaldo did not come home that night. And as it happens in these cases, that act had consequences.

He put his memories aside. Again, he heard the voice.

"Do it, do it!"

They certainly did it. They were celebrating life.

The same "Do it, do it!" that brought him to the past brought him to the present.

Arnaldo saw the tattoo on his own wrist. He didn't know what it was doing there.

The broadcast that day seemed more like a media show than a gathering of people related to science. The biohackers were showing live CRISPR-Cas9 experiments on their own bodies.

David, one of the men on display, looks more like a cyborg than a man. He has implanted several chips that allow him to simultaneously measure body temperature, movements, heart rate, blood oxygen level and the functioning of some organs.

NELSON BUSTAMANTE & CARMEN VICTORIA PARDO

Andreina has shown the navigation system she has installed in her body. Now she will not get lost anymore. Another shows with pride how this advanced technology has given him a stronger musculature.

There is no age. They intervene their own biology, taking a shortcut to achieve better results. Seeking to conceive a more perfect man.

When the show ends, it gives way to a debate. They exchange ideas and show the developments in the process leading to cloning.

Kevin emphasized the importance from a scientific point of view of having the bones of John, Jesus' cousin. He knew that power "could do all kind of things."

Horrified at everything he heard and saw, Arnaldo wondered what he should do.

Talk to the police?

Report them so that they could be located and imprisoned?

Tell his superiors what they were up to and present the evidence Pilar had given him?

Sometimes, tribulations are part of God's plans. We are not always aware of that.

He chose to honor the hierarchies.

He asked for a new hearing. It had been six years since the legal proceedings had been initiated for trying to stay in Rome.

Truth also has a price. The price Arnaldo would pay would be very high.

12

After the press and Ariel were silenced, Lee had nothing to worry about. He was safe and the only thing he had to do was work on his investigations and find a way to clone Jesus.

Thus, calmer and feeling protected, Lee resumes his investigations.

Apparently, he was using the same procedure that, years before, allowed for Dolly's cloning. It was differentiated only by small adjustments.

However, his labor was not bearing any fruit.

It was time to see things from another perspective.

In order to have a different result, he could not be doing the same things.

He needs John the Baptist's bones. He believes that a sample of that DNA could bring another perspective to the project. He has decided to call those in power to make the impossible possible. They said that they were there for him. It was time to prove it.

Lee takes his cell phone. Normally, he does not use it. Before, he used it to talk to his mom, but since her death the device has been useless to him.

He rings Wang, one of the Asian financers. He would have never done this unless he was out of his mind. He feels agitated.

His hands are sweaty. He breathes deeply. Listens the line ringing.

Finally, the phone is answered.

"Mr. Wang! This is Doctor Lee speaking."

"Doctor Lee, what a surprise! I was sure whether to pick up. It's the first time you've rung! So, tell me."

"You told me that if I ever needed anything I could ask you for it," said Lee.

"Sure, how can I help you?"

"The bones of Jesus' cousin were found in Bulgaria. I think it could be useful for us if we had access to them. There are other scientists with the same purpose as us. In fact, I have no doubt that they already have them. We cannot be left behind. If those truly are John the Baptist's bones, we would have Christ's DNA."

"Do not worry about that! I will make sure that you have what you need in less than 72 hours."

"Thanks!"

"Is that all?"

"Yes."

"Perfect, then!"

Like a master who rubs his lamp, and the genie who grants his wishes, Lee got what he wanted. After 36 hours, the package arrived.

With everything at hand, it was time to achieve the long-desired result.

In his laboratory, he has transferred the DNA from Jesus' and John the Baptist's blood to adult somatic cells.

The sample also includes a cocktail of proteins and nutrients. He energizes them repeatedly with electrical shocks.

There is some progress!

The embryos seem to be responding. Only for a few seconds. They do not seem to stabilize. Still, nothing has been materialized. He has to keep trying. He must discard whatever is preventing him from carrying out the formation.

Hours and hours.

Observing and analyzing.

That is one of Lee's virtues: patience; being persistent until achieving the wanted result.

"You'll get there," he assures himself.

He does not give up.

He does not want to make the same mistakes that have arisen in animal cloning. After Dolly, many have been born with problems and, in this particular case, there is no room for error. Of any nature. He decides to take into account all the biomedical deliberations that the case calls for.

Lee is not only interested in cloning.

He wants perfection.

And along with it, revenge.

CHAPTER IX

THE BEGINNING
OF THE END

1

The hearing Father Arnaldo asked for has a date and time.

It is not as soon as he thought it would be, and time seems to pass slowly.

He compiles more information about *Code Christ*. This helps him keep his mind busy with other things and not think much about the hearing.

Since he first entered the deep web, he has not been able to stop joining the meetings. Listening to them is madness. It exacerbates his despair. But the best way of knowing the enemies is to keep them close.

Perhaps this is due to the morbid fascination that some events trigger in the psyche, but he wishes they broadcasted 24 hours a day. Even with his investiture, Arnaldo is not an exception. He has to dig deeper; to know what their plot is. Every step of it. This arouses his curiosity.

Kevin knows that Arnaldo is now part of *Code Christ*. That he is connected. That he is following them. He was the one to give Arnaldo the immediate access after seeing his application.

When that happened Kevin was graphically comparing the results from some tests he ran. He was with Rik in the clandestine laboratory.

Usually, when someone submits an application to access *Code Christ's* community, the name of the person pops up at the top of the screen along with the ringtone of a slot machine.

As soon as Kevin read "Arnaldo Romero" he quickly opened the application.

"Wow! A little priest, in these parts!" said Kevin out loud.

"What are you talking about?" said Rik.

"An old friend who I never expected to see here," said Kevin.

Rik approached Kevin. From the place he was standing, he could clearly see Kevin's screen.

"I met this man some years ago. We were working on the cloning of Dolly the sheep. He wasn't there for long, but we had the chance to share a lot. He is a man of science, and part of the Catholic Church. Currently he is at the Vatican," explained Kevin.

The sentence "Currently he is at the Vatican" made him think. He turned his chair around to look at Rik's face.

"Wouldn't it be a transgression to have someone from this religious entity in our community?" he asked.

"Absolutely! *Touché* for the Church! Besides, what brought him here?"

Kevin turned his chair around once more, now facing his computer screen. He clicked on a link. Some writings and research popped up. In a corner of the screen was Arnaldo's picture.

When Rik saw it, he could not get over the shock. He knew him. He knew him very well. His brother from his juvenile gang. One of the first members of his clan, so to speak. He decided to keep it to himself.

"I'm going to contact him! There is no way someone can resist the temptation of being part of history," said Kevin.

Rik would do the same. The only thing is that Kevin would not know it until years later.

Contrary to Kevin's thoughts, what has encouraged Arnaldo to join Code Christ is his sense of urgency to tear down everything that is going on behind the scenes.

Their clash seems imminent.

2

It is nighttime.

Rik is sitting on the couch trying to watch TV next to his accidental companion from that week.

The cell phone light comes on. It is in silent mode. The reflection makes Rik turn to see who is calling. Again, and again the light flickers. He doesn't answer. His hands start to sweat.

"Hey, baby, I think that screen that keeps turning on is your phone. Somebody's calling you!"

Rik knows it is Kevin.

"Aren't you going to answer?" She insists.

"It's from work. Today's Sunday. They shouldn't fuck with me!"

The light comes on again. Again, and again.

"They keep insisting, it must be important. Why don't you answer, baby?"

"It's none of your business. Who are you to meddle in my affairs? Why do you care so much about me answering the phone?" said Rik, raising his voice in annoyance. "And don't call me 'baby'!"

She took her things. Then she stood up. She slammed the door with all her might as she left. Rik threw the TV remote control on the cabinet, punched the wall, and walked out into the yard.

'They're all the same!' he said to himself as he lit a cigarette.

He had broken the internal protocols of *Code Christ*. That is why he avoided the call. He was an extremist, not only as a *grinder* within the biohacker community but as a human being. He considered violence to be a valid way to defend ideologies. His was being mistreated.

Psychologically he was conservative and dogmatic at the same time. These are common traits of the type of mind where only one truth exists: their own. Anyone who did not share his opinion became his enemy. That was why he was so similar to Kevin.

After Kevin announced his intention to clone Jesus, Rik had decided to change his strategy. He began to create new areas of integration with the members of the group. He did not confront them but showed them the power of freedom and personal transcendence.

To go against Kevin, you must also go against Nuremberg. Thus, he indirectly incites the collapse of large pharmaceutical companies and power-grabbing agencies.

His discourse has a fairly simple basis: with CRISPR-Cas 9 there is no longer any need for multimillion-dollar laboratories. It is inexpensive and within everyone's reach. Man is the master of his destiny and can improve his environment; he can be "the creator of his new self."

His charisma and closeness create a sense of belonging to the group. With his speech, he literally "brainwashes" them even more.

In every conversation, he emphasizes that they are "the beings called" to bring perfection to animals, plants, and whole of humanity. He invites the overthrow of power.

He no longer uses the deep web. Anyone can log on to codechrist.com and request access. He sells CRISPR-Cas 9 kits so anyone can experiment with science and technology. He has created a new universe and meeting space.

He also asks them to meet on Twitch, the live video streaming platform that attracts close to 30 million views daily. In a matter of months, the growth has been dizzying. It is no longer a space closed to a few. Everyone has access. *Code Christ* has become a public group that is gaining followers by the second and Rik, once again at the forefront, is the leader of this movement. He has regained a space of power and belonging.

He calls himself "The Envoy."

A big trend is starting to appear on social networks. Men, women, children, animals... All with their bodies tattooed with the *CC* seal. A cross that once again speaks of liberation, but this time, through the extermination of the monarchy's dominion over science. The hashtag *#iamcc* spreads through the networks and permeates the streets. In a matter of weeks, he has turned heads once again.

Kevin was unaware of what Rik was doing. Protocols had been broken. As soon as he found out, he looked for him intensely. He wanted explanations. Deep down, he wanted to eliminate him.

As Rik sped up to smoke his cigarette, his mind was rekindling every time he had felt less than important. The many slights of Kevin. The insults. Every moment in which he had played his life down.

He filled himself with that hatred to finally take the phone call. There was no longer anyone on the other side.

He dialed. Once. Twice. Three times without a response.

He got angry.

"Why is he not answering me now? Does he feel so important that the world should pay respect to him?"

He lighted another cigarette. He breathed in the smoke, trying to calm down. The cell phone's screen came on again. He took a deep breath. He answered.

"Hello!"

"What the hell did you do?" Kevin shouted annoyed.

"I don't know what you're talking about"

"Are you playing dumb now? Why the hell is our community now public, and why are we trying to get rid of companies that support science? Did you forget the people who finance this are the same people you are going against?"

"Let me speak frankly: Fuck off! Fuck that shit! Those people poisoned your brain. They bought you off with their dirty money. They don't care about a new way of understanding science or democratizing so that man takes responsibility of his destiny. They only care about continuing to control us, just as they did with you."

"What are you saying? The cloning of the Son of God is around the corner!"

"Then go clone your fucking mother!, Stick your god, his son, and his whole family up your ass!" Rik shouted.

"Rik, you better stop this or you're a dead man! I swear it!"

"Watch out, you may end up being the dead man first!"

Kevin's intelligence and astuteness were losing strength because of his uncontrollable impulses. With his emotional flashes, he could ruin everything that had been meticulously built up over time.

Monsters can indeed be created through everyday nature and without science interceding. He was not aware of that.

Sectarianism had overwhelmed Rik's mind.

A process of intolerance that had increased as time goes by.

A hatred born out of nowhere.

A psychopathology that becomes a bomb ready to explode in your face at any moment. Putting in check an underworld, through which a man's dream of glory may be literally buried with him underground.

That was about to happen.

3)

—December 26th, 2012.
St. Stephen's Day. One of the first martyrs of Christianity.
Accused of blaspheming against Moses. Sentenced to death
by stoning.

The day of the hearing has finally arrived.

Arnaldo is nervous. He has been praying on his knees every day. He has rehearsed many times what he will say in the hearing. He has to be careful.

He woke up in the middle of the night, agitated. He has been praying for the Virgin's intercession. He is ready for what is to come.

At least, that is what he believes.

He crosses himself when entering the building. He opens the door. Surprisingly, he is once more face to face to Cardinal Domínguez.

As they say, "Gold is tried in the fire."

"Good evening, Cardinal! I didn't know that the hearing was with you."

"Good evening, Father Arnaldo. Yes, it is with me. Are you surprised? Which new transgression have you committed?" he commented sarcastically.

"With all due respect cardinal, I have some information that I would like to share. I believe the Holy Father should be aware of it. The Church is in danger. A group of men, with the power to do so, is looking for the creation of a sole and universal Church. This plan includes destroying our Church."

"Wow, Father Arnaldo! I think your problem is worse than we first thought. All of this for something that we already know since the constitution of our Church? There's nothing new in saying that they want to eliminate us. Did you really study? Otherwise, I do not understand how they granted you the priesthood," he said with irony. "May I remind you that conspiracies against the Church have always existed? I just did not realize that one of them was so close to us."

Arnaldo was trying to keep calm. He swallowed and took a deep breath.

He took the USB drive out of his pocket. He rushed to give it to the Cardinal. With anxiety in his voice, he was begging to be heard.

"Please, cardinal, here is the evidence! These people meet in a group called Nuremberg. They are financing scientists to work on Jesus' cloning. They have a big community, and the power, money and means to achieve it. I know the person in charge. He worked in STURP. They are the ones who stole John the Baptist's bones. Here you have the proof you need of their plots..."

The cardinal did not let him continue. He approached Arnaldo. He looked at him directly in the face and snatched the drive from Arnaldo's hands.

"Of course, I'll have a word with the Holy Father: to ask for your removal due to serious mental issues! The Church will never be destroyed! Do you understand? You are a heretic on Holy Ground! The Devil himself disguised as a man of God. Do not ever waste my or the Church's time with your ravings. Do us a favor and have some dignity, renounce the Church!"

Arnaldo desperately continued trying to talk to him, but Cardinal Domínguez did not let him. He turned his back to Arnaldo and handed the drive to one of the bishops accompanying him.

"Destroy it! But, before that, throw holy water to it. Maybe then Satan will leave us in peace! I hope this 'priest' stops fucking around."

Arnaldo kept trying to speak but it was impossible.

He raised his voice, full of impotence, and shouted at the Cardinal:

"I demand you to listen to me!"

"You don't demand anything of me at all!" replied the red prelate.

The cardinal stepped out of the room, not bothering to hide his rage and disdain. Seeing Arnaldo made him sick to his stomach. He wanted to make him disappear. Once and for all.

Arnaldo requested other hearings. He tried to reach the Pope directly. Internal doors started to close.

It seemed that Cardinal Domínguez had got what he wanted.

Arnaldo's helplessness made him vulnerable. His inner fight was restless.

"Why? What can I do? Just what?" he asked himself.

He was going through an ordeal that seemed to have no way out, and evil was winning the battle.

"Father, if I'm wrong, give me wisdom and open my eyes. I don't want your Church to be destroyed!" he repeated all the time.

A few days later he received a notification. A spiritual sentence that marked his soul. He had been excommunicated. Same as St. Athanasius or Mary

MacKillop, the first Australian saint. Without any conditions. Without any right to reply.

The notice was simple, laconic, and forceful.

Canon 1339 in paragraph 2 establishes the automatic or Latae sententiae excommunication of Arnaldo Romero for the act of physical violence against Bishop Ismael Domínguez.

"Physical violence?" said Arnaldo while reading and screaming with impotence. "What is this? A lie, a fucking lie!"

It was his word against the bishop's.

Arnaldo knew that no matter how much he protested, it would be useless.

After he finished reading the notice, feeling devastated, his hands were shaking and the letter fell on the floor. He tilted his head. Once again, he moved his hands towards the cross hanging on his chest.

He was overcome with uncontainable helplessness. A state of desolation that would only be the preamble of what was to come. He could not get over his shock. Everything was convulsive. The darkness within him was like a thick mist, preventing him from seeing the road in front of him. Unable to know if there was a path or a ravine. The only way to find out was by going forward.

He could not fight the battle from the inside.
How could he from the outside?
The answer was between his hands.

4

—May, 2013.

With Rik, everything has gone too far.

His rhetoric is sectarian and socialist. He leads a struggle in opposition to the oligarchy and the authoritarianism of the rich. He attacks what is most important to Kevin: the economic power that is sustaining his dream of cloning the Son of God.

Rik now leads *Code Christ*. Kevin is no longer part of it. What began as talks about the power of science and the freedom of the use of our bodies has evolved into a cult that calls for more transgressive goals.

They behave like a large brotherhood that recruits proselytes through the web, chat rooms, and their social media accounts. It has outgrown Twitch. The followers seem to be mesmerized by Rik's preaching. He indoctrinates them with a speech that initially articulates breaking the tyranny of the rich and personal freedom. They are called to the ideal of a "better" life which is only attainable through "surrender" to the mission aiming to save humanity.

Local *Code Christ* communities have been created. They operate as churches that spread their message through digital media.

Rik emphasizes that they are in a supernatural condition. He makes them believe that they are "The Chosen Ones." Nature calls them to be free, to be masters of their destiny. They are selected among everybody else to improve their environment, and to be "the creators of their new self." Creators of the new world.

That is why they can do whatever they want with their body, with their mind; in order to aspire to perfection. Transmuting the power that has been conferred to them, to go as far as altering the organisms of animals and plants.

The cross tattooed on their bodies is a permanent reminder of liberation. The signature of their alliance... #*iamcc* is their form of social belonging. It empowers them to feel that they are in charge of their destiny.

Some followers have been conferred the title of Superior Brothers of *Code Christ*. They are disciples who share the message. They see in Rik the image of the person chosen to lead them to liberation. A special messenger who has opened their eyes to the devil of the world: the masters of the valley. Evil personified.

They are convinced that this monarchy only seeks their personal benefit. It can't be any different. They control the economy, technology, public health, finances, politics, communications, and even men who have not yet awakened. In other words, they control everything.

For the members of *Code Christ*, they are the target. The demon who must be fought in order to cleanse the whole of humanity.

The movement is supported, on the one hand, by the contributions of some sponsors with money and by the sales that are generated on the web with the CRISPR-Cas9 kits. But more importantly, on the other hand, it is supported by its followers. They are called to support it financially.

NELSON BUSTAMANTE & CARMEN VICTORIA PARDO

This contribution helps the chosen ones to "add points" to their individual salvation. But also, to the collective one. For each contribution, the disciple receives a link on the webpage where he can include the name of up to ten of his close ones that he would like to "save." The more points they accumulate, the closer they are to salvation.

According to them, this breaks the individualism that characterizes the masters of the valley.

In *Code Christ*, they think collectively.

All for the good and the salvation of humanity.

The transactions are done electronically, helping to support the entire infrastructure and allowing them to continue spreading the message.

Absurdly, they obey Rik and the superior brothers. Not only do they help with contributions, but now, they have gone a step further. They are called upon to be in the streets. They promote marches with slogans that incite the dismantling of the power of the big ones. They organize acts of violence against the networks of power. Their unbridled greed moves up to another level.

The green light Kevin needs to carry out his threat. It is not in his interest to be linked to Rik.

He must be stopped at all costs.

He realizes that a monster was created.

Since Rik tests any new technology or device on his body before everyone else, Kevin has thought of including arsenic in the gadgets that Rik puts on himself. A simple and easy way to eliminate him for good.

However, he thought it twice.

He did not want to get his hands dirty. Let others do it. Those who know how to do it. He wasn't going to give up his day job.

He took his phone. He made a video call. On the other side of the line, was Dimitriv Basov.

"My friend, what a pleasure to see you! I'm surprised you called," said Dimitriv. "Everything alright with our plan?"

"Hello, Dimitriv! Let's say it's a courtesy call," said Kevin, smiling.

"Tell me, how can I help you?'"

"My ex-partner has created a community that's attacking the interests of Nuremberg."

"How?"

"He has close to 100 million fanatical followers who have joined him at a dizzying rate."

"So many?"

"Yes, and in less than six months. His rhetoric speaks of banishing the existing hierarchy and creating a conspiracy. He manages all the information about you. Remember I told you he was my partner. If no one stops him, this could get out of hand at any time. His network is spreading and growing."

"What is his name? And the name of that famous community he created?"

"Rik. Leader of *Code Christ*."

"What do you suggest?" asked Dimitriv.

"What do you think would be best in this case?" replied Kevin.

"Don't make our lives a misery! You focus on our business. I'll take care of anything that might disrupt that."

That's how Rik disappeared. Just like that. Without a trace.

Weeks of fruitless searching.

An emptiness that gradually dampened the euphoria of those who followed him.

A month later, his body was found in a wasteland in a nearby town.

The police could not find the perpetrators. They were not interested. The conscience of the forensics unit also had a price.

This is how, sometimes, some chapters of life are resolved.

There are people who do not like the grey, nor the lukewarm.

The Bible says that God will spit these people out of His mouth.

The positions are black or white. Hot or cold.

You are either with us or against us.

The warning Kevin had given him came true.

Rik was a dead man.

5

Fortunately, Arnaldo kept the key Pilar gave him and copied the information contained onto a USB drive. He was not sure how it would help him. In any case, he kept it with suspicion.

Everything seemed to be coming together to plunge him even deeper into the abyss. While he was trying to get over the shock of his excommunication, an unexpected call made him collapse.

"Father Arnaldo, there has been a tragedy... A fatality!" said Antonio, sobbing. "We just have been informed that they found Pilar's body. They found her beheaded near the church where John the Baptist's bones were. Father, her eyes were taken out!"

"It can't be! It can't be!" said Arnaldo.

He crumbled. The phone fell on the floor. He started crying. He felt as if God had abandoned him. He had sunk. Sunk into the deepest point.

"God, what is this? Where are you? Where?" said Arnaldo in despair while looking up.

That woman had become his friend.

The pain of her death clouded all his senses. He took his things. Headed to the airport. He had to get a ticket to Sofia, Bulgaria.

Almost two hours of flight and many hours of uneasiness.

He knew that Pilar had nobody else, so he took care of all her business.

The coroners from Bulgaria warned him about the state in which they found the corpse.

He mourned her. He watched over her for a night. It was only him and the priest from Sozopol, who buried her.

Arnaldo no longer had the authority to do it.

When he returned, he felt as if everything was up in the air.

He could not have imagined that he would fall even deeper.

While in his room, he heard the sound of a text message.

It was from his mom:

Hijito, I didn't dare call you, but I have some news that will bring you sorrow, just as it did us. Your friend Margarita is in God's arms now. Pray for her, pray for the little girl and pray for us. We are going to be praying for you. The girl is OK. We love you.

How does life suddenly go away in a second?

For Arnaldo, God had moved.

The Church was about to collapse.

He had been excommunicated.

Pilar, murdered.

Margarita had just passed.

He thought of his grandchild. The only thing that kept him standing.

All of this was a torment to Arnaldo.

A spear stuck into his soul.

As the seconds passed by, he was overcome by spiritual aridity. An uncontainable rebellion in the face of the setbacks that had befallen him.

He seems to be trapped by a suffocating sensation, depressing his soul. Draining it. He wishes to run away and erase everything that troubles him. But that is impossible.

The chaos he saw all around caused him to sink deeper into despair.

6

That man of God knew he urgently needs to find refuge. Everything that has happened stuns him. He crosses himself in front of the wooden crucifix of the small apartment he now lives in. It looks like the one that watched him from above in Santa Magdalena Jicotlán.

He is restless. He takes the rosary in his hands. He knows it is a powerful weapon. However, he is unable to concentrate. It makes no sense to remain there. He goes out.

He wanders, looking for signs. He takes a deep breath and cries. He dries his tears. What a huge void!

He asks himself where God's voice is.

It has been a long time since he last heard it. Now he doubts if he really ever heard anything.

He decided to walk through Via della Stazione when he passed in front of St Martha's Chapel, also known as the Holy Spirit Chapel. It was a small temple located between the residency and the Leonine Wall.

He decided to go in.

It's a small chapel filled with triangular arrays made of four thousand different-colored marble pieces. The marble from the altar, floors, pillars, and the copper ceiling have that shape, evoking the Holy Trinity.

He has been there on other occasions, but this is the first time he is all alone.

He kneels down while appreciating every detail around him.

How many times do we look over the details of what we see every day?

A golden pigeon stands out in one of the apses. In front of the holy table, some Latin text can be read: "Holy Spirit, come and renew the heart of your followers."

"Just what I need," said Arnaldo out loud.

The Most Holy is exposed; it looks as if Jesus has been waiting for him.

Even during his crisis of faith, Arnaldo tilts his head. He takes the crucifix from his neck into his hands, as has become custom for him lately. He invokes the one who fights against the spirit of darkness. In the exact place he felt his soul resided.

"Oh, Holy Spirit, beloved of my heart..."

He stops. He cannot go on. The weeping makes it impossible for him to keep going. He tries to breathe. He cannot. He tries to calm himself.

A breeze comes out of nowhere.

Strangely, there are no open windows. A smell of roses permeates the atmosphere. In the middle of this manifestation, Arnaldo starts feeling accompanied and sinks into his pain.

"What is the reason for all of this, Holy Spirit? I don't know what to do in this uncertain moment! Enlighten me, guide me, give me strength, comfort me. Tell me what to do, give me your orders. I promise I will subject to anything you want from me and accept everything you allow to happen to me. Let me know your will."

He stays there, without speaking any other word. Whimpering.

He dries his tears.

He looks up.

He looks at the crucifix behind the altar. The Christ made of metal that is hanging in there looked as if it were changing before his eyes. He rubs them to reset his vision. A hand smoothly touches his back.

His friend Giacomo is there.

Arnaldo stands up. He hugs him. He bursts into tears. He is not afraid of being vulnerable.

"I'm unfamiliar with your sorrow, brother, but everything will be okay!" says Giacomo. "You are with the best of friends. If you want to talk about what's going on, you can count on me," said Giacomo.

"I know that, and I am more than grateful," replied Arnaldo.

There is a long silence.

Arnaldo takes a seat on one of the benches.

"I'm in no rush. If you want, I can wait for you."

"I would love that! And thank you once again. Please just give me a few more minutes alone."

"Take your time. All the time you need. I'll be in my office. I'll wait for you there. I don't have much to do today so we chat calmly."

And so, later on, they did.

As if he were an open book, Arnaldo told him everything that had happened. Pilar, her death, his meetings with Cardinal Domínguez and his excommunication.

He also told him about Nuremberg, their plans and the possibility of the Church vanishing.

"I'm moved. By the injustice. By the way that we sometimes react as a church. We have a time bomb right in front of us, and we're refusing to see it. Do you think I'm crazy, my friend? I feel like I have to do something but at the same time I wonder if I should just leave everything as it is."

Giacomo did not show any sign of surprise.

"I know exactly how you feel and what you are talking about. More than you can imagine.

There are always things that can stretch our ability to be shocked. I know about Nuremberg. My grandfather was one of its forerunners."

Silence took over the environment. Arnaldo's hands started sweating.

Who was he talking to? Was he friend or an undercover foe, infiltrating the Church?

"I come from a wealthy family. I can assure you that to begin with, they actually had a noble purpose. There are still people in the group that think that way. It takes all sorts to make a world. Money alongside power can derail even the noblest of goals."

"Your grandfather was actually in Nuremberg?"

"Not only him, but my father as well. What Pilar told you is true. I grew up listening to the stories of the agreements reached at those summits. Years later, I went to a couple of them. When I heard what they were discussing for the first time, I was disgusted. As for my father, he thought that my interpretation of the summits was a distortion of their goals. I argued with my family. I distanced myself from everything. That day, I decided to have a fresh start in life. That's why I started looking for a job in Rome. I wanted to contribute what I knew to the Church to protect it from the inside,"

Arnaldo was astonished. He did not know what to say.

The world is definitely very small. Everything has its time and everything beneath heaven has its final hour.
It seemed like the final hour had arrived.

"Do you remember when I told you about the chronovisor and I suggested activating the machine?"

"Yes..." replied Arnaldo.

"I wasn't joking."

Arnaldo was not expecting this.

"My position has given me the privilege, so to speak, of being not only in front of the chronovisor but also hundreds of marvelous things that the Church keeps with great suspicion."

"Why don't you just speak directly? I don't understand what you're trying to tell me..." said Arnaldo impatiently.

"I know what Nuremberg is looking for. That is why I thought about the possibility of using the machine and going to the past. If it works, can you imagine Jesus himself helping us save His Church?"

Life was definitely taking an unexpected turn.

An unpredictable chance was knocking on his door.

"We lose nothing by trying. I wasn't joking either when I talked to you about the future. About bringing Him back," said Arnaldo. "What I'm about to tell you goes against any norm, but wouldn't it be more powerful bringing Him to life today? Giacomo, this may sound crazy, but we could bring Jesus back. Be part of his Second Coming. We can clone him. I know how to do it."

Giacomo was shocked by Arnaldo's statements. He never expected to hear something like this from Arnaldo's mouth. Arnaldo kept going.

"I will ask you the same question. If Jesus were here today, who would be better than Him to save His Church?"

Arnaldo's idea was not as crazy as it seemed.

For Giacomo, it was an interesting turn. He had heard about a couple of scientists performing tests to make this a reality.

"Did you know that Nuremberg is financing a couple of scientists to do this?" asked Giacomo.

"Yes. I know about them. I have been to some of their meetings. They seem to have advanced a lot in their investigations. We must do something. Those men could create the Antichrist himself."

"I thought the same thing!"

After a brief pause, Giacomo put one last card on the table. The one that would complete the puzzle. A proposal undoubtedly powerful.

"For some strange reason, God put us together today. I trust you, and I have this feeling that, although it may sound disruptive, I'm certain this is what we have to do. If the problem is financial, let me tell you that that won't be an issue."

It was the only problem. Without looking for a solution, it had already been resolved.

Arnaldo wasn't at the Vatican anymore. He had the time. The chronovisor existed. They just needed to see if it worked. He had the blood and the body of Jesus and the knowledge to embark upon one of the most controversial projects.

Above all, the love he had for God was so huge that he was feeling eager to be with him all the time. Arnaldo smiled.

"Count on me. The clock is ticking," said Giacomo.

"When do we start?"

"Yesterday."

Everything was falling into place.

From that moment, a new chapter started to be written.

It was probably the final one.

CHAPTER X

THE TRUTH
REVEALED

1

Awar is at the gates.
Like in every war, there are double agents undercover in the enemy's headquarters. Ultra-secret plans disguised among truths and lies. Traitors. Spies.

Spies such as those described in the Bible, like those sent by Joshua to Jericho. Or those who took part in the secession war. Spies who wander among us nowadays.

Without them, without their names, events would have been different. For good or ill.

What would have been of Great Britain against Nazi Germany without Juan Pujol García? The Spanish double agent that cheated Hitler, better known as *Garbo*.

What about the Second World War without Virginia Hall? According to the Gestapo, the most dangerous of the Allies' spies.

Anatoly Stuling is involved in this war. Code name: William Murrow. He has spent many years in counterintelligence. Keeping an undercover and secret relation with members of the different cabinets from Nuremberg. Hunting dissidents.

He has traveled from Moscow to the United States, from Great Britain to the Middle East. He makes them think that he is on one side, but in reality he is on the other. His identity varies, but everyone knows him as "The Angel."

A lady-charmer.

His charisma makes him have a hypnotic effect on them. He seduces his informants. Women that are in power or work close to it.

But this war is different that any other.

His strategy is to decant Nuremberg's list. He is close with people who, radically and frontally, have declared themselves enemies of this powerful group. He has also stalked and investigated them.

He has an enviable list of key contacts. Important documents that, once photographed and copied, have been returned without raising suspicion.

More pieces of evidence added to what Helena left behind.

The operation he is carrying out is known as *Revelation*. It means "removing the veil." This is also the name of the last book of the New Testament. The one many talk about.

The Book of Revelation.

Would these be the times mentioned in there?

«Ye shall hear of wars and rumors of wars... Nation shall rise against nation, and kingdom against kingdom... A beast with seven heads will rise».

A beast with seven heads.

There are also seven central axes that make up the Nuremberg Group. Seven areas of vital importance: political, economic, communicational, military, scientific, religious and technological. All in one single group. One single power.

Pure coincidence?

What is true is that they have an omnipresent control that gives them the privilege of publishing half lies, creating fake news, making truths become obscure. Making public opinion believe them.

The threads of this silent beast are threads of power that control the world.

Anatoly has also infiltrated Rome. He has undercover spies there. People who are close. Very close.

The information he has gathered about the so-called "lords of the world" aims to destroy, once and for all, the silence surrounding them.

The evidence he has is overwhelming. He feels he has everything to make the eyes of the world to turn and condemn them. To make the veil fall.

There is no doubt about these people's intentions: absolute control. In every aspect. The masterly game of geo-power.

With what Anatoly has in his hands, he could make the very highest tremble.

However, something seems off.

The phone of the headquarters of the American secret service rings. It's a call from Washington Airport. In immigration they have arrested a man who has all the characteristics of the one they are looking for. The General Director only hears:

"We have a gift! Anatoly is here."

"You already know what to do."

In a matter of seconds, the airport is filled with armed agents. Combat units. They have surrounded him. He has been captured.

Despite this, the man is calm.

Although his description coincides with the one from the man they are looking for, his documents show that his name is William Murrow. It is not the first time he has entered the U.S.

They have called in several experts to interrogate him. However, he had learned a good deal from Markus Wolf, the espionage chief from East Germany. He trained his agents by saying that it was impossible for them to be incarcerated unless they confessed. To endure and keep calm. So did Anatoly. He denied everything. He kept calm.

They could not prove he was the person they were looking for.

They had to let him go.

"The Angel" was on the loose.

Despite his intelligence and knowledge, he cannot imagine what is about to come.
Nobody can.

2

—April, 2013.
After Anatoly's masterful escape from the security units, there is no doubt that the man has been very well trained. But he is not always as lucky.

After a few months of final preparation, together with his team and with the advice and protection of his friend Vladimir, Anatoly delivers the first blow to Nuremberg. He has managed to contact several editors of major world newspapers who have not yet submitted to the hegemony of the tycoons. He has handed them the evidence.

In the articles they are preparing to release, they point out the evidence that incriminates several of the group's members and openly denounce the existence of the plan that is already underway:

The creation of a virus that aims for the extermination of 75% of the world's population.

A single worldwide government.

A new church, sole and universal.

Absolute control.

It sounds like madness.

But it is not. Just like every other process, it has taken its time.

This powerful group has been meeting for many years, preparing everything silently to checkmate the world at a precise moment.

In the documents there is, among other things, detailed information related to the new church that is being created and, below this, several premises. These include annotations that Nuremberg has internally established and that were left as evidence of their plans and movements.

These are some of the premises:

1. Shake all religious foundations.
Every pre-existing denomination will be eliminated. The small denominations will disappear.
Note: The imploding of religions in order to create the new and universal Church is increasingly imminent.

2. Use the infinite resources of the universal mind.
Through its connection to the mind, humankind will achieve the maximum extent of its union with the sacred realm.
Note: This connection is underway. It is conducted with mass surveillance programs which will allow absolute control over the planet and its inhabitants.
3. Advocate for knowledge of humankind itself.
Men should aspire to a wide comprehension of the facts in order to imbue themselves with the knowledge of the universal mind.
Note: Men must believe that they are thinking for themselves. Their thoughts will be controlled through the manipulation of everything they consume. Their thoughts have not been their own for a long time.

This new Church has no God.

They themselves are the gods.

It proposes the power of the mind as an extension of the universal psyche. In this lies the universe itself.

As in every religion, this one also has its sacred book.

To access it, the person has to be initiated by being marked on its right hand.

A small cross.

Paradoxically, everything coincides with what appears in the Book of Revelation before the seven year tribulation.

"...And he causeth all, both small and great, rich and poor, free and bond, to receive a mark in their right hand, or in their foreheads"
Revelations 13:16

Pure synchronicity?

Their cosmogony details the steps to follow to reach what would be the nirvana of Buddhism. The final goal. They call it *The Panta. The Whole.*

They profess that, just as a drop of the sea is not the sea but contains the whole sea in itself, man is only a particle of the universal mind that contains the whole.

In their sacred book they mention the great men who have accessed the universal mind and achieved mastery over it. Jesus, Buddha, Krishna, to name just a few. This way, they will attract followers of all the pre-existent religions.

It is a manual. A perfect guide in which rites and ceremonies cohabit, exposing to humanity the infinite potential that resides in every human being.

However, not everyone knows that the forces that are manipulating them are malicious.

This 'sacred book' speaks of the world submitting itself to a social cleansing. Only a few will be the chosen ones to stay, and they will then be able to enhance the power that resides within them. Those who do not survive are guaranteed eternal life in *The Whole. The Panta.* Their deaths will be a blessing, an offering to the universal mind.

The truth is that the lords of the valley control this reality.

Divine commands do not come from heaven or from the universal mind, but from them. From hell itself.

If anything is exposed to the eyes of the publishers and the world, after reading the evidence in detail, they must have other interests.

They represent a model that appears to promote life but is marked by death. Drenched in blood.

A worldwide game. Extreme.

So perfectly conceived it shows another side of reality. In appearance, a more promising one.

Within hours after all the Nuremberg information is published, small media owners try to contact Anatoly to talk about what is exposed there. He is not afraid anymore. He faces the music.

In his latest statement, Anatoly Stuling appeared as himself mentioning that he has received threats.

Indeed, it was the last time he was seen in public. No one knows his whereabouts.

Some think he is as good as dead.

But when it comes to high-level spies, everything fits into a strategy.
Not everything is as it seems.

3

"...and the elements will be dissolved in flames, and the earth and all that it contains will be disclosed."

2 Peter 3:10

In the media reporting the news, there is a lot of confusion.

Following Anatoly's alleged death, Edgard Wooden, a former US Government employee in charge of computer security at the CIA, has also decided to publicize information that compromises governments and incriminates several of Nuremberg's representatives.

He has leaked documents showing how the national security agency, along with other European agencies, monitors and keeps track of every step of its citizens. This corroborates some of the evidence that Anatoly possessed.

The information reaches Rome. On the one hand, Arnaldo feels relieved, but on the other, he fears for his life. If the newly publicized information is true and no one is left out of this surveillance, he is on the list.

Cell phones and other devices are under the radar of the ones in command. They control everything. Edgard Wooden exposes how people have not yet realized that they themselves have brought home the devices that feed on this data. Every word they say is being recorded and algorithmically entered into their network.

Thanks to this move by this computer genius, information on three of the mass surveillance programs used by Nuremberg to control the entire planet is now public. He has unmasked them. He has brought the intelligence network beyond them to the forefront. As expected, the press seeks to corroborate the information, which is denied on national television by the President of the United States himself.

Anatoly's research now generates more interest.

The press, both written and audiovisual, devotes entire articles to the subject. The media, which are controlled by the Nuremberg management, cleverly emphasize that all these events are a strategy aiming to destabilize the world as part of conspiracy theories.

Very few emphasize the hidden truth that is now being unveiled. Social media is filled with funny memes.

Man's ingenuity never abandons its efforts to escape the snowball that is coming and that may soon become an avalanche, sweeping away everything in its path.

Some have realized the seriousness of the matter. They are dismayed.

If true, there is no escape.

There are rallies in several countries. Protesters calling for basic freedoms around the world and respect for privacy. It would seem that everything is getting out of hand, but it is not. It is part of the plan.

Without realizing it, each of these men and women have exposed themselves in such a way that they have become a perfect target.

At the first opportunity, they will be the first ones to be eliminated.

They are the traitors.

In New York's Fifth Avenue a tall white man dressed in jeans and white t-shirt, wanders from one corner to another. He has blue eyes, as deep as the sea. A long beard. Unkempt. He is carrying a sign with a big cross drawn over it. Inside the quadrants that form the cross, in the upper left and lower right quadrants is written a small letter *c*. The same symbol as *Code Christ* uses. One of the sides of the sign reads:

THE SECOND COMING OF CHRIST IS IMMINENT!
THE 7 YEARS OF THE GREAT TRIBULATION
BEGIN.

His has a happy expression on his face. As he walks, he shouts the contents of his sign out loud. The pedestrians look at him out the corner of their eyes. Some cross to the other side of the street.

Others do not even notice him and walk by, engrossed in their phones.

Edgard Wooden is hidden in his girlfriend's flat. She is not there. His phone starts ringing. On the screen, her number. He picks up.

"Hello, Andre, darling," said the voice on the phone.

"Edgard Wooden? This is Anatoly Stuling."

He does not understand what is going on. Anatoly knows how to hack the lines and make another name appear on the registry. He laughs.

"Anatoly Stuling? It can't be."

"I am honored to have outwitted the man in charge of CIA security," says Anatoly.

"But..."

"Yes! I know! I'm not dead as many think. Nice to meet you."

"The pleasure is mine," answers Wooden.

"I'm sorry I can't do it in person, but I would like to congratulate you for your bravery. Making the decision to release that information mustn't have been easy."

"It mustn't have been easy for you either. You inspired me in some way," said Edgard.

"I'm going straight to the point. I like protecting valuable people. I guess you're making arrangements to get out of the country. The Swiss government can provide shelter. So, take your things right now and go. Do it quick because they're after you!"

At that moment he heard someone opening the door.

He didn't have time to do anything.

It was already too late.
They were there for him.

4

Faced with the great crossroads that life presents to believers, there are two types of human beings: those who do things their own way and those who consider that it is God's will that guides them.
What happens when life dictates you a path many times and you decide to deny it to follow your own?
Does a man's life have a pre-established script?
What would our life be like if we were certain that the steps we take are the right ones?

In appearance, it was a day like any other in Huasca de Ocampo, a magical Mexican town surrounded by a beautiful, wooded landscape and cobblestone streets. Full of old farms with accompanying stories of elves.

A picturesque village. Modest. Peaceful. Just like in Santa Magdalena Jicotlán, nothing happens here.

It is a special place. This is the first community that Father Arnaldo has been assigned to after his ordination to the priesthood. His parish was named St. John Baptist.

In the life of this man chosen by God, as in everyone's life, nothing will happen by chance. Every name, every detail, every person, every moment, is marked by signs. If he knows how to interpret them, he will discover a whole new world through which God talks to him.

It was no coincidence that he had been assigned to this community.
St. John Baptist had something for him.
Something that Arnaldo would maybe understand in the future.

That Sunday he was excited. It was the first time he would meet his parishioners, give his sermon and be able to give communion as a priest.

The night before he was nervous. He practiced the homily several times. The rooster had not yet crowed when, in the solitude of that simple church, built by the Augustinian friars in the 16th century, Arnaldo was rehearsing his Mass. He knelt in the gloom, illuminated only by two huge candles lit on either side of the altar.

While he was praying, he went into a kind of mystical ecstasy.

The sun's rays began to penetrate through the four small windows on the upper right side of the temple. It was then that Arnaldo came out of his trance.

He got up feeling refreshed. It was almost 7:30 a.m. He happily rushed to open the main gate. On the church's outside, at the top, was in relief an image of St. Michael the Archangel.

"You too. Protect me," he said, looking up.

St. Michael the Archangel is the guardian of the Universal Church. The same one Arnaldo would try to protect.
There is no doubt.
He was listening to him.

A couple of children came running towards the church. Playing, laughing, running faster by the second. They were about 8 years old.

"Good morning, Father!" they all said at the same time while looking at each other.

"I said it first!"

"No, I did!"

They competed in a healthy way. They kept laughing while trying to catch their breath after the race.

"Good morning, boys!" said Arnaldo.

"Nice to meet you, Father! My name is Rodrigo!"

"My name is Arnaldo too!"

"What a beautiful coincidence!" said the priest. "Nice to meet you! The pleasure is mine."

"Here, my mom sent you some *tamale* cakes!" replied Rodrigo. "If you don't like them, you can give them to me. I'll eat them because they're the best!"

"*Tamale* is my favorite, but I can share," said Arnaldo.

They were the altar boys.

With their excitement contained, they went in. They helped him prepare everything for the big banquet. It was ten minutes to eight in the morning when the church bells began to ring.

Within minutes, the village parishioners were inside, seated in their dark wooden benches. They could smell the sublime scent of roses, incense and myrrh that suddenly invaded the space.

It was a church without columns, decorated with altarpieces of paintings of saints. It was adorned with passages inviting people to journey through. Jesus' life and side altars that mixed wood and baroque.

The Gospel of the day spoke of the Annunciation to Joseph.

"He was a righteous man, and the righteous are those who hear the word of God and put it into action."

In this way, Arnaldo invited his parishioners to be like that carpenter from Jerusalem, open to listen to God's messages.

He also talked about the trials that Joseph faced. Of the importance of obedience and results.

At that moment, God was not communicating with those present.

God was talking to him. About what was to come.

The greatest thing happened at the consecration.

He lifted the host and at the instant of the sanctification of the body of Jesus, he saw how a spot of blood appeared in the center. He remembered Father José Luis, the priest of his childhood. His heart was racing. His breathing began to falter. He was trying to see his hands.

Had he cut himself like his old childhood friend?

During that sublime moment, he was not the priest or the scientist. He was the vehicle God had used to manifest His power and grace.

Without understanding the reason for the beauty manifested through him, he nervously placed the host on the paten. He examined his hands again, unnoticed. He left it there. Subtly placed on one side. The living body of Christ. Latent. He did not say a word.

He took another host for the communion. He was shaking. The parishioners thought that it was because it was his first Mass. They did not see anything.

When the Mass finished, he put the small piece of flesh in the monstrance. He didn't know what to do.

Just as Joseph was, he was being tested.
Just as John the Baptist did, he would need a clear sign to confirm who the Messiah sent by God was.

Arnaldo didn't understand that before his eyes was the clearest of the signs. It was no coincidence that the parish where he started his priesthood had John the Baptist's name.

It is said that many long to find a divine sign, a supernatural revelation. They wander in search of some sign that will give them certainty of what is to come. Few are the fortunate ones on whom this grace has been conferred.

Arnaldo's life was full of events that, in the eyes of some, had a supernatural filter. Much more than imagined.

"Arnaldo, son, my bleeding heart waits for you. Don't let me down."

That bleeding heart shouted in burning flesh that there he was.

He was witnessing that God spoke through things. That Jesus' miracles were happening day by day. In different places. He's still alive.

"Could this really be a sign from God? What does it mean? What does he want from me?"

That is why he became a researcher on that topic. He hoped to find rational answers to this series of supernatural manifestations he'd experienced.

That is why he didn't hesitate when they called him to be part of the Pontifical Academy of Sciences.

That is the reason why he escaped to be alone.

He did understand that it was not a coincidence that he was part of many eucharistic manifestations.

Arnaldo felt he did not deserve that grace. He didn't tell anyone what had happened. He kept it silent.

That was a secret that weighed heavily.

A secret that would be a cross of guilt that he would carry for the rest of his life.

There was a perfect plan.

He'll have to accept it if he wants to become God's right hand. But free will also play its part and can change the course of events.

The history written for Arnaldo could be about to change. And with it, that of humankind.

5

After Arnaldo and Giacomo's conversation, it was time to get down to business. It was the very next day. There was no time to spare.

Once more, they met at Giacomo's office. Behind closed doors. As men of faith, they agreed to pray before starting to work and put everything in the hands of the Son of God.

They began by developing a detailed plan to start the experiments: where to set up the laboratory, the materials, the strategies, and the actions to be undertaken. Everything, absolutely everything, until it was complete.

In Giacomo's office there was a folder that caught Arnaldo's eyes. He did not dare to ask what it was about, but he thought he recognized it. The papers that were piled up covered part of the front cover and he could only read, upside down, three of the letters. *Oma*. No matter how hard he tried to remember where he had seen this before, it was impossible.

Facing teamwork also put them to the test. Sometimes they had diametrically opposed ways of looking at things. They argued about the right way to start everything.

They decided to see if the chronovisor could work for them. Sometimes the atmosphere became heavy. But something always made them aware of this. They calmed down and continued.

Arnaldo tried several times. Enough times to question what they were doing.

"This is a waste of time! Complete madness!" he thought.

They had to find another way. Maybe a more traditional approach. Similar to Arnaldo's way of thinking. Giacomo's joy and support filled Arnaldo with the optimism he needed, although several times he had to battle his own demons.

Was he really doing the right thing or was he ending up sinking his soul into hell?

Questions were constantly going back and forth in his head.

However, the illusion and hope of knowing that they could be an instrument in God's hand encouraged them to continue, even in the midst of uncertainty. The project they had on their hands was bigger than them.

They were about to begin everything in this new trajectory they had set out on, when, in the middle of the night, Arnaldo woke up with a start. Once again, the dream. That dream. Was he asleep or awake?

Jesus was talking to him. From his heart, blood, light and water emanated. They were like springs that gushed ceaselessly. The Messiah constantly repeated to him the phrase he had heard since he was a child: "Arnaldo, son, my bleeding heart waits for you. Don't let me down!"

The vision did not end there.

Suddenly, Arnaldo saw how Jesus extended His hand to touch his heart. It went through his body.

Arnaldo began to feel a great pain. A piece of Christ's passion.

With love, Jesus again withdrew His closed hand. Jesus opened His hands before his eyes.

The crucifix was there. Open.

A heart was beating heavily. His beating heart.

"My bleeding heart waits for you," repeated the voice with infinite sweetness. "I leave before your eyes the answers you need. The path you are looking for. I am right here, next to you. Look again, do not be afraid."

In moments, that heart was transformed into a naked child. Around them was nothing but a sea of pink with petals opening like buds.

"I love you. This is the proof of my love for you and for mankind," He spoke.

As He started talking, a cloud came over them. As in the scriptures, the heavens opened in two. From above a deep voice said: "This is My beloved Son, with whom I am well pleased; listen to him!"

Arnaldo was silent.

He wondered again whether he was asleep or awake.

Out of nowhere, an immense hurricane approached, spitting upon Arnaldo with the forces of air, water, earth, and fire.

The devil himself was possessing him.

From inside that cyclone, he began to hear another voice, announcing one of the passages of the apocalypse:

> *For there will be a great tribulation, such as has not occurred since the beginning of the world until now, nor ever will.*
> *The period of time that God has declared is 70 weeks. But before that, the tribulations. 7 years. A time for God's judgment to be brought upon unbelieving man. Visions and prophecies will be fulfilled.*

Arnaldo saw the fire. The church burning. There were fights and wars. Children being born and dying. The voice spoke again.

> *Everything will be overthrown and also rebuilt, but this will happen in the anguish of the times. They will destroy the sanctuary of a principality to come. A cataclysm that will only rebuild Rome if man opens his eyes and discovers what is now in front of them. A hidden river will be the spring to drink from. A river of wolves that will only be destroyed through love.*

The speed and the thunderous sound of that hurricane, in which the words *Roma* and *Amor* could be heard echoing, sweeping everything in its path, made Arnaldo think that his end had come. The most fateful.

He saw his life pass in a second. His childhood. Father José Luis. Getaways with friends. Margarita's love. His first day in the seminary. The moment he arrived in Rome. The mystical experiences in his life. The body of Christ guarded in the crucifix. His scientific life. Pilar. Cardinal Domínguez. Giacomo. The daughter he never met. Guadalupe.

The hurricane swept him away.

He felt like he could no longer breathe.

With a loud scream, he expired.

Silence. Complete silence.

The force was still moving around him. With him. It took him to the eye of the hurricane.

It lay him down there. Inside there was calm. Peace. A little girl. His granddaughter.

He opened his eyes.

It was a strange mixture of emotions.

It had been so real!

He was sure that what he just witnessed was the book of his life.

That hurricane was the demons that followed him.

The hidden lies were inside it. The secrets that ate away at him. His daughter. His grandchild. The fact he never saw her.

His story ended with her. With Guadalupe.

Seeing our lives and coming face to face with our failures is shocking. This was no different for Arnaldo.

Curiously, he began to feel that before taking any steps to initiate cloning, he had to sort things out.

First things first.

He had to go back to the source to heal his past and present.

He was not working at the Vatican anymore.

It was time to make a trip.

One that would give him a new vision.

A new way of seeing love.

6

"Let the children alone, and do not hinder them from coming to Me."

According to the evangelist Matthew, those were the words Jesus said to His disciples when some children tried to approach Him and the disciples tried to stop them.

That is why the heavenly kingdom belongs to people like them. Children always tell the truth, and they live in awe and spontaneity. Remaining a child is the biggest challenge of existence. Jesus knew it well.

It was something Arnaldo was about to experience.

The dream he had awoke in him the need to reconnect with that lost side of him. He wanted to be free and spontaneous like children are. This feeling was accompanied by the need to approach the purest thing in his life. Guadalupe, his grandchild.

He did not want to overthink it.

There are things to be done today and that's it.

Tomorrow would be too late.

The next day, he decided to give Giacomo an early call. He had to talk to him. He had made some decisions over night.

"Good morning, my friend!" greeted Arnaldo.

"Good morning! Did you fall out of bed?"

"Actually, I have important news to tell you. I know we have a lot to do, but before, I have to do something very important. I am going on a trip. I will be back in a week."

"What are you talking about? Where are you going?"

"To fulfill my duty."

"I don't understand!"

"I'm going to my hometown. There's something that I should have done a long time ago. I can't explain it to you right now, but I promise I will when I get back."

"Are you okay?"

"Completely. Trust me."

Six hours later, Arnaldo was leaving the Leonardo Da Vinci International Airport, on his way to Mexico.

The first thing he did when he arrived was kneel before the feet of Our Lady of Guadalupe. He wanted to start his crusade with her blessing.

He stayed a couple of hours at the Basilica de Nuestra Lady of Guadalupe. Long enough to instill in him the strength he needed to face things and walk like Jesus, with the truth in front of him.

He didn't give any warning. He wanted to surprise his parents.

He arrived to Santa Magdalena Jicotlán just before the evening. The village seemed to be stuck in time. Everything was the same as Arnaldo remembered. The square, the wrecked benches, the school. The only change was that the little kids wandering around the streets were different.

He stopped in front of his parent's house. He knocked on the door. The excitement of seeing them again was immense. He clearly heard the voices coming from the inside.

"Guadalupe, my darling, go and see who it is. Your grandpa is taking a nap, he won't hear anything!"

"I'm coming, Grandma!" said the little girl with a sweet voice.

"If it's Mrs. Rosa, open the door and let her in. If I go, the food will burn," said Ana.

"I'm cooooominnnng!!!"

Rushing with her dog, she approached the door. She was jumping, trying to see through the peephole and making Chocolate, her dog, jump alongside her.

"Who is knocking?" asked Guadalupe.

"Someone who loves everyone living in this house very dearly," replied the voice.

Without knowing who was speaking, she opened the door.

She had seen that face many times. There were pictures of this man all over the house. With the innocence and cheerfulness that characterized her, jumped onto him to hug him.

"Uncle Arnaldo!" she screamed with excitement as if she had ever seen him in person.

A rush ran through Arnaldo's insides.

"Who is this beautiful princess?"

After hearing this, Ana quickly turned off the burner in the kitchen. She rushed to see if what she was hearing was in fact true. That voice! Her son's voice!

"I'm Guadalupe! Don't you remember?"

Arnaldo started crying while looking at her.

His heart wanted to tell her that he wasn't her uncle, but her grandfather. He wanted to ask for forgiveness for all the years he was absent. For having never met his mom or taken care of her grandmother.

"The little girl is gorgeous!" he thought. "With only six years, she has that fresh beauty that Margarita flaunted."

So many things went through Arnaldo's mind!

"Grandma, Grandma! It's Uncle Arnaldo!" Guadalupe kept shouting.

With her arms extended, Ana came running full of excitement. When she saw her son, her eyes could not hold back her tears.

"It can't be! I can't believe it! What a beautiful surprise! Child of my soul!" she said, her voice shoked with tears as she filled him with kisses.

There is no greater joy for a mother than to embrace the one she had in her womb.

That instant sealed, with love, thousands that had been lost.

Arnaldo tried to remember the last time he had seen her. Many years had passed.

This is how time is, harsh.
That is life. Brief. Ephemeral.
It goes by fast and we do not realize it.

They remained fused in that embrace while Ana, in tears, continued to shout with happiness. Long enough for Hugo, despite his deafness, to be woken up by the commotion and go out to join the party at that moment.

"Uncle, uncle! I can't breathe" shouted the girl while being stretched by Arnaldo's arms.

Arnaldo stepped back a little. He lifted her high as he laughed. He placed her on the floor and with his two hands he grabbed his parents' faces. Filled them with kisses on the forehead.

He finally went in. There he could see the same old cushions upholstered with flowers, a little more yellowed. The same photos on the wooden shelf where the crockery was kept for special occasions.

Finally, after a long time, it would be taken out for dinner. Everything seemed to have stopped.

"Why didn't you tell me, boy? I'm old enough to die of a heart attack! I cannot bear strong emotions like I used to!" said Ana, smiling. She could not hold her excitement inside.

"If I had told you, it wouldn't have been a surprise. I wanted to surprise you!"

He turned to see Guadalupe. Looked at her right into her eyes.

"You are the most beautiful girl in the whole world!" he said.

"She is the joy of the house!" said Arnaldo's father.

Carefully, Ana approached his ear as she whispered to him.

"This is your friend Margarita's grandchild, darling! May she rest in peace! She has been a blessing for this old couple."

"I know, mom. We can talk about it later," said Arnaldo in a low voice.

Ana brought him a hibiscus tea and they all sat in the living room to talk. Guadalupe sat on Arnaldo's lap and kept hugging and kissing him. She stared at him, and he was enraptured by her childlike tenderness.

They told him everything that had happened in the village.

"How are things going at your work?" asked his father.

"Right now, I'm not in the position I was. Let's just say that I've been assigned another special project."

"Mmmmmm... And what's it about?" asked Ana.

"This is all more related to science. I will tell you some time."

He didn't give her any details. Parents' intuition never fails, though. They suspected something was up.

Guadalupe fell asleep in his arms. It was not long before he took her to her room and put her to bed.

"I have something to tell you," he told his parents.

They sat comfortably.

"First of all, I want to apologize. I don't feel like I've been a good son. Although we always stayed in contact, I became distant. I didn't even remember how much time had passed since the last time I visited!"

"Don't say that, son! You have your obligations, and we are aware of that... We are proud to have a son who is a priest. A man consecrated to God. As a father, now you have lots of children to keep an eye on."

That shook Arnaldo. He felt even worse.

The time had come to let go of the heavy burden on his back.

"Mom, it's not okay! Even with the Guadalupe issue, I should've come and talked to you. It shouldn't have been done through a phone call."

"That little girl has been a blessing," said his father. "We are happy to have been able to help your friend Margarita with her grandchild."

There was a silence.

"She's my granddaughter," he replied.

This was how he told them his story with Margarita. The way in which he found out, twenty years later, that he had a daughter. Everything that had happened in his life since that moment.

His lack of courage to face it at the time had led him there.

After emptying the inner baggage he had been carrying, the man faded away in tears.

"I had no one to ask to take care of her. I should have told you the truth, even more after my investiture. I don't know what came over me, but I regret everything profoundly. I should have told you."

His parents approached him with love to embrace him. They cuddled him just like when he was a child. His mother started humming that lullaby she always sang.

The lizard is crying.
The lizard is crying.
The lizard and the lizard
with little white aprons...

She cooed to him with the love that only a mother can understand. She was also crying her heart out at the sight of her son's pain. His father tried to calm him with warm hugs.

"Shhh my son, don't worry! Everything is all right, it's okay! It hurts me to know that you've been carrying this heavy burden," his father also said with tears in his eyes.

If there was one thing the Romero Lopez family could do, it was knowing how to put themselves in the other person's shoes and walk with them.

That embrace would fill Arnaldo with the strength he needed to continue his higher purpose.
To forgive himself.
That was the forgiveness he needed the most.
That day he understood how God was able to sacrifice his son for the world's salvation.
He would have to do the same.

7

Forgiveness is healing.
It liberates. It gives renewed strength.
Before God and before himself, Arnaldo has regained his freedom.

He did not know how, but he had agreed with his parents that the next step would be to tell Guadalupe who he really was. To ask her for forgiveness.

As soon as morning light came through the window, Guadalupe jumped out of her bed and rushed to greet everyone. She walked through the colorful corridor opening and closing doors. Looking for her grandma and grandpa.

"Let me see if they're here..." she said.

She heard voices in the kitchen. She went out running with Chocolate, who was behind her, barking. With the candor, sweetness and spontaneity that characterized her.

"Goooooood morniiiiiiingggg! Guess who it is?" she exclaimed mischievously. "The joy of the house is already awaaaaake!"

That was her usual greeting.

They were all gathered around that colorful central table, drinking the freshly brewed coffee that was so good for Mrs. Ana. With all the excitement and contained joy, Guadalupe entered the kitchen.

"Grandmaaaaaa, Grandpaaa!! Uncle Arnaldoooo!!!! I'm really happy you're still here," she jumped onto him, giving him a kiss.

If there is one thing about Ana, it is that she's not very patient.

Ever since Arnaldo commented that he wanted to tell the girl the truth, she had been worried. So, like a good mother, she took advantage of the moment to do things her way. The most natural of all.

"Honey, he is not your uncle! He is your grandfather!" interrupting her with sweetness and naturality, without giving many explanations.

"My grandfather? I didn't know that, Grandma! Sorry, thennnnnnn, I will call you *Litooooo*. Good moorning *Lito*!" she said instantly.

Just like a teacher, Grandma explained the situation.

"He is the father of your mother, that is why he is your grandfather."

"Aha, now I understand!"

"Come on and give me a good morning kiss," said Ana as she also approached the girl to give her a kiss.

"And where is mine?" asked Arnaldo's father.

"Sure, *Grandpaaa*! Did you think I would forget about you?" she answered, laughing.

From that moment on, Guadalupe started referring to him as *Lito,* just like that.

That touch of naturalness from Mrs. Ana took a weight off Arnaldo's shoulders. Everything began to flow normally.

For Arnaldo, that trip to Mexico meant a reunion with a part of himself that he had forgotten. He felt free. He understood better the parable of Jesus that encourages people to be like children. Every time he had the chance, he threw himself to the floor to play with his granddaughter. They jumped over puddles. They counted sheep and discovered the shapes hidden in the clouds.

He spent hours making up stories with her. All of them magical, where God was a superhero whose love protected everyone and defeated evil.

He used those moments to educate her about faith. He talked to her about Jesus. The child who was born in a manger and came to save the world. A shrewd, curious, intelligent little boy like her, who grew up carrying a message of love to everyone.

Guadalupe was attentive and curious.

"*Lito,* have you ever seen God?" asked Guadalupe once.

"Yes."

"Reaaaally?" she said, opening her dark brown eyes wide in amazement.

"Yes! Really! And I'm going to tell you a secret," said Arnaldo while whispering in her ear, "but promise me you won't tell anyone."

"I promise!"

"Do you know where I saw Him?"

"Wheeeere?"

"In your eyes..."

"In my eyeees?!" she answered with wonder.

"Yes... I think he hid there so everyone who looks at you will know that you are the apple of his eye."

Guadalupe was fascinated.

"Can I tell everyone?"

"I do not think it's necessary. Anyone who looks at you will notice it!"

God was in her eyes.

Since then, that restless girl could not stop asking her *Lito* questions. The type of questions that adults do not always know how to answer.

"*Lito*, what happens to people when they die? Where do they go?"

That is why Arnaldo liked being like children more and more.

"When a person dies, there is a huge party in heaven! God is happy because another son has come home. To meet with him. That's why there is a super party!"

"Are there balloons at the party?"

"Yes! I think there are! Of thousands of colors, music, types..."

"That sounds great, but I will feel sad if God decides to come for you and Grandma and Grandpa to take you to heaven," she said. "Death is ugly!"

"Death is not ugly, nor is it something bad. Probably you will feel sad as you say, but that person is going to be with God. All of us have a day and a time when we'll have to leave. When you think about that, imagine the most beautiful party that God can prepare to celebrate that the person has finally arrived in His presence. From that moment on, let's say the person still lives but in another way. They become eternal."

"Ooohhh! So, that means they're still alive?"

"They will always be every time you think about them. They will be in your heart and in all your memories."

"What if we make a box to keep the memories in?"

"I love that idea!"

This is how Guadalupe made her box of memories.

There she would keep everything that represented a beautiful memory for her. Notes, flowers, small pieces of paper with drawings and even a special bottle that would be filled with all the kisses and hugs from her grandparents and her *Lito*. That way, on nights when she had trouble sleeping, she would open the magical bottle and fall fast asleep, filled with those big hugs and all the love contained in a jar.

The week went by very quickly and they made the most of every day. Guadalupe's box of memories was full in a short time.

Unfortunately, the time had come to say goodbye.

Arnaldo promised to come and see them at least twice a year. He would call them more often. With Guadalupe he made a pact: he would take her to see Rome very soon and, if possible, she would visit him every so often. A promise that made the ties between them grow even stronger.

Days after Arnaldo's return to Rome, some of the girl's great-uncles appeared. An unrecognized daughter and son of Margarita's father. They wanted to find the whereabouts of his sister and niece. That caused a stir in Santa Magdalena de Jicotlán.

Comments were heard everywhere:

"Did you hear the news about don Gilberto's sons?"

"Sure! Who would have thought? With their little 'it wasn't me' face... It was terrible!

"And poor Juana being cheated on since who knows when!"

The grandparents did not take it very well. They did not know their intentions. They had no choice but to introduce them to Guadalupe. Whether they liked it or not, by blood they were her great-uncles.

"I don't like any of this, Hugo! Suddenly, some uncles appear."

"Keep calm, woman. The little girl will always be with us. Stop the jealousy."

The wheel of life turns endlessly.
For the grandparents.
For Guadalupe.
For everyone.
Nothing is forever.

8

Arnaldo came back renewed.

Everything he experienced in Santa Magdalena Jicotlán with his family inspired him to continue.

The moment he arrived in Rome, he called Giacomo. He wanted to tell him why the trip had been so sudden. He also was dying to tell him all the doubts that had come up regarding their project of bringing back Jesus.

They meet in a cozy restaurant called Il Bocconcino. It was a peculiar *trattoria,* very near Saint Clement's Basilica. From the large window of the door, you could see all the way in. It was a beautiful day. They decided to sit outside on a warm, open terrace.

Arnaldo was an open book.

For the first time, he didn't hesitate to tell his life story. He felt free. He was less burdened by his sordid past. He could talk about why he decided to make that sudden trip to Mexico. He even told him about the dream he had the night before the flight.

"How are you feeling?" asked Giacomo after listening carefully.

"At peace. Calm"

"Then, there is no doubt you did the right thing."

"I agree. It's amazing how we can lose our lives in a lie. Not showing your face. Not doing the right thing.

A brief silence.

"Talking about doing the right thing, I was asking myself on the flight back if the idea of cloning Jesus is the right thing to do. I have many doubts," said Arnaldo.

"I blindly believe that God brought us together for a reason. It is no coincidence you went to Mexico and when all this happens, you feel truth is with you. I know the path will be difficult, but doing everything we can to save the Church cannot be a mistake."

He was forceful.

There was no room for further doubt. Just as he had made the decision to make amends for his mistakes, the time had also come to definitely move forward. He had to trust his instincts, but, above all, he had to trust God.

NELSON BUSTAMANTE & CARMEN VICTORIA PARDO

"Say no more. The time has come!" he said without hesitation.

It was to take action.

They didn't waste a second. That same week they rented a space that would serve as their research center. The equipment had arrived. They only needed to install them and start the tests to make sure everything would work perfectly.

Giacomo had already conducted some interviews with collaborating colleagues. He was very selective in the process and took advantage of Arnaldo's arrival for a second opinion. They had to be very cautious and agree with the selection.

There was a lot at stake.

The plan and strategy they had devised was in place. The real day zero had arrived.

Giacomo could not be absent from his duties at the Vatican archives and, anyway, when it came to science he only knew the chemical formula for water. His support was of a different nature.

Arnaldo initially stuck to the steps that had made Dolly's creation possible. With a piece of the transubstantiation of the Eucharist, he sought to reproduce the DNA of Jesus in order to insert it into a plasmid and obtain recombinant molecules.

He tried to obtain as many of them as possible in order to do multiple tests.

Attempt after attempt.

Nothing.

"If this is His blood and we are following the processes, what's wrong?" Arnaldo asked Giacomo.

Giacomo was ready for a different kind of answer.

So, one day it arrived with a sealed box.

"I brought you something, partner! I do not know if this will be useful, but I hope it helps with something."

He handed him the box with a note. A friend had sent it to him.

We trust that this sample of the bones of Jesus' cousin will help you to obtain Christ's DNA. We remain anxious and watchful for the Second Coming, and how this good news will be received. We trust the Lord. May it be the joy and hope that these times and humanity need.

Arnaldo felt that Giacomo was not being careful. They had agreed to keep the project secret.

"Who have you told about this? Didn't we agree not to say anything?"

"Trust me. I'm here to give you all the tools you may need that can help us. There are still people in the world who can be trusted."

"Just two years after the bones disappeared, it was the last day I saw Pilar. I feel weird holding part of this relic in my hands."

"Please, think about this as a scientist. The important thing is to evaluate whether it will be useful to the project."

He was right. Arnaldo had no other options. The sample he had in his hands was undoubtedly valuable.

Would he use it?

The problem was that trying to incorporate both DNAs rather fouled the sample.

What is purer than the living, beating DNA of the very heart of Jesus that was in the piece of the Eucharistic miracle?

He gave up with the John the Baptist issue.

What he had from Jesus was more than enough.

However, achieving sequence amplification through electrical impulses, fusions and cell divisions was not yet possible. The result obtained could be summed up in four words: *failures and more failures.*

Arnaldo knew that the project he had embarked on had a high probability of failure. In the face of the unstoppable and unforgiving time that continued to advance without the desired fruits, the cloning of Jesus was a mystery that remained unanswered.

He felt a constant pressure. He knew that both Kevin and Dr. Lee, whom he learned about from a friend of Giacomo's, were working on the same thing. They were probably using the same procedures.

Something was still missing.

There was a variable Arnaldo wasn't taking into consideration. But he wasn't getting anywhere.

A slow time for him, in terms of what had been achieved overall.

An accelerated time in other areas.

During those years, Arnaldo not only watched the seasons go by and his granddaughter grow up. Many changes also took place in the world.

Instability and tensions within the European Union intensified.

The Russian Federation expanded.

Socialism in Latin America became a plague of death.

The global economic meltdown had no reverse.

Religions began to suffer transformations and losses.

For Nuremberg, these were steps that tipped the balance toward their new world order.

They were pulling the strings as they pleased increasingly more.

The world was in complete and absolute chaos.

The Second Coming of Christ was becoming more and more urgent.

Soon, a silent purge would put everything in check. The worst was yet to come.

9

When Lee is immersed in something important, his brain has the ability to completely block out any distracting elements. His focus is absolute. It is the only moment where fears are overshadowed.

He was in his office looking at the board he had created on the glass walls. Rereading the formulas. The procedures. He seems to have found a new window. Another possibility. He calls his partners. That time he stayed all day.

His eyes are looking up as if inside his brain he were checking again the procedures of the new strategy he is about to share. Finally, the genius comes out.

"What if you could get the nucleus introduced into the zygote to somehow reprogram the cell and make it behave like an early embryo?"

Everyone is left thinking.

They review how they could make this possible. If someone could see their brains, they would probably get lost in the infinite connections that were starting to form.

Suddenly, Lee seems to find an answer.

"If we manage to prevent certain epigenetic modifications, we will surely manage to minimize the possibility of restricting the potency of DNA... Of course! That's it!" he said asserting something he had just discovered. "This way there should be no failures and the perfect human cloning will take place without mistakes!"

He became excited as he heard himself speak. He started to raise his voice. A result of the excitement of the moment.

"Okay! Okay!" once more, he seems to have found another alternative. "Colleagues, we may continue to use induced pluripotent stem cells, but, with these chemical modifications, they may guarantee our potential fetus to be perfect. All hands on deck! Let's achieve this and see what happens when they're in vitro and we transfer them to the artificial ovule!"

One of the scientists interrupted him.

"Excuse me, Doctor Lee..."

"What is it?" he replied, uncomfortable after being brought out of his excitement.

"What if we reprogram directly? We haven't tried that yet. We could try and see what happens."

"I don't understand, explain yourself better."

"I thought that, to save us from going through the intermediate stem cell stage, we could convert, for example, cells into neurons."

Lee pondered the idea. It sounded interesting. Challenging. Indeed, another possibility. Deciding to work with other people had not been a bad idea after all.

He stared into his partner's eyes. It seemed that, for the first time, he was really looking at someone. However, it wasn't like that. In his head it was him and only him.

"Divide into two groups. Let's try both and see what happens," he said.

He turned his back and went back to his office.

A new way of doing things had just begun.

10

Just before the beginning of the pandemic that confined the world, Guadalupe went out to spend a weekend with her Great Aunt Imelda and her husband, Vicente, in Zacualpan. She had many friends there. It was December and, for the first time in her life, she would not spend Christmas with her grandparents. Regardless, she called them every day. With each conversation she reminded them of how much she missed them.

She came back a day before classes started. It was already dark; it was almost seven o'clock. The lights from the two lamps in the living room were lit. Everything was silent.

"Grandmaaaa, Grandpaaaa, I'm here! It's me! The joy of the house! Did you miss me? You did, didn't you?" she said as she threw her bag on the floor and rushed toward them to hug them and give them the usual nose greeting.

Nobody answered.

She looked for them in the kitchen and the balcony. Finally, she found them in their room. Half-embraced. Sleeping.

She approached them to wake them up. But something was different. Their faces seemed translucent. Their resting was not temporary. Their sleep was deeper than that. An eternal one.

Guadalupe realized that her grandparent's love was so big that they had made the decision to leave together. She approached them to hug them. She stayed next to them. Her eyes shed buckets of tears that soaked the sheets and flooded the floors, but could not soothe her soul.

They were the first love Guadalupe has memory of having felt. She stayed like that for several minutes. Hours maybe. She got up and looked for her box. She opened the jar of kisses and hugs.

"I do not want to spend all of them, but I need at least a few," she said while looking at them.

She imbued herself with them. That little girl magic still worked.

She kissed them. She hugged them. She said goodbye.

Finally, she stood up and walked towards the living room. She picked up the phone. Dialed. A sleepy voice answered the phone.

"Mom! Is everything okay? Why are you calling at this time?" said Arnaldo after seeing the number on his phone. Ana was the one who always called him from home.

"*Lito*... It's me, Guadalupe..."

"Hi, love," he replied, not noticing her crying.

"Can you hear the party in heaven?" she said, deeply sad. "Grandma and Grandpa were the guests of honor today. They decided to part together, *Lito*! God was waiting for them!"

A void took over Arnaldo. An inner emptiness shook him.

He had always spoken of the joy of meeting the Lord after death. Of eternal life. He knew that now they were feeling much better.

But in the end, Arnaldo was just a man.
And in man selfishness prevails.

11

Manipulating genetic material can be a blessing or have lethal effects.

Devastating ones.

In the wrong heads or hands, CRISPR-Cas9 is a dangerous instrument. By allowing alterations to genes, it can, therefore, also induce the risk of these effects can be activated or deactivated.

In the limitless world that Mullis and Davis coexist in, the project of cloning Jesus continues to go further beyond. In the madness that accompanies the genius within them they have decided, after many discussions, to transgress, even further, the boundaries of what is permitted.

"Do you think it will work?" asked Mullis.

"I carried out all the tests with rats. Everything indicates that it will," answered Davis.

"What did you do?"

"I made a culture medium by borrowing some genes from the planaria and the lobster. Two of the few animals that bear the genes of regeneration and immortality. I incorporated them in the rats and their organism responded greatly. They adapted it as part of their own DNA!"

"That is great! Wonderful!"

"Have you ever heard about Henrietta Lacks?"

"Ummm... maybe , but I' m not sure."

"She was a woman who died of cancer at 31 years old. During the process, the doctors took some samples of her cells. These cells are still alive and replicating non-stop. This has been going on since 1951."

"But cells can only survive after a limited number of separations... That's impossible!"

"Exactly. That's why Henrietta's cells are so special. Hers are still alive. They are known as the HeLa cell line, from her initials. In fact, it was what gave birth to the first immortal cell culture."

"I know what you are talking about! Do you have access to them?"

"They are spread throughout many laboratories all over the world. I have a lot of contacts. These cells have been used in more than 70,000 experiments. Why don't we see what happens when we combine the DNA of these so-called immortal animals?"

"That's brilliant. The truth is we've got nothing to lose."

"Or... we could gain a lot. For instance, going down in history as the men that brought Christ Himself back to life and made him... Immortal!! Not even God managed that."

They spoke with cynicism and arrogance.

"Immortality made possible, not by an all-powerful God, but by an all-powerful science," Kevin said haughtily.

"The myth overthrown!"

They have decided to keep this information hidden. Only they know about it. In the tests they have developed to bring back the Messiah, they have incorporated this powerful ingredient into the DNA strand.

Mullis' fascination went beyond that. Just the thought of the perpetuation of species, in an untainted and now also immortal form, became a temptation that escaped all rational thinking. His brilliant mind transgressed boundaries.

He delighted in imagining future offspring who could copy the perfection of an immortal, tailor-made Christ.

The one who conquered death.

"Keep the commandment without stain or reproach until the appearing of our Lord Jesus Christ, which He will bring about at the proper time; He who is the blessed and only Sovereign, the King of kings and Lord of lords, who alone possesses immortality..."

1 Timothy 6:14-16

Were they being part of God's plan for humanity?

Mullis dreamed day and night of the moment when the cloning of Jesus would become a reality. He hated the Church. He rejoiced in the thought that it would be a low blow to this institution. He saw himself in dreams extracting live cells. Inserting them into thousands of embryos conceived in laboratories. Improved ova and spermatozoa. He saw them dance. Merge. Fertilize themselves in front of them. Become immortal.

As immortal as he wanted his legacy to be.

Despite all the ongoing investigations financed by Nuremberg, neither Kevin nor Mullis could have imagined what was about to happen.

The reports with the group's plans, which Anatoly made public in 2011, were already on track.

In the world-wide sphere, the economy was being hit. The Sino-American Cold War, which had been brewing over the years, had big changes on the horizon. Some economists warned about the economic deglobalization and Balkanization that was knocking on their doors.

One of them was economist and New York University professor Nouriel Roubini. Better known as *Doctor Disaster*. He predicted the Great Depression of 2008. For 2019 he warns of a major economic debacle by 2020. But he spoke in economic terms.

And it all came, in an unthinkable way.

~

—Wuhan, China, December, 2019.
A new virus in humans, which causes respiratory disease,
is beginning to spread rapidly. The information known
is limited. Lockdown begins to be imposed, little by little,
inside the Asian city.

On the Chinese social network, Weibo, Dr. Li Wenliang, an ophthalmologist at Wuhan Central Hospital, warns about the spread of the virus and is accused of spreading rumors. On January 20, China closes its borders and declares an emergency.

Two months later, the rest of the world has to do the same.

A global pandemic has broken out, bringing the planet to a standstill and locking humanity in their homes.

Some say that this virus has been created in a laboratory. That it is a biological weapon. Fear is generalized. Everywhere is locked down. Journalists from the major networks begin to transmit the news from their homes. The streets become empty.

It is said that the elderly are the most vulnerable, but this virus knows no age. Day by day the number of cases and deaths increases. Public health begins to collapse.

Was this the massive cleanup they were hoping to initiate at the Nuremberg Club convention, in that room B, in 1997?

A large-scale plan.

While the world went into lockdown and the eyes of science were focused on finding a cure for the virus, Kevin and Mullis continued to conduct the tests necessary to make the experiment that would radically transform humanity viable.

But rebellion comes at a price. Sooner rather than later it must be paid.

Paradoxically, for a man of science like Mullis, the virus issue was more of a strategy than something real to worry about. A smokescreen for hidden purposes.

Although everyone was warning about the fast spread of the virus, for him, the lockdowns and use of masks were exaggerated. The center did not stop its activities, and everyone took their precautions. Except him.

He began to experience generalized malaise. Shivers. A high temperature. He did not say anything about it. He had also had some breathing difficulties. He worked fatigued.

"Are you feeling okay, Mullis?" asked Kevin.

"I didn't sleep well. It's probably a flu-like illness."

"You haven't got the virus, have you? You should go to hospital."

"Are you mad? This will go away."

"Don't take this the wrong way, but I would feel better if you went home. Besides, you can't work in this state. As soon as you're feeling okay again, you come back."

And so, he did.

As the hours passed, the discomfort and hardship began to worsen. Against his will, Mullis had no choice but to go to the hospital.

When he arrived at the emergency room, he wanted to run back.

Everything was Dantesque. Stretchers full of sick people everywhere. Nurses and doctors running back and forth. Widespread confusion. Total chaos. For the first time in his life, he knew what fear was.

He was transferred to one of the improvised rooms. The respective tests were performed. Results: Positive for COVID-19.

His condition worsened rapidly. He was transferred to intensive care. Intubated. Twenty-three hours later, that man of science died alone at California General Hospital. There was no time for farewells.

Without knowing, his financers were his executioners.

After a few days, Kevin called Mullis. He didn't find him. Nor did he look for him to see if everything was all right. He preferred to take shelter and protect himself.

"Lest the old man gets the virus and infects me. If he's alive, he'll show up... if he got it, let him die if he wants to!"

All of Mullis' research remained in the hands of his disciple.

With his death, his dark and despicable past vanished, as well as many controversial ideas and experiments in which he participated, in the name of science, ending other lives.
They say that those that live by the sword die by the sword.

12

Mankind begins to feel the birth pangs before the Second Coming. The pandemic situation is frightening.

—March 13ᵗʰ, 2020.
The diocese of Rome decides to close all its churches.
The chaos spreads everywhere. Parishioners around the world feel they have nowhere to stand in the emptiness that fills the streets. Gradually, other bishops' conferences around the world do the same.
No one comes out unscathed.
In a matter of days, the world is closed.

Arnaldo, like many believers, does not know what to do. He wonders how all this is being managed internally in the Vatican. What it would be like to be there at that controversial moment. It was a difficult moment for everyone. Faith was the only instrument he had to cope with what was happening.

Since his excommunication, he went to Mass daily. Not as a priest but as a parishioner. He did not take communion. Out of respect. But there he was.

The fear that is experienced not only threatens institutions, health and spirit. It also greatly affects the economy. The labor and economic crisis that the world begins to experience widens the social gap. Most citizens have seen their living standards decline. There is nothing that can be done.

The reality is that death does not distinguish between one person or another according to the number in their bank account. Death begins to be experienced at all levels. Human frailty is exposed.

The situation has become critical.

Arnaldo and Giacomo decide to heed the call and remain in quarantine. They close the laboratory. Indefinitely.

The days become longer. He does not know what to watch, who to talk to. How to use his time. It was in that space of uncertainty that Arnaldo was reunited with a part of his soul that had been sleeping.

The year almost ends. That November day, the sky had dawned bluer and brighter than usual. The deep glow gave life to those days where death was everywhere. In the privacy of his modest apartment, he decided to break his self-imposed sentence.

To recover his daily appointment.

To meet daily with Jesus as a priest.

He opened his small balcony to celebrate a private and intimate Mass.

A different kind of ceremony.

He developed the stages of the liturgical ritual.

The neighbors, leaning out of their balconies, began to follow the religious ceremony with fervor. They felt calm as they tried to listen to the word.

But as he reached the consecration of the body and blood of Jesus, Arnaldo stopped.

He looked down. He placed his wedged hands on his chest. He remained like that for a few minutes.

He cleared the table.

Out of respect for the Church, he did not go on.

With just that action, he felt closer to God.

The neighbors did not understand why the priest stopped right there.

The same ritual was repeated every day. At 9 a.m., Arnaldo started Mass. The neighbors went out to their balconies ready to listen to God's message. He began to read the scriptures. The sermon.

He always finished the Mass at the same point and closed his balcony.

"What a strange thing to do, Giuseppe," said Mrs. Rosa. "The same every day!"

"I agree, Rosa, but at least he talks nicely. We can start the day with some peace."

Listening to the scriptures allowed them to at least find hope amid the long days of quarantine.

"We will wait for tomorrow, Giuseppe!"

That daily encounter Arnaldo had strengthened the love he felt for Jesus even more.

He started reading and investigating everything he could about assisted reproduction techniques.

The quarantine had to be extended. Cases of infection and death were increasing.

One of those mornings, the reading was from the book of Daniel.

From the time that the regular sacrifice is abolished and the abomination of desolation is set up, there will be 1,290 days. How blessed is he who keeps waiting and attains to the 1,335 days!

But as for you, go your way to the end; then you will enter into rest and rise again for your reward at the end of the age.

He felt voices talking to him again.

He finished his private ceremony. He closed the balcony.

"From the time that the regular sacrifice is abolished... go your way to the end... you will enter into rest and rise again for your allotted portion."

Would he really rise again for his reward?
On the contrary, he felt he was being sacrilegious.
He did not celebrate any more ceremonies.

The state of quarantine forced by the pandemic was mentally dangerous. The enemy is cunning. Its actions permeate minds and create tormenting obsessions in them.

Although he had reconciled with his past, he felt unworthy of forgiveness, which grieved him and caused a deep sense of oppression. So much so, that he could physically feel a dagger stuck in his heart.

Once again, a new battle is beginning for Arnaldo.
But this one has a time limit that he has been unable to read.
One thousand three hundred and thirty-five days.
Three years and six months.
After this period, the prophecy would be revealed.
The one he could not understand.

13)

Something unusual was happening in Comala, a municipality in the small state of Colima, located some ninety nine miles south of Guadalajara and surrounded by groves of trees.

Comala was always filled with magic, legends and stories. There lived Luis, Guadalupe's great-uncle. She had gone to spend some holidays with him and her cousin Paula. But what ensued that afternoon in the church hall was out of the ordinary.

The world was starting to recover after the pandemic.

The first ones to leave quarantine were the young ones. They met in squares and open places. People gathered in small groups and tried to go back to normal.

That day, Guadalupe was with her cousin and friends in the square. Although the afternoon had been clear-skied, a shocking downpour came out of nowhere. It was uncommon in that town.

They ran down the cobblestone street trying to find a place to take shelter. Closest was the San Miguel Arcangel del Espíritu Santo Church, Comala's only historic monument.

It was built in 1884. Its gleaming white structure makes it stand out among the surrounding farmland. It has a beautiful quarry stone arch and above the entrance is a sculpture of St. Michael the Archangel, the guardian Angel of the Lord, of His Sacred Heart and of the Eucharist.

In Hebrew Miguel means: "Who like God?"

He is the enemy of Satan, which is why he is also known as the Chief of the Armies of God.

The gates were open. Despite being soaked, they decided to go in. At that instant, a thunderous sound shook them. It was the church bells. They seemed to be welcoming them.

The reality is that it was six o'clock and, as in almost all towns, they usually ring at noon, at that very time in the afternoon and on Sundays to announce that Mass is about to begin.

They were startled by the resounding peals, but then the peals brought them to their senses. They were in a sacred place. They stopped running. They crossed themselves while laughing and looking at each other. They did not stay in the nave of the church. They went to one of the parish halls.

The white plastic chairs were somewhat dirty. It has been a long time since anyone had been there. There was also a wooden podium, a guitar in the corner and three paintings hanging on the wall. One had an image of John Paul II, another was of the Divine Mercy and the other was of the Virgin of Guadalupe.

Before the pandemic, this was the place where the children met to do youth pastoral work and organize community activities.

What was going to happen that afternoon was beyond our imagination.

At the beginning, they only talked, but the sound of the rain was so loud they barely could hear each other.

One of the members of the group picked up the guitar. He was a virtuoso with a special gift. He had never studied music, but he was able to play any instrument he was given by ear. As soon as he played the first cord, the sound of the rain started to soften. They started singing.

It was a time of total revelry. The boy was able to play any song they named perfectly.

"Another one, another!" they said each time a song ended.

"Any ideas?" someone else would ask.

"Tell me one, just one!" exclaimed the boy with the guitar.

"Let's see if you can keep up with this one," challenged Linita.

Her voice was beautiful, angelical. She decides to sing a praise. It sounded so lovely! They listened to her, hypnotized. Mesmerized.

Suddenly, José started moving irregularly in his chair. It seemed like he was drowning in his own saliva. The music continued. Only one of them had noticed. Little by little, the young man seemed to enter an ecstatic, frantic, almost hypnotic state. His mouth began to curl up as he spoke, unintelligibly, in a language no one knew.

"What is wrong with José? What is happening to him?" shouted one of them, scared.

The music stopped. There was silence.

Their hearts started to beat faster.

Guadalupe was scared like everyone else.

"I should have stayed home," said one of the boys.

"He seems possessed," said Paula. "It's like he's somewhere else."

"Let's get out of here!" shouted one of them.

"Are you crazy? We can't leave him here," said Guadalupe.

"What's he saying? What's he saying?" asked one of them at the same time.

Such was the uproar and commotion that the parish priest, who was a little deaf, heard them. He ran to see what was happening and where the sound was coming from. Entering the living room, he found the children startled. Scared to death. Trying to understand what was happening.

Juanpa, another of the boys, said that he had started to feel a fire burning inside him. Guadalupe felt the same. At that moment, Andrés also started to feel ecstatic. He was experiencing the gift of interpretation and prophecy. Looking directly at Guadalupe, he said:

Listen, O daughter, given attention and incline your ear:
The King will desire your beauty.
He is your Lord, bow down to him.
It is He who keeps for you a space at His right hand.

It was the second time that the priest had experienced something similar.

But he was not scared at all.

These were *charisms of revelation*. The Holy Spirit had become present and filled the room. That was why heat ran through them all and burned them with its fire.

Charisms are special graces from heaven that God gives to bless others. An outward manifestation of one of the gifts of the Holy Spirit. From the apostles to the present day, the charisms are still in force.

According to the biblical account, the apostles began to fulfill the mission that Christ had entrusted to them on the day of Pentecost. On that day the Holy Spirit descended upon them.

Suddenly, everything ceased.

When that magical and supernatural moment had ended, the parish priest approached them, trying to calm them down. He explained to them that they were not demonic possessions or anything like that. That there are different spiritual gifts and that they had simply been an instrument.

The gift of miracles, wisdom, tongue, faith and healing. And many others. He took the opportunity to tell them about Padre Pio, who, since he was eight years old, had been experiencing charisms of vision.

"Padre Pio talked to his guardian angel and to other people's angels. He also had the gift of prophecy; he spoke with the Virgin Mary and many attested to the miraculous healings he performed. His stigmata accompanied him for fifty years and a scent of flowers emanated from them."

At the end of the story, he asked them not to miss Mass on Sunday. He wanted them to give testimony of how, in the San Miguel Arcangel del Espíritu Santo Church in Comala, the same Spirit of God was present.

"You have homework! Please read the First Letter of Corinthians, chapter 12. It will help you in your testimony!"

The moment he stopped speaking, the rain stopped completely.

They returned to their homes elated, recounting what they had experienced.

That Sunday they attended Mass, as the priest had asked them to do. During the homily, he explained how we are all parts of the body of Christ. All this was to be used as a link for the testimony that the young people were going to share.

He invited them to the podium. Before giving them the floor, he read the last verse of the letter he had set the children as homework.

God himself says in the scriptures:

> *"But earnestly desire the greater gifts. And I show you a still more excellent way."*

"Let's look forward to them!"

They told their story before the eyes of the parishioners who marveled to hear them. When they had finished, the priest asked those present to stand up. He felt in his heart a deep desire to pray for the sick. He raised his hands. He asked the congregation to do the same.

After a few minutes of mystical effusion, from the back of the church a shout of delight filled the atmosphere with celebration and joy.

"I've been healed! I've been healed!"

It was the paralytic of the village, who was now walking.

"Miracle! Miracle!" claimed some of them.

At the following Mass, the number of attendees tripled. That day too about ten sick people were loudly proclaiming that they had been healed.

The rumor was spreading and with it the number of people arriving increased.

The third week was madness. Since they could no longer fit in the church and there were people gathered in the street, they even had to look for auxiliary sound.

A blind woman was there. She had come from one of the neighboring towns when she heard the news of what was happening in Comala. The priest asked her to come with him.

"Please, extend your hands over her!"

At that moment, one of the village elders started to shout that he had seen her in his dreams a few days before. God had told him that, when he saw that woman, he should tell her that she would regain her sight.

She opened her mouth to proclaim her inexplicable healing to the four winds in amazement.

After the priest spoke about Joel's prophecy, the most fanatic women decided to print it out and paste it everywhere. In this way they would remember that Comala was being blessed.

> It will come about after this that I will pour out My Spirit on all mankind;
> And your sons and daughters will prophesy, Your old men will dream dreams, Your young men will see visions. Even on the male and female servants I will pour out My Spirit in those days...

> *Joel 3:1-2*

Some young people ran to tell of their special revelations. Marcela, Gabo and Eloísa said, like the Shepherds of Fatima, that angels had appeared to them and asked them to pray a lot for what was to come.

Luisa, the little girl with honey-colored eyes, said that the Mother of God had even appeared to her and that she had spoken to her.

Thus, in the midst of that outpouring of miracles and healings, the news spread everywhere and even began to be replicated in the surrounding area like an avalanche.

Prodigies, outpourings of the spirit and charisms were the main theme of almost every radio station. The most skeptical tried to divert attention. They said that this was an invention of the people and attributed it to the contagion of the masses. As expected, between believers and non-believers debates flared up.

On one of the radio programs they talked about Héctor, an old man from the province who even claimed that, like St. Teresa of Jesus, he had had visions of purgatory and that he was able to talk to some of the oppressed souls there.

"I know that man! He is my neighbor! The man suffers from dementia!" said one of the radio listeners angrily. "How can they call themselves journalists if they go along with those things?"

Héctor's daughter lived in the US. After his father told her the story and acquaintances warned her that he now he really had gone mad, she decided to take him to live with her.

What they never knew is that, after that, his memory was better than ever.

Guadalupe went back to the house of her Great Aunt Imelda and her husband, Vicente, in Zacualpan. She had been living with them ever since the death of her grandparents.

She arrived anxious to tell them everything.

Her anxiety was doubled since her aunt was effectively an atheist. She did not like talking about God, religions, miracles or prayers.

"Come on, girl! Don't start again with those stories of yours. Don't start!" she usually told her when she brought up the topic.

Since Guadalupe moved in with them, that kind of conversation always came up. She felt a special curiosity. She could not help it.

When she was seven years old and visiting her great uncle during the holiday season, she could be found in their room, sitting on the floor on a pile of sheets and reading religious books. Her *Lito* had sent them as she had requested.

She wanted to know why each religion had a different God.

"My *Lito*'s God is 'the best'. You'll see when you meet him!" she said.

Her aunt had no other choice but to accept it.

She thought the little girl was "weird." She was always very mature, suspicious, curious and sharp-witted, as well as sweet and intelligent. Their conversations were at another level. Not at all normal for someone her age.

She was literally in love with that figure who seemed to be from magical fairytales. The man from the stories her *Lito*, Arnaldo, told her. The superhero who did everything for love. The one named Jesus.

What Guadalupe did not know was that the manifestations were not only happening in Comala, but also in Zacualpan. Pentecost was present, and the charisms were still alive. What is happening has no explanation.

"If only you'd been here! You have no idea of what happened! Those things you like have turned the village upside down! Maybe you are right, and God does exist!" her aunt said with surprise as soon she saw her enter.

Guadalupe could not believe it.

She did not even have time to tell her story first.

In the streets of Zacualpan the cries of Father Félix can be heard. He rambles back and forth alerting everyone about what is going on.

"Everyone, everyone, please listen! The Darkness also uses the same tricks and easily sneaks in to manipulate you. Open your eyes! Do not be fooled by fake prophets!"

While some cry out to the Lord of Wonders, others fear the wonders of the Lord.

Now it is Guadalupe who cannot get over her astonishment.

14

"For false Christs and false prophets will arise and will show great signs and wonders, so as to mislead, if possible, even the elect."

Matthew 24:24

When God turned Moses' staff into a snake, the Pharaoh's sorcerers were able to do the same.

God or the devil?

Two polar opposites.

The same act. Two very different intentions.

How can one recognize the enemy's traps?
Can they be avoided?

Since these manifestations began to take place in Comala, many people in the surrounding towns have risen up to warn of the dangers to come.

Tomás, the priest from Chapala, was one of them. He was dismayed by all the news he heard, and, like Father Félix, he urged his parishioners not to let themselves be carried away by this fascination with the inexplicable.

Their doubts were reasonable. Satan also has the power to perform miracles.

In the Book of Revelation is written:

"They are spirits of demons, performing signs, which go out to the kings of the whole world, to gather them together for the war of the great day of God, the Almighty."

"Listen to God's voice and not the devil's!" said Father Tomás.

Even in these cases, fanaticism has two sides.

While some ran to spread the good tidings, Father Tomás did the same, but to sprinkle holy water on those who said they had been healed.

"I command the demon within you to go to the foot of the cross! With this water I bless you in the name of the Father, the Son and the Holy Spirit!"

Just then, they received that blessed bath.

He was convinced that by doing this and wielding his crucifix, he would bring out the demon within them. Even if they opposed.

"So, Father Tomás, are you going to keep doing this? Leave me alone and look for another person who has demons to exorcise!"

This was followed by a sermon.

"Brothers and sisters! Open your ears to God's voice! In the scriptures it is written that the lawless one will appear, made by Satan, performing miracles, signs and false wonders. Do not listen to or believe what they say. It's the work of the devil."

Faced with so much scolding, holy water and reprimand, the church of Chapala began, little by little, to become empty.

For some it was the Epicurean paradox.

Who is right?

Does God want to prevent evil? Why can He not?

But in the spiritual world, everything, even the most sordid, can be part of God's plan to meet his children.

Guadalupe was no longer the six-year-old girl Arnaldo saw the last time they met. She had grown up. Not only in size but also in her deepness of thought.

The communication they had was enviable. She never stopped questioning him to know in detail what he was working on. To know about the things he was experiencing. He had no problem in presenting himself as an open book.

However, Arnaldo was very reserved and jealous regarding the information he handled on the cloning project. It was a well-kept secret.

That evening, Guadalupe came back to Zacualpan and was anxious to talk about her experience, not only to Imelda, but to her *Lito* too. Of course, with the bombshell news of the aunt and her near conversion, her grandfather could wait.

As soon as day broke, she rushed to get ready for class. She took advantage of the early hour to call him and give him the super news.

"Good morning, *Liiiiiiito!* You won't believe it!"

The great piece of gossip. It was not only what she had seen but also about her Great Aunt.

She was so excited that she narrated everything in detail. That contagious energy made Arnaldo reconnect with his own mystical experiences.

"*Lito*, I swear! It was incredible! I can't explain everything I experienced those days. After what happened at church and the village, I felt as if I was being carried! And for Aunt Imelda to tell me that this was also happening here... I meaaaan... You believe me, don't you *Lito*? You can ask Cousin Paula, I'm not crazy or anything! She was there too. I wish you could've been there!"

"Of course! I believe you! This is how things work with God!"

Arnaldo suddenly felt an unexpected outburst of honesty. He had to tell her what he had also experienced.

"Can you keep a secret?"

"Of course!" she replied.

"You know what? I can understand you very well because I've also witnessed some marvelous manifestations that have no explanation."

"Really, *Lito*? What happened?"

"Do you want to know?"

"I'm dying to know!" she said, excited.

Arnaldo told her about the miracle that Jesus had allowed him to experience in the Eucharist. In doing so, he also relived the pain of the times he had doubted His presence and denied Him.

"Don't let anything else make you think it's not from God! It's Him knocking on our doors. The fact that you witnessed it is a grace from heaven." he said, saddened, but happy at the same time.

Guadalupe was fascinated. The clock kept ticking and it was nearly time for her to go. Nevertheless, she decided hold on to the magic of the moment. It would have to be late.

"One hour more, one hour less, what difference does it make?" thought to herself.

"Wow, *Lito*! What beautiful things you're telling me! It must've been really special. It's beautiful being able to feel Christ so close!"

"It won't be long until we'll be even closer, princess!"

"Why do you say that?"

It was at that moment that Arnaldo realized what he had said and done. A mistake that could cost him dearly.

"Could you keep another secret?"

"Of course, *Lito*. I'm like a tomb."

"My degrees have allowed me to be close to many experiences of that kind. I have told you about them. As a scientist and priest, I've been witness to a particular mixture where faith and science sometimes collide, and at other times don't. Do you know what brings them together?"

"The truth?"

"Exactly. The truth. Accepting it is difficult at times. The day I understood that, I stopped working at the Vatican. In fact, even in an institution like that one there are half-truths, but not because of the institution itself, but because of men."

"It must have been difficult for you..." said Guadalupe with a saddened voice.

"At first it was a very hard blow. But were it not our faith, I would have been swallowed up by the darkness."

"How did faith help you?"

"God makes use of everything. I have no doubt about it. In that difficult moment, I remember reading something that fell into my hands out of nowhere. It was a speech that Pope John Paul II had given to scientists and students, speaking about the ideological crisis of the time. Eventually I learned it by heart, as it had touched me directly. He said:

> *"In order for crises to be overcome, the Church advises not prudence and caution, but courage and decisiveness. There is no reason not to side with the truth or to adopt an attitude of fear before it. The truth and all that is true constitutes a great good, to which we should tend with love and joy. Science is also a path to the true, for in its reason is developed; that God-given reason which, by its very nature, is not determined towards error, but towards the truth of knowledge."*

"That was the same morning I ended up at the Chapel of the Holy Spirit. The same place I met my friend Giacomo, the prefect of the Vatican Secret Archives... The day that changed everything..."

"What changed, *Lito*?"

He decided to go all in. To put all the cards on the table. To trust her grandchild.

"Do you remember our pinky promise?" he asked.

"Sure!"

"Because, today more than ever, you cannot break it."

"Of course, *Lito*! Don't worry. What is it then?"

"The day that text fell into my hands I had been excommunicated. I talked about a lot of things with Giacomo. That day we decided to go a step further. I remembered what I had read earlier. There were words that echoed inside me: *courage* and *decisiveness.* 'All that is true constitutes a great good.' 'Science is also a path to the true.' 'Reason is given by God for the knowledge of truth.' That day we wanted to be an instrument in His hands. We are doing everything we can to clone Him. To bring His son into the world, for a second time."

Guadalupe did not know what to say. It was the last thing she had expected.

"Cloning Jesus? How is that possible? *Lito*, what are you talking about? How can you be doing this? A man like you..." she said with indignation.

"There is a group of people looking for the same thing. The cloning of Jesus. They have no good intentions. They want to create the Antichrist himself. They have the DNA of his blood and one of his kin. Scientifically speaking, it is possible."

"Oh my God! This is unusual... it sounds like science fiction!"

"It sounds like it. But it isn't, princess. These are people with a great deal of power who also have a plan in place to reduce humanity, to take over everything, to eliminate the Church. The pandemic was always part of their plan. Giacomo can attest to this. His family was even part of this group."

Dazed, Guadalupe listened. This had puzzled her.

"I have questioned this many times. There is something inside me that tells me we are doing the right thing. Jesus himself said that He is the way, the truth and the life. We decided to follow Him. That is why we are in this process of bringing him back."

"Do you have that DNA too? Where did you get it?"

The questions in Guadalupe's head were going faster than her mouth could say them and quicker than the answers she could get.

"Remember what I told you about the Eucharistic manifestation?" said Arnaldo. "For I have a piece of that living, beating heart of Jesus. I've had it for many years."

"How's that?"

"I felt a call standing in front of one of these demonstrations and took a portion. I don't even know why. I kept it in my crucifix. Surprisingly, it's still alive.

"Did you steal it?"

"I can't explain it. It may sound like that. But now you can also understand that there are things that only fit into the category of 'miracles'."

"I don't know what to say, *Lito*..."

She stayed in silence.

Inwardly, her emotions had transformed from uncertainty, to anger, and to an unexpected peace that she could not explain. She could only imagine being face to face with the superhero she had been told about since she was a child.

"If anyone knows my love for Jesus, it's you! Believe me, if I didn't know that His Church was in danger and that the need for his return was so imminent, I wouldn't be doing this."

He paused.

"You know what? It must be beautiful to be able to have Jesus as close as you do now!" she said, deep in thought.

"He is also close to you, next to you... Do you remember that He hid in your eyes?" he said sweetly. "I believe he's asking us for courage and decisiveness so that His flock does not get lost."

After a long pause, she replied.

"*Lito*, I believe in you! I can only ask Our Father to guide you!"

"To guide us!" he said.

He felt at peace.

"Amen, princess! Amen! Just remember that I'm doing this for Him."

They closed the call, both with a strange feeling inside.

Arnaldo has no idea what is to come.

15

Arnaldo's confession had aroused Guadalupe's curiosity. She talked to her *Lito* daily to see how things were going. She didn't want to miss any detail. Not one.

"What have you achieved?"

"Why didn't it go well?"

"What could have failed today?"

"How are you going to bring Him back?"

"Is it really going to work?"

On the one hand, the questions Guadalupe asked Arnaldo questioned his methodologies, but on the other hand they forced him to search harder for the answers.

He told her how they obtained those recombinant molecules. As if talking to another colleague, he discussed the speed of electrical impulses, cell fusions and cell divisions.

"How do you know if the DNA works? How do you make it fit?" she asked.

"That's both the biggest challenge and the biggest question. We're reproducing, in the laboratory, what would be mature eggs from an ovary. This is where we haven't got it right. We are evaluating several options for fertilization."

"What if they look for a woman to be the recipient?"

"It's too risky. In every sense. That's why we are evaluating alternative solutions where a real egg is not involved.

Just as Arnaldo was looking for solutions, Guadalupe thought about alternatives.

Giacomo also opened up to share some things he had kept secret. He decided to give Arnaldo a report he had been keeping under wraps for some years.

"I want you to read this carefully. If anyone can decipher and understand all of this better, it's you."

"What is it?"

"A revealing report. Almost like a diary of projects where science is involved. It was given to me by a friend who had an interest in Nuremberg. He sought to slow them down. His father had been murdered for taking this report."

Arnaldo recalled seeing the report in Giacomo's office. He kept it in a private safe in the Vatican archives. It was the last place they would look if they wanted to retrieve the document. That was why the man had given it to him.

That was the day Arnaldo told him about what had happened to Pilar. However, Arnaldo was trying to remember where he had seen it before. It looked familiar.

He took the report.

The cover read: *"Progetto ROMA - Nuovo secolo, Nuovo uomo."*

He read the title over and over again. Suddenly, he remembered the moment he had seen it for the first time.

"Of course! On the table in the library!" he said out loud.

"What are you talking about?"

"I was pretty sure I'd seen it before. But until now, I didn't remember where."

"You know about the report?" asked Giacomo, astonished.

"Yes, I'm sure I have. I just remember seeing it in your office, but also on one of the tables of the Vatican Archives. That was the day we bumped into each other for the second time."

He stopped for a moment.

"Does the man who was in the library when we met for the second time have anything to do with this?" insisted Arnaldo.

"Yes. How did you know?"

"He had it on the table that day. The title just caught my attention. That's why I remember it."

"What it contains is very important" said Giacomo.

Arnaldo opened it.

The report provided information on specific projects in the scientific field that Nuremberg was developing.

In their biosafety level 4 laboratories, they created everything from lethal diseases in test tubes to artificial viruses. In giant, earthquake-proof bubbles, the viruses mingled freely inside.

Nuremberg had started in the 1950s. Club of Rome in 1968. However, the report stated that the first human coronavirus, then called HCoV-229E, had been successfully isolated in 1966. There were tests with rodents. CoV alpha and Beta-CoV. Suggestions to perform subsequent tests on bats were also outlined there.

That science manual recorded the steps for the creation of a bacteria Its name: Anthrax. And the creation of a new strain of a virus they would call bird flu.

"When you review it, keep in mind that they had this report in 1997. Check the dates of the previous annotations."

Arnaldo could not get over his shock.

It matched what Pilar had given him. Even events that happened long after this report was stolen.

"Who was the man who gave you this?"

"The only thing I can tell you is that he knew more about me than I knew about myself! He knew about my interest to protect the Church from the inside. He even knew why I broke apart from Nuremberg and from my family. He planned everything masterfully just to meet me. Paradoxically, we became friends. We met each time he came to Rome. One day, he told me the truth. Maybe that is why he gave them to me. They were looking for him. After that, he faked his death."

"Where is he now?"

"I don't know. His biggest dream was to bring down the Nuremberg Group. Somehow, he managed to do it. He brought things to public light, generating an internal breakdown. As I said, check it calmly. In addition, there are nomenclature and evaluations that are beyond my understanding. I think it's important for you to read it. The plan that has been in place since the end of the last century is still underway today and is detailed there."

"*Progetto ROMA - Nuovo secolo, Nuovo uomo,*" read Arnaldo out loud. "Why would they have named a science-related report 'ROMA'?"

"Perhaps because they know that, with science, they seek to detonate ROME."

Like a reflection, that word would hide more than one answer.

16

Arnaldo could not get over his shock.

"It's amazing! All this was planned! What else exists that I haven't yet deciphered here? What has emerged since then?", he said out loud.

All of this made him more impatient. And he had only read one part of it. He had to accelerate the cloning of the Son of God.

"How can we create the perfect egg? How can we make fertilization possible?" he asked himself.

He found it controversial to think of a Second Coming without an angel to warn Mary. Without a Mary who would surrender her womb as a sacred vessel. But the risk was very high. He had to be created in the lab.

His phone rang.

Like every day, it was Guadalupe.

"Hi, *Lito!*"

"Hi, princess!"

"How are you? How's it going?" asked Guadalupe.

"Good, as far as it goes."

"What's new?"

"I can only tell you that these Nuremberg people have more planned than you and I can imagine."

"Why do you say so?"

"I'll tell you another day. It's a long story and I have lots of work to do, honey."

"Don't worry, *Lito*. Could you solve the eggs issue?"

"Not yet. But we're working on it."

Suddenly, a question shook all of Arnaldo's foundations.

This can happen with the simplest things.

"*Lito*, could my eggs work?"

Arnaldo was left completely cold. Shaken.

He wanted to erase from his mind what Guadalupe had said.

But words, once spoken, cannot be taken back...

He continued as if she had said nothing. Guadalupe interrupted him.

"*Lito*, I asked you if my eggs would work," she insisted.

Silence.

It was a window Arnaldo was not willing to open. It is one thing to use a woman's eggs or machines that can simulate them, but it is quite another if that woman is your granddaughter.

"They would. But we can't do that," he answered drily.

He tried to change the topic. To hang up the call. She interrupted him again.

"*Lito*, listen to what I'm about to say. Ever since you told me how Jesus was alive in your hands, I wondered what it would be like to have Him back among us. How I could experience Him that closely. I have given it a lot of thought since then. Why don't you use my womb? You've talked about a sacred vessel, use mine."

"NO!" he shouted with all the denial of what this implied.

"Why not?"

"No, and that's that!" said Arnaldo, wanting to draw a line under this conversation.

"Give me an answer that convinces me," she insisted.

"I said no! Besides, you are just a kid! It makes no sense," his tone of discomfort increased.

"I remind you that I'm almost 18! Who better than me to keep all this safe without anyone saying anything?"

"I said no! End of story, Guadalupe!"

"Tell me when and I'll be there" replied Guadalupe as if she hasn't heard what Arnaldo told her before.

Arnaldo became increasingly exasperated. That possibility did not exist. It could be anyone but her, his granddaughter.

"If you keep insisting, I'm going to hang up," he said.

"Are you really going to hang up on me? At least tell me you're going to think about it."

Another silence.

"Tell me, *Lito!*"

He had no other choice than to say he would think about it.

He did so to calm things down. His mood. She was calm.

Confident about what she was saying.

He hung up.

Cloning Jesus was one thing. Involving his granddaughter in the equation was quite another.

There was the report.

On the table.

The answer he was looking for was that close.
However, Arnaldo still could not see it.

17

After the conversation with Guadalupe, Arnaldo chose not to answer her calls. He needed time and space. It all tormented him.

Guadalupe kept insisting. She had gotten the idea in her head that she was a paintbrush in God's hands. She felt a deep desire to experience Jesus. To have Him close. Just like his uncle had done on certain occasions.

She called him insistently. Not once not twice, but several times a day.

"He better answer, even if it's out of frustration!" she said every time she picked up the phone.

With each unanswered call, a text message.

> *Lito, remember that you're the adult here. Behave yourself.*
> *Call me.*
> *Lito, don't be selfish. Allow me to experience Christ as you do.*
> *Lito, Jesus needs a mother...*

If there was one thing the girl had, it was perseverance.

Arnaldo had not discussed what had happened with anyone.

"When there's nothing good to say it's better to keep quiet," he repeated to himself.

Inside, it was eating away at him.

~

—April, 2024.
Arnaldo was stunned. Doubly stunned.
On the one hand, he was avoiding her. His granddaughter.
Guadalupe.
On the other hand, he was trying to avoid his thoughts on
the subject.

That day, Giacomo had stopped by the laboratory on his lunch break. Arnaldo decided to tell him what had happened. He needed support. His answer confirmed that the world had indeed gone mad.

"Arnaldo, my friend! That's delightful! You have to take her word! I think that's beautiful!"

"She's my granddaughter! Don't you understand?" he said, bothered.

"Exactly! Look at it this way... Your granddaughter can be God's chosen one. The sacred vessel of our time. What a sublime sacrifice! Somehow it's like you're handing your granddaughter over to Him."

"You can't be serious. Are you actually my friend?"

"What are you afraid of?"

"She's my granddaughter..."

"If there's one man who has his eyes fixed on Jesus, it's you. And when that happens, nothing can go wrong. Let go of fear... You will walk on water as Peter did! Why not?" insisted Giacomo. "Think about it!"

He could not hang up as he had done with Guadalupe.

It was impossible. He was in front of him.

This could not be happening. No.

He wanted to run away.

He was not saved by the bell, either.

Fortunately, Giacomo's phone saved him. It rang.

He had to return urgently to the Vatican Archives. He had scheduled a meeting that he had forgotten about. They were waiting for him.

It was perfect. More than perfect.

Arnaldo felt stifled.

There was no doubt that telling him about Guadalupe had not been such a good idea.

There was only one way out.

Prayer. Kneel. Prayer.

He took his Bible. Looking for an answer, he opened it randomly. Once again, as in the times of pandemic, Daniel's prophecy fell into his hands.

> *From the time that the regular sacrifice is abolished and the abomination of desolation is set up, there will be 1,290 days. How blessed is he who keeps waiting and attains to the 1,335 days!*
> *But as for you, go your way to the end; then you will enter into rest and rise again for your reward at the end of the age.*

Same text.

Different kinds of isolation.

This was an inner one. More severe.

Was this the daily sacrifice spoken of in Daniel's prophecy?
Was everything happening with Guadalupe part of the horrible sacrilege the prophet referred to, so that at the end of time the reward would be reached?
Whose reward?
Arnaldo's?
Guadalupe's?
The Church's?
Humankind's?
Who was to persevere?
1,335 days. Three years and six months before the big day.
It was impossible to know.
Impossible to even sense.
Such are God's ways: crooked but straight.

All the more reason. Prayer. Kneel. Prayer.

Fulfilling God's will in our lives can be terrifying. It requires an extra dose of love that is not always easy. Love involves sacrifice, that may be painful; and many hearts have become hard over time. That is why our soul does not always find its way back home.

In the midst of so many questions being asked with so few answers available, Arnaldo decided, after his intimate encounter with the creator, to remain silent for one more minute. That instant when nothingness seems to reign.

Between Giacomo and Guadalupe, his psychological and spiritual foundations were being shaken. He was left with no choice but to drop his attitude. To accept that he was the real adult here. He missed his granddaughter.

"Hi!" said Arnaldo.

"Hello, my dearest *Liiiiiito!* The old man finally deigned to call!" Guadalupe replied mischievously when she heard her grandfather's voice. "Did you think about it? How are we going to do it? What are we going to do, hey?" she said, giving no time for answers.

The voice of love weakens the walls.

"Hello, princess! God bless you," he answered while smiling at Guadalupe's comments.

"Hmmm... let me guess. Are you calling to tell me that you bought me a ticket to go come over?"

"Are you going to keep insisting? I already said no! That option isn't possible."

"This old man hasn't thought things over very well... No, nooo!" she said, imitating her grandfather. "What about it worries you?"

"Guadalupe, you're barely 17. Your life has just started. You have to study. Having a child is an extremely important decision that can change everything. I can tell you that! I want something else for you..."

"Is there anything better than being the one to bring the Messiah back?"

Arnaldo's foundations moved.

"*Lito*, listen... It was you who taught me to love Jesus! To know that he is alive in the Eucharist! His flesh and blood are there. Your stories are what's inspired and guided me. All those miracles I witnessed show me the power of God in a tangible way. Why are you denying me the grace?"

A long silence.

Divine grace is a gift.

You know it has manifested itself in your life when you are more than you could ever be with your strength alone.

And Arnaldo's conviction had been disarticulated.

"*Lito*, are you still there?"

"Yes," he said in an inaudible voice.

"So?"

"I said NO!"

Even if you deny it a thousand times, when something is meant to be, it will be.

By hook.

Or by crook.

CHAPTER XI

BIRTH

1

—*Argentina.*
Monday 10th, November, 2025.
7 p.m.

It is apparently a normal day like any other. However, thanks to the impact of social media, from that moment on, no day would ever be the same again.

A powerful marketing campaign carried out three months ago called for people to "tune in" to witness an event that would shake the world.

A group of youngsters have got together for a barbecue. They are listening to music. Chatting.

"What time is it?" asks one of them.

"Almost seven!"

"Seven? Bro, it's almost time! Hey, Claudia, turn the music down," shouted one of the guests. "I don't know about you guys, but I'm gonna watch the news..."

On the screen there are three men and a woman. They are dressed in white robes. They have ID cards around their necks. It is clear that they are in a laboratory. Shelves. Test tubes. Chemistry equipment.

One of them is the chief. The others are behind him.

The main one has straight, dark hair that is starting to go gray. He has a well shaped beard. He greets the audience charmingly. Closely. He commands respect.

"My name is Dr. Kevin Davis. I'm an American scientist, former employee of NASA and lover of CRISPR-Cas9 technology. It is an honor for me to share with the world the news that will change the way we see science. For more than twenty years, along with my team, I've been working on a project that has taken the quantum leap that mankind so desperately needs. Human cloning. But not just anyone. We wanted to test the infinite possibilities that we have in our hands."

Inside a giant incubator, a perfectly formed fetus can be seen. It is floating inside of what could be a kind of amniotic fluid.

"Dear audience, right in front of your eyes is the almost-completed cloning of the man who for many is the most important person to ever live: Jesus Christ."

In a matter of seconds, the video is the main focus on social media all over the world. In the Vatican, they do not want to believe it. But they know that it is true.

"We had all the elements required to clone the Son of God. An advanced nuclear transference technology was developed. As reliable as in vitro fertilization. Our research has borne fruit. Today we celebrate science! This isn't about religion. It's about science. Today, humankind has become invincible."

Everyone was looking astonished.

In Arenales 2460 street, Argentina, a young couple could not get over their shock.

"This man's lost his marbles!" said Lucía to her boyfriend.

"He's completely mad! Maybe he's a relative of the crazy old man that lived here," says Matías while they kept staring directly at their tablet's screen.

Kevin continued.

"Very soon we will change the history of science. We didn't want to be selfish. We wanted you to accompany us. We wanted you to be part of this birth."

Kevin's desire to go down in history was as strong as that of the Russian man who had sent the whole of humanity into a tizzy a few years earlier with his unquenchable thirst for power.

"You might be wondering how this is possible. I took advantage of new genetic modification techniques such as CRISPR-Cas9. I obtained a sample of the blood on the Shroud of Turin. We had the bones of Jesus' cousin, John the Baptist. This technology has allowed me to modify the genome and alter sections of the DNA sequence. I have cultured pluripotent embryonic stem cells that were inserted months ago into a nucleus-free egg. That is what you see in there!" he said, pointing towards the transparent structure. "The faithful copy of Jesus Christ... finally, immortal!"

2

—California.
Six months earlier.

Lee continues.

He has multiplied the DNA contained in the piece of the Shroud and performs, simultaneously, all the tests.

His state of anxiety has been growing. His financers are angry. Another group of scientists has succeeded before him. The formation of the most desired fetus is in process.

Unexpectedly, two involuntary movements manifest themselves. Once again, his nervous tic appears. He had it when he was a child. He thought it had disappeared. It hadn't.

"Everything okay, Dr. Lee?" asks one of his assistants in the research center after seeing his involuntary and strange movement.

"Yes," he answers drily, trying to control his body.

He goes to the restroom. He locks the door. He observes the tic that now threatens, as it did when he was a child, to turn him into a target of bullying and attention. He cannot stop looking in the mirror.

He breathes to control himself.

He breathes.

And he breathes.

Each time the tic becomes more pronounced.

He gets exasperated.

Suddenly, a scream comes from the other room. They start calling Lee desperately.

"Doctor Lee, Doctor Lee!" they shout.

The girl who was assisting him runs off to the bathroom. She knocks insistently on the door.

"Are you inside? Doctor Lee, please, come out!"

Lee opens the tap and washes his face. He tries to keep calm. The tic becomes more acute. He cannot stay in there.

"I'm coming! I'm coming!" he gets exasperated.

"You have to come out, quick, please, quick!"

He breathes again. He steps out. He heads towards the main hall. Scientists and assistants are gathered around one of the laboratory-created eggs. Everyone is celebrating.

"Congratulations, Doctor Lee! The egg has been fertilized!"

3

—*Rome.*
December, 2024.

Arnaldo still cannot find what he is looking for.

God, according to him, is still not answering him.

He is sitting in the laboratory. In his office.

Uses a fake glass wall as a whiteboard. There he writes down everything that is pending.

Since Giacomo gave him the report he kept with zeal a couple of years ago, Arnaldo had the word *ROMA* written in one corner of a window in his office. Just to remind him to review *Progetto ROMA* in detail. To decipher the nomenclature, research and plans that were detailed there. He kept it in a safe.

From that moment on, that word had been written there on the glass. Alone. Left behind. Forgotten.

Guadalupe had not failed, in any of her daily calls, to remind Arnaldo that she was there for the project. For him. For Jesus.

He kept denying the possibility.

He worked with the pure sample of Jesus' flesh from the Eucharistic manifestation. He had done so many tests that only a tiny particle of the sample was left. Without a sample, there was no chance of bringing back Jesus.

Arnaldo was worried. He had not told Giacomo about the magnitude of the problem. He clung to his faith in the hope that in an instant everything would become possible.

He knew that his days to try and complete the project were numbered.

That afternoon he stared absorbedly at the whiteboard. He compared formulas. He was looking for the answer, the key. He needed to guarantee the success of the project once and for all. At most, the sample, still latent and alive, would only allow for a couple more attempts. Three, if he was lucky.

"I'm missing something here. Give me your eyes, Lord. Give me your eyes. There's something I'm not seeing!" he said as if he were praying. But he was working.

He stood up. He needed to clear his mind. He walked around the laboratory. He returned. Suddenly, like a flash, he saw that word reflected in the glass. *ROMA*.

He managed to put together in his head everything that had always been in front of him.

That flash was a revelation.

According to mythological legend, the greatest empire of the ancient world, ROMA, was formed thanks to the intervention of Luperca. The she-wolf that served as a mother for Romulus and Remus and rescued them from the imminent death that awaited them after they were thrown into a river.

It was those twins who founded, years later, the great ancient civilization.

The term *loba* comes from the Latin *'lupa'*.

Guadalupe means 'hidden river'. It comes from the Arabic root and the Latin *wuad al luben*. *Wuad* is 'river' and *lupus* is Latin for *'wolf'*. River of wolves. Of she-wolves.

What was the hidden thing that Arnaldo could not see?

God gave him his eyes.

He read the word again. In his mind and in his soul the letters were rearranged. ROMA equals AMOR.[1]

It was always there.
The missing ingredient.
The answer to his questions.
LOVE.
Nothing more perfect than LOVE, as the Bible says.

---

[1] In Spanish, ROMA can be read backwards as 'AMOR'. The English translation of this word is 'LOVE'. Thus, Arnaldo connects the word Rome with Love.

He thought for a moment.
What kind of love is the purest?
A mother's love.
There it was. The real sacred vessel.

Still in awe and bristling at the revelation, he picked up the phone.

"Hello, *Lito!*" answered his granddaughter with a sweet voice.

"Hi, love!"

"Are you calling to tell me you thought about it?"

"When can you come?"

Silence.

"You were right. Jesus needs a mother. I have no doubt. He has chosen you!"

Guadalupe's screams could be heard throughout the town.

The answer was always right in front of their eyes.
The time had come.

4

—California.
November, 2025.
Sunday.

The uproar over Kevin's announcement was epic in magnitude.

It was thought to be exaggerated, but that was not the case.

What at first seemed like a rumor is now a reality. No one, even in their best dream or worst nightmare, could imagine what was about to happen.

The scandal has generated multiple extraordinary sessions inside what was originally the site of the Roman Emperor Nero's circus. Some cruel spectacle seems to be revived in which it became customary to torment Christians.

And boy was there torment!

At first, within the Church, they fought because they had not been able to stop it. They had known this for a long time. The Church had become a lot weaker. Arnaldo had warned them.

In an elegant Vatican office, Cardinal Ismael Domínguez follows the news from his computer.

"Sons of a bitch! Fuckkkkkkkkkk!

The walls rang with the cries of the prelate. They know that what is coming is not Christ; but a laboratory monster.

What they did not know was that there were three of the same experiments going on simultaneously.

Can science surpass God Himself?

This violates an international norm approved by the Council of Europe on January 12th 1998, which prohibited the cloning of human beings.

They broke the rules, the norms, and ethics itself.

Scientists were quick to speak out. Friends and detractors met. The international community went into a state of alarm.

The news has spread and has moved all nations. From Rome to the general public. It is the only topic of conversation. In a matter of hours, it has started trending worldwide. The cloning of the Son of God seems to be near. For some, it is already a fact.

With great caution, the leaders of the Catholic and Protestant Churches appear in different media, revealing themselves before the step that is about to be taken imminently. In less than one month the new Messiah would be born.

The great tribulation spoken of in the Bible seems to have arrived. Good and evil are at stake in an unprecedented bioethical, moral and religious war that is about to change human history.

There are protests in many places. A great theological and moral debate on reproductive cloning is established in various instances.

Some limits have been crossed.

One can't be playing God.

What is on the horizon is a violation of human rights and dignity.

The only reality is that it is already underway. There is no turning back. It is man against himself.

Was it true?

Was God manifesting in all this?

Where does the truth lie?

Many wonder if this was part of the apostasy spoken of in the Bible.

"For this reason you also must be ready; for the Son of Man is coming at an hour when you do not think He will."
Matthew 24:44

"This is only the beginning of what is to come. Science has succeeded. We'll see each other soon," stated Doctor Kevin while ending the transmission.

The Parousia was real.

The modern version of the Son of God was on the way.

Meanwhile, in California, Dr. Lee accelerates the race to achieve the fiercest revenge of all.

The red line is about to be crossed.

5)

—*California.*
May, 2025.

"We did it! We did it!" they kept shouting.

Lee's nervous tic has miraculously disappeared.

Through the transparent glass that holds the egg and the artificial placenta, a small formation can be seen. An embryo that has been forming for weeks now.

One of the researchers is engrossed. He had never seen anything like it. A miraculous and unusual achievement. While everyone's eyes are on the artificial machine, Albert turns to one of the central multiparameter monitors. A special device that allows the internal heart rate to be measured. The register is oscillating.

He increases the volume.

In the room, the sound of a beating heart is heard.

The presence of life.

Everything is flooded with jubilation.

Lee's face is transformed.

However, the time to claim victory has not yet come. The goal is near. He would rather wait for the formation to finish.

He approaches it and observes the fetus through the glass.

"Your time is near! My time is near!"

There are many months left.

The countdown begins.

6

—Rome.
December, 2024.

St. Thomas Aquinas described miracles as "things that are divinely performed outside the order commonly observed in nature."

Sometimes more is happening around us than we are willing to see. That is what had happened.

When Arnaldo told Giacomo about the conversation with Guadalupe, he also joined in the jubilation.

"Delightful! Amazing!" he shouted like a child.

Arnaldo also felt that joy inside him, though it was difficult for him to express.

"Okay, okay! We have to think about the ideal plan and do everything right. Remember, she is my granddaughter. My granddaughter! ...God, shed light over us!"

It was not clear whether Arnaldo was just talking or praying.

There they had everything they needed to obtain pluripotent stem cells. Guadalupe would travel to Rome to have some of her eggs extracted. In the laboratory, through electrical current, they would make the cells enter the egg. Then, they would be transferred into her. That would be the path they would take.

There were many more variables. The plan was to do it all in one step.

As a scientist, Arnaldo was aware that a human clone could superficially resemble the individual it came from but that, in its essence, it could differ drastically in the characteristics that defined it, such as personality, intelligence, talent and character.

With Guadalupe involved in the cloning process of Jesus, there was no room for failure.

Now, even less so.

Three days after her grandfather gave her the news, Guadalupe arrived in Rome.

As scheduled, the first three months were used to do tests on her. The tiny particle of life that Arnaldo still kept seemed to be waiting for her. For that woman.

Once fertilization took place, it was only a matter of days before they would know if it had been successful.

~

—June, 2025.
Guadalupe has been in Rome for six months already. She is three months pregnant. Time enough to make sure everything was going in the right direction. Arnaldo wants her to stay. She, as stubborn as a mule, says that it is time for her to go back home.
No one can convince her otherwise.

"I want to give birth in Mexico! Don't worry!"

Arnaldo knows deep down that Guadalupe's decision is the wisest. For her safety. At least for the first few years.

In this way, without them realizing it, the humility of the birth would repeat itself.

For him, she was the modern manifestation of the Theotokos.

Even against his own wishes to protect her, he had to let her go.

And so he did.

She went back home. Happy.

With her inner satisfaction. Double satisfaction.

According to the estimate, the baby would be born in early 2026.

(**7**

—*California.*
December 17th, 2025.

Lee's time has come.

The fetus is ready.

Everyone is stunned by the great event.

They watch as Lee opens the incubator and disconnects what would be the umbilical cord.

He takes the baby in his arms. Lifts him. The child starts crying.

It is the most anticipated cry in Lee's life.

"Congratulations everyone! We did it!"

Those were moments of great celebration. But noise always torments Lee. He had already had enough. It was not long before the party was over.

"Thank you, everyone! The day is over! Go and have some rest, we'll see each other tomorrow! Ah, Sophia!" he said to his assistant. "Before you go, please make sure to dress the baby and put him into that thing you bought."

Her maternal instinct, help her to prepared everything for the birth. Clothes. A little basket. Formula milk. A small, sky-blue blanket. Lee did not have time to think about those things.

Now only the two of them are in the laboratory.

Lee and the baby.

He approaches him. He picks up the miracle of science in his arms.

They cry.

Lee does it out of the excitement of having surpassed God Himself.

The baby does it because he is a newborn.

And, just maybe, because He knows what is about to come.

Lee opens a bottle of Dom Pérignon Rosé Gold. One of the financers had given him some for when the fertilization was successful. It was reserved for a special occasion.

"For you to celebrate with your team once you succeed!" the financier said.

Without a doubt, the moment was special.
On this occasion, even his approach to drinking changed. Before, it was his way of evading his surroundings. That day it was his way to face them.

He opened it.

He poured himself a glass.

Lee grabbed the bottle Sophia had left ready and clinked it with his cup.

"Cheers!"

He leaned.

He did not give Him the formula.

He drank the first glass of champagne.

Then the second. Then the third.

The child kept crying.

He opened a second bottle.

With it came not only that alcoholic fermentation with an aroma of orange peel and dried fruits, flavored with notes of redcurrants and wild strawberries. What also bubbled to the surface was the ghosts of his past, released by the amount of alcohol already coursing through his veins.

"Stop crying, you brat!"

Those were the exact same words his father told him that night.

The night of the storm, the thunder and lightning.

The night he peed himself.

When his father killed himself right in front of his eyes.

The night he swore to meet with Jesus, face to face.

The night of revenge.

Outstanding debts would be finally settled.

8

—California.
December 21th, 2025.

A group of scientists has received a last-minute call. They are invited to witness a milestone of science. They will be witnesses to the most controversial of all experiments.

Kevin can wait no longer.

The day has come.

The guests know the place very well. There are security guards inside and out. They arrive happy, joyful. They have encoded IDs hanging from their necks, giving them to access that restricted area. To get in, they have to scan their fingerprint.

They take the elevator. 3rd floor.

When the doors open, the jubilation inside can be seen through the transparent walls.

In the center is the machine. The impressive source of artificial life. A device emulating a maternal womb. Specially designed for this purpose.

They enter. They are welcomed effusively in the midst of the party. Everything is ready. They were waiting for them. That *cortège* of men in white robes surrounding the incubator.

Since Kevin made the announcement almost a month ago, various authorities have tried to find his whereabouts. They are not able to. No matter how hard they try. Nuremberg is behind all of this. They have planned everything.

They are the ones who manage all the information. The big networks. What is consumed on social media. They did it their way. Every step of this transcendent event is planned.

"Men are like sheep. Establish a routine for them. Indoctrinate them. There they will be," said one of Nuremberg's leaders.

That is why Kevin is live at the same time through various networks. People tune in. They want to see the fetus live. In motion.

"It's Christ" say some while crossing themselves after seeing him on their phones.

"It's a demon!" others scream.

The big show is about to start.

"Everything ready, Dr. Kevin?" asks one of the scientists.

"Yes! All ready!"

They turn on the devices.

It's 8 p.m.

The transmission begins. They are live.

"Humankind! All of you! Dr. Kevin greets you once more. The big day has come."

9

—Mexico.
December 24ᵗʰ, 2025.
11 p.m.

Since Guadalupe told him that the baby made her go pee frequently, Arnaldo decided to take an earlier flight.

He had thought of going on the 22nd to surprise Guadalupe but, between the bad weather and the shock of Kevin's news, everything was delayed. He had already organized everything with Imelda and Vicente, however, that day, all the flights in Rome were canceled. The snowfall was terrible. Few times had such bad weather been witnessed.

He finally arrived at the Benito Juárez International Airport on the 24th of December at almost 8 p.m. He still has to rent a car. It will take him four hours to reach his destination.

The bad weather is everywhere.

The rain is torrential.

Some say that they are signs from heaven.

Zacualpan is a small mining and artisanal town located in the south of the state of Mexico.

According to the Codex Mendoza, the hieroglyphic that represents the coat of arms of Zacualpan means: *"where valuable objects are kept."*

In the streets the joyous atmosphere can be felt. The parties in town seem to go on forever. Despite the crisis, everyone is celebrating, drinking and getting drunk.

It's a national holiday.

It is also raining cats and dogs in that town used to a cool and dry climate. Strangely enough, temperatures have been high, and the heat is almost unbearable.

"This is because of global warming," says José, between beers, to his friend Vicente.

"It must be that, compadre!"

In this small town everyone knows everyone else.

Guadalupe is rushed to the local outpatient clinic. She is soaked. Since her water broke, her labor pains have accelerated.

She is welcomed to the sight of cheap plastic chairs. They serve as an antechamber to the entrance of the main surgery. The healthcare center is in very poor condition. Instead of doors, there are hanging sheets.

"Is someone there? I can't stand it anymore, please!" screams the girl.

She is wearing a white dress. Her brown hair is tied back in two braids that fall over her shoulders. Her brown skin seems to glow. Her lips look fuller than usual. It is the effect of pregnancy.

From inside, a hoarse voice shouts that she can come in.

In the town, the party continues under the heaviest rain that the town has ever seen.

In the corner of a ranch, between beers, music, and the commotion, José tells his friend:

"I insist, all this rain must be because of global warming."

"It must be that" answers Vicente. "By the way, compadre, where is Guadalupe? Her *Lito* told me she was coming, but she hasn't arrived."

Inside the outpatient clinic, the nurse has a tired face. Traces of alcohol perfume the atmosphere. He understands she is about to give birth.

"Girl, what sort of date is this to come and give birth? You're lucky I haven't left."

He takes another shot of tequila. He sits her on an old and somewhat rusty stretcher. As he prepares everything he needs, a strange smell of roses permeates the place and spreads, little by little, through the village. It goes around every corner. Few notice it. They let the warning that the gust brings go past.

A new scream shakes the place. The labor has started.

Guadalupe screams and tears stream down her face. As he places her on the stretcher, he realizes that the baby has crowned. All that remains is to push.

"Oh my God, you're almost ready!" says the nurse. "There is no time to tell the doctor!, Anyways, he is at the village's party. Be strong, breathe!" says the young nurse.

But she is not able to concentrate. Fear has taken over her. He holds her hand firmly and looks into her deep brown eyes and he tells her to breathe once again.

"Come on, come on! Push, kid, push! I see its head, it's coming!"

10

—California.
December 21th, 2025.

Kevin has captured the world's attention.

"Yes! The day has come."

The number of viewers increases. And increases. And increases. It is absurd.

Outside, the street is hot. Everything is too controversial. Whether they like it or not, it is the trending news of the moment.

Everyone is talking about it: Catholics, Jews, Muslims, Buddhists, believers and non-believers. In every corner of the world. In all social strata.

"Be witnesses, from wherever you are, and together with the men and women who are with me today, of this definitive step for humanity."

Kevin approaches the main device. The fetus is inside, moving. It seems to know its time has come.

"Ready?" Kevin asks rhetorically to make the show more exciting.

He presses some buttons on the side of the device.

Mechanical hands come from two sides.

They grab the fetus.

They take him out little by little.

Kevin presses another button.

A flexible tube is the umbilical cord. From one side, some automatic forceps approach and cut the long extension from its root. Now, nothing connects the baby with the device.

What seems to be the amniotic fluid is withdrawn through the lateral tubes.

Air comes into the device.

"Is he breathing? Is he breathing?" asks Kevin, worried.

Silence takes over the atmosphere.

—*New York.*

Holding a sign in his hand, a tall white man loudly announces that time is up.

> *THE SECOND COMING OF CHRIST IS A FACT!*
> *JESUS IS ALIVE!*
> *THE WORD OF GOD HAS BEEN FULFILLED!*

Science certainly seems to have won.

On some street corners there are growing groups of fanatics who, after hearing the news, have come out to gather and pray in the middle of the city.

~

—Zacualpan.

"Mom, mom!" shouts a girl while jumping out of bed and rushing to share the news. "They cloned him! They cloned him!"

"Who?" asks her mother.

"Jesus, mom! This is getting exciting!"

"Oh, my daughter, don't say that, it scares me! It must be a false rumor...!"

"Look, look!" she says while showing her the phone.

"I'm not going to look at anything! Go and throw that thing away!"

The woman crosses herself. As soon as she got close to the phone, she got goosebumps.

"You have to be really sick in the head to play these things and get into such a fuss! These people have no scruples. They are playing God. Let's pray that the tables do not turn and that what they've created is not the Antichrist himself!"

In the background, the voice of Simon, Isabel's father, can be heard.

"Well, let's stop being prudish, it wouldn't be a bad thing if it were really that Jesus, hopefully He can fix this mess!" he replies out loud. "You tell so many stories about all this science stuff, woman, yet you forget that it's thanks to science that we are here. Or do you not remember that without the scientists, after that virus, you wouldn't be here to talk so much rubbish? Isabeeeel!" shouts the man. "Bring me that thing, I want to see it!"

"She's better off not talking to you!" says Maritza. "Isabel, don't mind your father, you'd better take out your rosary. Come with me to pray!"

"You know what? Don't worry, love, I'll look for the news on my own phone."

Since Mrs. Maritza found out about Guadalupe's pregnancy, she decided to start a campaign to discredit her.

"What a way for a girl to fuck up her life!"

She even reproaches his daughter for her friendship with Guadalupe:

"I'm going to tell you something, Isabel María. I don't like you even speaking to that girl. You'll thank me later. You do not want that kind of friendship!" she says every time she has the chance.

In a corner of the room, there is a small table with several saints. She picks up a box of matches. Lights the candle. The wick is about to run out; it is the same one she uses every day at the beginning of the rosary and that she blows out when she finishes praying. The basin is discolored. It belonged to her great-grandmother. It was part of the heritage that had been passed down from generation to generation.

They cross themselves.

"Where two or more are gathered in my name, there I am in their midst," Maritza says to begin the prayer.

The true Messiah was really close.

12

—California.
December 17th, 2025.

Lee was in front of the child. His creation. He looked at Him non-stop. He started talking to Him.

"Where were you? You never showed up."

He poured another drink. He drank it immediately. He put the glass down.

Why use it if he was going to drink the whole bottle anyways?

"I told you to stop crying!"

The crying was making him desperate.

It began to rain heavily. It was pouring down, even thundering.

"Aren't you the Son of God? Are you hungry? Come on then, show me your power!"

Monsters do not forgive.

"Aren't you going to tell me why you never showed up? Where are your power and greatness? You know what? This is how I wanted to see you! Defenseless. Just like I was. Just like my mother was. Crying, like I was. Like my mother was. Immobile, like she was. Like I was. Peeing yourself. Like I did."

Claps of thunders shook the place.

"Are you scared? Huh? Aren't you gonna answer? Let me tell you something... I've been waiting many years for this moment: You are a shitty God! A really shitty one!" he said while screaming at him and shaking him. He shook him hard. With brute force.

He was drunk. As drunk as his father was that night.

Life is cyclic.
So are its events.
So are its demons.

13)

—*Mexico.*
December 25th, 2025.

"Come on, come on! Push, kid, push!" insisted the young man to Guadalupe.

One more push and the sky seem to open.

The rain stops.

A deep silence invades the place.

There is no noise.

Arnaldo finally arrives to the village, hurrying.

There is no one at Imelda and Vicente's house.

Everyone is celebrating.

No matter how hard he looks for Guadalupe, he cannot find her.

He has a hunch. He knows the time has come.

Intuitively, he heads for the outpatient clinic.

He goes in.

That scene is lovely.

Guadalupe has the baby in her arms.

The little creature does not stop crying.

"*Lito*, what are you doing here? How did you get here? How did you know?" said Guadalupe, tired but astonished. "Come... Meet Emmanuelle!"

Arnaldo was astonished.
He cannot manage to say anything.
His eyes cannot believe it.

14

—*California.*
December 17th, 2025.

Lee realized what he was doing by attacking the child.

The monsters came to pay him a visit again.

He went to the desk.

He took the gun. His father's gun. His only memory.

He headed towards the room where his son was. Yes. His son. He had created him.

Before the eyes of the baby, he asked for forgiveness.

"God doesn't exist! He never did!"

He pulled the trigger.

The baby stopped crying.

Forever.

He put the gun in his mouth.

His ghosts ceased to exist.

Forever.

15)

—California.
December 21ᵗʰ, 2025.

Kevin is watching tensely.
They do not know whether the baby is breathing.
The compartment is opened.
The artificial hands pick up the baby.
A cry is heard. Finally.

Everything has aligned.
Light and darkness meet in the same environment.

Kevin also feels the air coming into his lungs.
The celebration is total.
"Friends, you are all part of this historical moment. The new Messiah is born! Meet Christopher."

16)

—Zacualpan.
December 25th, 2025.

Arnaldo cannot believe it.
The Church is doomed.
Science and evil have won.
The course of history has taken another turn.
Forever.
"How could I have fucked this up?" he thought.

Emmanuelle is a girl.

INDEX

PAQUIDERMO
libros

This book was finished and
designed in March, 2023.

Playing God
will continue...

Made in the USA
Monee, IL
05 April 2023

30780541R00233